Between The Doors

For Sam, world's best TA.

Between The Doors

Wes Peters

Apprentice House
Loyola University Maryland
Baltimore, Maryland

First Edition

Printed in the United States of America

Paperback ISBN: 978-1-62720-004-2
E-book ISBN: 978-1-62720-005-9

Design by Katherine M. Marshall
Cover photo by Katherine M. Marshall
Design editing by Alex Namin
Section icons by creative commons - attribution (CC BY 3.0) the noun project

Published by Apprentice House

Apprentice House
Loyola University Maryland
4501 N. Charles Street
Baltimore, MD 21210
410.617.5265 • 410.617.2198 (fax)
www.ApprenticeHouse.com
info@ApprenticeHouse.com

for my mother

Contents

foreword

Between the Doors is a fantasy story, replete with castles and towers, lords and ladies, magic and wizards, even zombies and "crawlies." Passing through one door, young Andrew Tollson, armed with an old revolver he has found lying by the wayside, leaves his New Jersey home and enters a fantastic realm of good, evil, and everything in between. When there, he becomes a gunslinger with just one round of six bullets at his disposal. Accompanied by his newfound friend, Nick, Andrew then embarks on an exhilarating series of adventures, acquiring four more friends on the way, as he endeavors to save this world from the evil magic of a dark wizard who controls and corrupts it. What happens to him is full of surprises, and you'll find his story a true page-turner.

Like all good fantasy stories, however, this one does more than simply tell a tale of faerie adventure. In its depiction of a parallel reality, it reveals something important, even essential, about our own world. In this case, that something is a truth found in a great deal of both realistic and fantasy literature. As old as the proverbial hills, it's the realization that, as Nick tells Andrew, home is "where we're all heading anyway."

The return home is something of a literary archetype, and as many commentators have observed, fantasy literature is at heart a genre of archetypes. Ursula Le Guin, a widely acknowledged master of the genre, insists that true fantasy needs be a "journey," with the trappings of dragons or knights, dungeons or witches, disguising the archetypes by seducing readers into participating in what she insists "are dangerous things." The danger, Le Guin suggests, comes from the fact that archetypes bring us as readers perilously close to home—which in fact *is* Andrew Tollson's story. The real journey in *Between the Doors* is thus not the physical one that Andrew, Nick, and their companions take, but rather the intimate, internal one that Andrew shares with us as we read.

If this sounds heavy-handed or oppressive, be assured that Wesley Peters narrates Andrew's tale with a deft hand. As you read, Le Guin's dangers will never seem much of a threat, the seduction or disguise provided by the story's fantastic trappings being simply too exciting. The plot's twists and turns prove riveting, the characters intriguing, and you will always want to know what happens next.

Yet all the while you also will know what ultimately has to happen next. As the book's title announces, there is a second door for Andrew, and us, to pass through. That's the door that passes back from fantasy to reality. Much as with J. R. Tolkien's Bilbo Baggins or L. Frank Baum's Dorothy, going through it concludes one journey and starts another one. "Why should I go back," Andrew asks plaintively at one point; "why can't this be home?" The answer, proffered by the novel's good wizard, is as profound as it is simple: "Because it's not."

Paul Lukacs
Department of English
Loyola University Maryland

ONE

Affairs in This World

chapter one
playing truant

I

The boy came home to one hell of a mess that day. Stillness and heat premature in the early spring season hung like ugly tension in the air. The river beside the road to his home in the woods ran shallow. The drought had plagued the woods for almost a month. Andrew could hardly remember the last time he had slept upstairs, where the stifling heat crept in through the windows and enveloped the second floor. He had resorted to sleeping in the cellar, where it was cool enough to grab a few hours of sleep—cool enough to wake up without being drenched in sweat.

The sleep Andrew did manage to get was spare, and would've concerned his parents had they time to notice. His effort in school had been, 'lacking of late', as his father would have said had he time to notice. He didn't. Work with the local water treatment companies had become a twelve hour daily endeavor, thanks to the drought. Andrew's father kept his son on track during this time of year when the weather improved and Andrew's mind wandered from his schoolwork. Yet David Tollson had to leave at 6 in the morning and didn't get back til the late evening. There was no one to help Andrew with his schoolwork, or 'lack thereof', as his father also would've said.

Andrew's father had no 'lack thereof' of work, however, so Andrew's truancy had gone unnoticed these past few weeks. His mother busied herself from sunrise to sunset, saving her gardens from ruin at the hands of the drought. Patricia Tollson had the finest garden in town. Rows upon rows of orchids, roses, and blue hydrangeas transformed the small lot the Tollsons called home into a castle courtyard. Helping his mother plant and tend these flowers implanted in Andrew a fierce love for nature from a young age. Flowers, his mother said, had a way of making a small life seem grand. *Perhaps,* thought Andrew as he walked past the rows of flowers leading up to the front door, *now that the flowers won't bloom, that's why mom seems so small.*

She certainly was not small today. Patricia Tollson waited patiently inside the kitchen, fidgeting with a pair of gardening shears. Andrew had heard her humming an old rhyme at the dinner table last night: *April showers bring May flowers.* An old rhyme had been circulating through her petite head all day: *April showers bring May flowers.* Well, it was May now, and she had spent all spring mourning her dead flowers and cursing her new flowers that wouldn't grow. *So what about May flowers? What if there are no April showers?* As the front door swung open and young Andrew walked in, Patricia looked up and met her son's eyes.

"Andrew, dear," she said. Andrew froze. "Won't you come sit with me?" The boy treaded slowly over to the high table where she sat.

"What's up, mom?" he asked, forcing a small smile. She didn't return it.

"Oh, just lovely, Andy. Do you know Mr. Scalza? Do you know Mr. Scalza, darling?" Andrew's stomach dropped to his shoes. Mr. Scalza was Nayreton Middle School's truancy officer. All of the days he'd skipped school and wandered along the banks of the Warren River were about to catch up with him. He had stopped going once the heat settled in and the drought started, in April. There was no point in sitting through school, which lacked air conditioning. The rooms baked in the valley below the White forest.

I'm a fool, Andrew thought. *I've been to school maybe four times in the last three weeks. Of course someone was going to notice!* Before he could answer her question, his mother continued. She looked down at the shears in her hands and dropped her voice.

"Mr. Scalza dropped in for a visit this morning. I was out gardening…" Her voice trailed off. Suddenly, Andrew was very afraid. He knew his mother wasn't just angry about the hooky. No, there were other things contributing to her fury, things out of his control. To the boy, life didn't seem so fair and grand at this point in time.

She continued. "Mr. Scalza informed me that your attendance has been less than satisfactory as…of…late." Andrew grimaced. The old bird-faced Scalza, he knew, would have used that phrase, 'as of late'. His mother was simply repeating his words.

"Andrew, do you know how hard your father and I work to send you to that school?" Patricia Tollson asked, her voice rising. Andrew realized he had hardly said a word in the entire conversation. She hadn't let him. He tried to speak now.

"Mom, I-"

"Do you know hard we work?" she cawed out. Suddenly, she was up out of her chair, and Andrew could see the dirt on her jeans and blouse as the sunlight struck her shirt. Yes, she had been gardening all morning. She slammed the shears against the counter-top, scarring the old wood.

"Your father," she spat, "works all fucking day and comes home after dark, too tired to talk, too tired." She held the shears in front of her, and with that the entire situation changed in

Andrew Tollson's mind. He jumped to his feet, backing away slowly from his advancing mother, a slow-dance with shears. She continued.

"So tell me, Andy," she said, still advancing. "How will he like to hear that you've been absent twelve times from school in the past month? Oh, I know. He won't care. He'll be too tired. *Too tired.*" Her eyes blazed.

"Twelve times, boy," she said. With scary speed she reached out with her other hand and smacked Andrew on the head. He stumbled but kept his feet beneath him, his eyes focused on the shears.

She's not herself, the boy thought. *What's gotten into her?* He continued backing away, aware he was almost at the door. The world spun a little from her blow on his head, but he knew if he could get out the door safely he could get away. He tried to calm his mother, as he passed the small porch chair by the door.

"Take it easy, mom. I—"

"*Don't tell me what to do!*" she screeched, lunging forward again. Andrew was ready this time, shoving the porch chair between them as he jumped backwards. Patricia Tollson's upper body connected with the chair first, throwing off her balance. Her legs were next; her knees, exhausted from gardening all morning, made contact with the legs of the chair. She let out a small yell and collapsed over the chair, tangled up in its legs. Andrew avoided the collision and turned around, throwing open the door. He sprinted off the porch and through the garden, hearing his mother curse as she threw open the door behind him, hot in pursuit. The heat hit Andrew like a wall as he flew through the garden.

"*Get back here, Andy!*" she screamed in a voice unlike her own. The chase ensued for a few seconds, but by the time he passed the stone wall that marked the front of his property, he knew it was over. Andrew saw the shears skid up the street past him. His mother had thrown them in a last ditch attempt to stop him. Now she stood in her garden watching him run up the street, panting heavily. She blinked away the fertile tears that accumulated suddenly in her red eyes.

II

Somewhere along the road Andrew decided he wasn't turning back. He longed for the open road, for something new—something that didn't stink of the drought. Andrew followed the banks of the Warren River. He figured he had to follow the heart of the drought in order to escape it.

The Warren River was long and rich. It ran southeast, perhaps to the ocean—Andrew couldn't recall exactly where it went. *Should've paid attention in Social Studies.*

"Shit, I should've gone to Social Studies." He muttered aloud, and laughed. It felt good to swear, to feel independent. His mother swore like a sailor; why shouldn't he be able to do the same? He turned off the road and onto the forest path that ran alongside the Warren River.

He strode along the path as the hot afternoon slid into early evening. Soon he'd be hungry. After a few miles the path parted from the river and wound back up the road. Normally Andrew took the path to the road and headed back home. Today was different. He could walk for days on end. Andrew continued along the river, abandoning the beaten path for his own path along the banks. The ground was dry and cracked; normally in the spring the water would be overflowing the banks from melted snow and rainfall. This year, no snow had lasted long considering the drought. The snow had melted, and evaporated, and the woods were dry. The world was drying up.

Andrew strode along the banks, headed southeast, and some invisible hand guided him forward. In his mind, he wasn't Andy Tollson but a gunfighter from the spaghetti westerns he snuck up to watch on the western movie channels. He no longer walked on the side of a river but railroad tracks, having just shot up some bandits holding up a train.

Doesn't matter how hot or how long the drought lasts here, thought the boy. *The law of the gun carries on, whether it rains every day or it's so stinking dry your piss evaporates in your stomach.* That was Andrew Tollson's say.

The boy continued walking downstream past dried stream beds and rotten marshes. The trees above him refused to bloom, and they begged the sky for something to drink. Andrew was lost in his little fantasy when he nearly stepped on another.

He would've walked right by the gun had the sun not caught the metal and shined. He stopped and looked at it. It was not a handgun like the Nayreton police wore on their right hips, but an ancient revolver, huge and menacing. It lay on the forest floor, untouched by the mud and leaves around it.

"Holy shit."

Pick it up?

Why not? The boy wasn't going to pass up an opportunity like this. He bent over and ran his hands along the old metal. Picking it up, he felt the weight of the weapon. The grips were weighted and heavy in his hands and yet Andrew thought the gun felt... natural. As if he'd held one a thousand times before.

He'd fantasized about the law of the gun before, dreaming of a time when gunfighters held reign and evildoers were no match for the heroes' draw. The boy mimicked this draw, snapping the gun to attention and feigning a shot. He jerked the weapon upwards in western fashion. He didn't dare the pull the trigger of course; what if it was loaded? At this thought he pulled back the hammer, and jumped as he heard the gun cock. He opened the cylinder, and felt weight within. There were six shells in the chamber, each unspent. He had found a six-shooter, with six shots.

"Freeze, punks! Make my day!" cried Andrew, feigning fire at six invisible enemies, his right hand slapping the hammer back with each shot. He didn't dare pull the trigger, though in his head he imagined a sharp report and flash, as his enemy gunmen fell helpless, one by one.

The boy snapped out of his dream. Whose gun is this? Why is it here? Should he even hold it? What if the owner shows up?

What if the owner had a bigger gun? Without thinking, Andrew pulled the hammer back again. Having fired his dad's rifle a few times at a range outside of Nayreton, the entire process came naturally.

Andrew searched the ground for extra shells or footprints. There was nothing to indicate any activity near the gun, only an imprint of dirt where the gun had lay in. It was if the weapon had fallen from the sky for him to pick up.

"How long has this been here?" the boy wondered. It looked ancient, like a weapon belonging to a western epic. Finally, the young boy felt the air grow still. He looked up and saw the cloaked figure up ahead at the bend of the river.

III

The sun had started its descent behind the tall hills to the east, and in the golden twilight the mysterious figure shimmered and shined. The figure was short and emaciated, cloaked in white and hooded so that his face remained hidden. He (or she) was only a hundred feet from Andrew, standing before the river's bend, but to Andrew the figure seemed miles away. There was something unreachable about this stranger; Andrew wondered if one step toward the figure might cause him to bolt away like a deer.

The stranger reached out his arm, and in his hand he held a long bamboo walking stick in his hand, white and slender in the fading spring light. Now he beckoned Andrew using the stick.

I can feel its pull, Andrew thought, his heart racing. *Why shouldn't I follow it?*

With the gun hanging loosely in his left hand, the boy began to walk toward the figure. He quickened his pace to a brisk jog as the cloaked figure turned toward the river. Instead of following the river and rounding the bend, the figure ran down the river bank and disappeared from Andrew's sight. Andrew hurried towards the bend, and by the time he reached it, he saw the cloaked stranger across the river, moving south in the forest. The boy looked north down where the river bent and slowly faded into the wooded horizon. At the bank of the river where Andrew stood the water flowed slowly but steadily thanks to the sharp downhill curve ahead.

The hooded figure, almost out of sight now, turned and beckoned again for Andrew to follow. The boy spotted a few rocks in the water he could jump on to cross the river, and prepared to cross. His mother's voice nagging in his head stopped him.

How would your father feel about you following a stranger in the woods? How'd he like to hear, after a long day's work, that some hooded drifter led his son deep into the forest at nightfall? Andrew pushed the voice out of his head. His father wasn't around to notice either way. Andrew didn't know who he resented most: his mother, his father, or the drought.

It didn't matter. The boy crossed the river.

IV

Andrew made it across the river without much trouble, and continued his pursuit of the cloaked man. He had an idea of where the stranger was headed, of course: due south. Andrew followed in his path. The terrain began to slide downhill at a suicidal rate, and Andrew had to descend sideways to avoid stumbling and flying forward. The slope continued for a few hundred yards, and while most of the hill was littered with trees and sharp rocks, the path Andrew took was clear of all impediments. It was if the cloaked man had cut the path clean. Despite the safe path, however, Andrew still led with his feet in front of him and his body turned to the side to counter the steep terrain.

After descending for what felt like hours, Andrew saw the bottom of the hill. Most of the terrain around him flattened, but his own path did not; it dove into a deep grove, shadowed by tall, thick trees. Andrew headed down into this opening, below the flat terrain. After a few seconds of descending he came upon stone steps that twisted and descended deeper into the earth. Andrew grabbed the earthen sides of the passage to slow his descent and straightened his body so he could safely run on the steps. The steps were narrow and thin, only large enough for the foot of a child. Andrew was thankful his feet were still small, but still he slowed down to a near walking pace to avoid stumbling.

The steps descended into the earth further and further til Andrew felt he was miles below the forest floor. The stairs ended with a stone wall with a small hole in the bottom, only large enough for a child to fit through. Andrew, not quite five feet tall, squeezed right through the opening. He came into the grove, expecting it to be shrouded in darkness as the staircase had been. However, several rays of light pierced through the darkness from the canopy above, illuminating the patch of green grass he stood on. Around him a circular grove, surrounded by thick oak trees, rose up to the sky. At the far side of the chamber sat a small, plump boy. He was staring at a tree at the center of the grove, with what appeared to be a sketch drawn into it. As Andrew drew nearer to the door he saw it was no sketch. An actual oak door stood in the center of the tree, begging to be opened.

V

The strange boy turned as Andrew drew near. He was clad in a dark green tunic and dark leggings, with a mess of curly dirty blond hair on his head.

"Hello," Andrew said.

"Hullo," the boy said, with a thick accent that reminded Andrew of some foreign film he'd seen about Ireland. The boy climbed clumsily to his feet, which were gigantic in comparison to the boy's body. Andrew gauged him to be no older than thirteen.

"Name's Andrew Tollson," said Andrew, stepping forward

and extending his hand as his father had taught him. As he stepped into the light, the strange boy gasped, catching sight of the revolver in Andrew's hand. The newcomer stopped dead in his tracks and bent down to one knee.

"Forgive me, sir," the boy said, his eyes staring down at the ground as he stumbled over his words. "Pleased to meet you, Andrew, son of Toll. You can call me Nickolas, Son of Smith, he of the field and the scythe. I... give myself to your service? Wait, I don't think that's it..." The boy trailed off and shook his head. "I don' remember it, no sir."

Andrew didn't know what to say. *He called me the son of Toll,* he mused. That amazed him the most. His father's name was David, not Toll. *Just where in the hell is this kid from? He's acting sort of weird.*

When *was this kid from?* Andrew realized was the better question.

In his silence, Nickolas, son of Smith, looked up. "Beg your pardon, sir, but isn't this where you usually say somethin'?"

Andrew shrugged. "I couldn't tell you."

Nickolas furrowed his brow. "Wish I knew how this was suppos'd to go... it's jus that I never met one of your kind before."

"One of my kind?" asked Andrew.

"A man of the gun, you know," Nickolas said, motioning to the revolver in Andrew's left hand. "You look young, but you must be one of them. Them of legend!"

Andrew raised his eyebrows and stepped back. "A man of the gun?"

"Yea!" Nickolas cried with a grin, and lifted his hands to the sky. "A legendary gunfighter!"

VI

Andrew Tollson was no gunfighter. He was adventurous, more than most boys his age, but he knew he was no man of the gun. In his head flashed images of gunfighters he knew, like Clint Eastwood, John Wayne, and Lee Van Cleef. Those were true gunfighters, serving the law of the gun and the law of the light. They enforced that law in the old west; could such knights of western cinema really bring peace in the modern age? Could gunslingers even exist in the 21st century? Andrew had his doubts.

Andrew remembered something his mother had said when he had started reading *The Adventures of Tom Sawyer.* "All good stories," she said, as he sat back on the porch and she kneeled down in the garden, "start when a character takes on a new part."

Andrew, nine years old, didn't get it. "When they step into somebody else's shoes, and leave their own behind," she explained. Her pale face was beautiful in the spring light, as her crisp brown hair blew in the wind. It hurt Andrew to think about now. Her words echoed in his head. Suddenly Andrew wanted to leave his beat-up Nike's behind in this grove and don a pair of cowboy boots. He straightened and addressed Nick.

"Rise!" He cried in his deepest voice. Nick looked up in surprise. "Rise, Nickolas, son of Smith. I accept your service and thank you for your blessing." Andrew felt ten feet tall. Nickolas climbed to his feet, his eyes locked on the gunslinger. The twilight beaming into the grove from the canopy illuminated Andrew's face as he beamed.

Andrew looked around. "Uh…" he shifted somewhat uncomfortably. "So… what is this place? Did anyone come through here?" He turned to survey the grove, expecting the cloaked stranger to pop out of the trees. He didn't.

Trees surrounded the grove, in a neat circle. No leaves littered the ground- the grass remained untouched and green. On the far side of the grove, not ten feet from where the boys stood facing one another, stood a door. The oak monolith was attached to the largest tree in the grove, though the door's frame exceeded the tree's girth. Andrew thought it had a funny look to it, as if someone had propped a door upright against the tree.

Sensing Andrew's eyes on the door, Nickolas shrugged. "Beats me," he said. "Not sure what this place is all about, sir. I've been alone here all day." Andrew had to conceal a smile as Nick called him sir. "To be honest, I just woke up 'ere. I'm beginning to think this isn't my world at ohl." Andrew furrowed his brow at the odd pronunciation of such a familiar word.

"What do you mean?" Andrew asked.

"Well, for starters, there's no guns in my world," Nick said. "Or gunfighters, none of 'em neither. We only tell stories of guns. They're just legends, not the real thing." Andrew eyed the boy curiously.

"How did you get here?"

At this question, Nick cast his eyes downward at his feet. Andrew stepped forward and put his hand on the boy's shoulder.

"What happened?" Andrew asked, his eyes burning with curiosity.

After a short moment of silence, Nickolas looked up, but not at Andrew. He peered into the deep darkness of the forest.

"I died. . .I think."

VII

He had been sitting there for some time before the gunfighter entered the grove. Nick had begun to grow hungry, and that was strange—he didn't think ghosts could eat. He had tried chewing on some grass, but it was bitter on his tongue and he spit it out. Grass tasted bad whether you were dead or not dead.

Nick, who had always been told he was slow by his parents (though they weren't so smart neither, Nick thought—not book smart at least), couldn't quite grasp what had happened, and what was going on in this grove. If he was dead, then why was he here? He pondered this for quite some time when he woke up in the grove that morning, and when he spotted the door his questions multiplied.

The door was locked, as Nick had discovered when he tried opening it earlier. *What lies beyond it?* The boy wondered as he sat in front of the door, feeling the grass under his hands and the hot still spring around him. Perhaps it was a door back to the living world, he figured. *That would explain why it's locked,* he thought.

If that was true, then should he get up and leave the grove? Would that make this new world he had woken up in the afterlife? That scared Nick, and he quit thinking about it.

One thing, however, terrified the boy even worse than the concept that this new world was some kind of afterlife. As he paced around the grove that day, waiting to come up with an answer or for someone else to find out an answer for him, he was suddenly struck by a horrifying thought: what if the door led to the afterlife?

Can't be, thought the boy. *Nobody ever said you enter the next life through a door, that's just silliness.*

"But then again," the boy reasoned out loud, "nobody

knows what going to the next life is like cause once you go, you don't come back."

So it was a definite possibility. After all, he *was* dead. Or was he? He was sort of confused about that too. Sure, he had fallen, fallen a hundred feet or more, higher than the boy had ever climbed in his life. As the wind had whipped at his face on his death fall from the Clock Tower, he had not screamed nor wet his pants. He had simply awaited the end. The crack would sound as his neck snapped on the cobblestone street below and the numb feeling would rush through his body as his spine shattered. He would've screamed, would've wet his pants, but the view of the rising world around him was too incredible for young Nick to do anything but stare in amazement as he fell and the ground rose up to meet him. He didn't think of the people he'd miss, or the fact that he'd never lain with a woman (he'd heard stories from the older boys, but could hardly believe that a man and a woman would do… that). All he could do was watch and wait for that final crack that would let him know that it was all over.

The crack never came, he reminded himself as he sat in the grove. Instead of hearing that crack, he'd woken up in this strange place. Though Nickolas had never been to school a day in his life, he knew that some things in life demanded proof. Especially, he decided, something as important as one's death. If he wasn't dead, that meant all bets were off. In that case, it wouldn't make sense that this grove was the entrance to the afterlife, and the locked door the exit of his world; it also wouldn't make sense that this grove was the exit of his world and this door the entrance to the next life. If he wasn't dead, though, how'd he end up in this grove? None of it made much sense to Nickolas. So he took a seat in the grass, and waited patiently for someone to figure it out for him.

VIII

Andrew stood before Nick, listening to his story and trying to sort it all out. Andrew knew that Nick wasn't telling it all. He could see, however, that Nick was traumatized from whatever had happened; whenever the boy began talking about 'falling' he would stutter and look away.

"Well Nick," Andrew said when the boy finished talking, "you're not dead. If you were a ghost, I couldn't touch you right?" He put a hand on Nick's shoulder, who tensed up at first, then relaxed. "See? You're not dead. You probably just dreamed the fall." Nick, however, shook his head.

"Alright, well maybe not. But one thing is for sure, Nick," Andrew continued, and gestured at the stairs behind him. "This world is mine. Above this grove, we're in the gracious state of New Jersey. Are you from New Jersey?"

Nick shook his head. "Never heard of it."

Andrew reconsidered. "Delaware? Maine? Maryland?" Nick shook his head comically at each of these. Andrew tried a shot in the dark. "Texas?" No luck. Andrew gave up. "Where are you from?"

"Ever hear of Sunsetville, sir?" asked Nick. Now it was Andrew's turn to shake his head. "I live outside, in the southern fields. My dad, Farmer Smith as most know him, owns a good plot of land northeast of Brymino." Nick straightened as he said this. Andrew knew now why the boy seemed so simple: growing up on a farm, Nick must have never been to school a day in his life. Andrew suddenly felt guilty about the past few weeks.

There's something bright about him though, thought Andrew, though he couldn't put his finger on it.

"Well," Andrew said, "let's get you home, Nick. I bet Sunsetville's right through this door." He strode over to the oak door, reaching out for the handle.

"It's locked though!" Nick called behind him. Andrew put his hand on the brass doorknob and a bolt of energy flew up his arm.

Andrew jumped, feeling his heart race in his chest. Suddenly, he was focused. Things that had bothered him all day, like the drought, his parents, and school ceased to matter in this moment. He felt a heightened attention on the present, and the gun in his left hand. It was a frightening perception of reality.

He turned the knob in his hand, and of course it turned. *It opens to me,* Andrew realized. He heard Nick's breath draw slowly behind him in wonder. He heard the birds quit chirping in the canopy. In this moment of time, the world was standing still, and he could feel it. He opened the door and walked through.

"Wait up sir!" shouted Nickolas from close behind. Andrew heard him but didn't turn. He stepped into the blinding light. Then he was floating. The world of New Jersey waned and faded behind him.

TWO

Affairs in Another World

chapter two
through the bowels

I

Andrew lurched forward and landed on his knees, reaching out his right hand to brace his fall. The world spun.

Nick landed beside him, and had less luck with his entrance, tumbling forward into darkness. Andrew had to cover his laugh with his hand, which he found still held the gun. That was good.

The smell hit him next. Andrew reeled in dizziness. From the darkness, Andrew heard Nick:

"Of all the places to end up, this shithole..."

They were in a sewer. Long stone corridors led in either direction, shrouded in darkness except where light streamed in through overhead grates. Andrew gazed at the grate above him, blinded by the golden sunlight. *It's sundown,* he thought. *Sundown in Sunsetville.*

"Hope you'll pardon my language sir—it's just that—"

"Don't call me that!" Andrew exclaimed and hurried over to help his friend. Fortunately Nick hadn't gotten any of the excrement on him.

"Well no sir, I wasn't callin' you a shithole, you see—we're in the sewer."

Andrew laughed. "No, not that. Quit calling me sir." He laid his hand on Nick's shoulder, as Nick's eyes widened to the size of dinner-plates. "I'm not a day older than you, Nick."

Nick looked away. "But, sir, it's just common respect. Beggin' your pardon of course… if you want though, I can stop. Sir."

Andrew lost interest in the boy's dawdling. He walked forward and wrinkled his nose. "So this is Sunsetville, huh?"

Nick hurried over to him. "Yessir, I'd recognize that golden light anywhere. Even the smell of shit can't ruin that crisp, golden, springtime air. Sorry about the language, of course." He continued. "I know this sewer pretty well, yep. I work down 'ere."

"Do you?" Andrew asked. "But you're just a kid!"

"Yes well, I've got to do somethin' during the day. My aunt and uncle are usually workin'. They want me to keep out of trouble and all," Nick looked around. "I knew this sewer pretty well, workin' with the maintenance men. Too often I'm knee-deep in…" he looked at the puddles of waste and murky water around him. He couldn't find a polite word for it. He continued.

"Of course, it's been knee deep since I've got here, three moons ago. Especially since it hasn't rained in over a year, that is."

Andrew turned sharply. "There's a drought in Sunsetville?"

Nick considered it for a moment. "If that's what you call it, then yes. The whole world's got a bad case of it." His cautious answer brought a grin to Andrew's face. "I never heard that word, though, but if druh-out" he sounded it in two syllables, "yeah, if this dry-out means the weather's hot and sticky all the time without rain, then that's what it is. Sir."

Andrew didn't say anything, thinking of his home. He'd thought he could escape the drought through a door to another world, but apparently that wasn't the case.

"And truth be told, the rain's stopped ever since *he* came," said Nick, talking more to himself than Andrew, who explored ahead. Andrew asked who *he* was, and received a few seconds of silence from Nick. When Nick spoke, it wasn't an answer to Andrew's questions.

"Look here, sir—it's a manhole. That's what we use to get in and out of the sewer, you know."

Andrew turned around, spotting the manhole on the ceiling. He flashed his friend a smile.

"Let's get out of this shithole, bud," he said, tucking the gun into the waistband of his shorts.

II

Andrew followed Nick, who leaped and grabbed the iron rungs of a ladder that dropped from the manhole. Before he had jumped Nick commented:

"I may not have a load of 'smarts' as my dad says, but I've got a compass in my head." He tapped his finger on his temple. "Fills up the room where my brain is s'posed to be, my dad also says. I know my way around, and if I'm right we're below the center of town. Well," he paused, thinking. "we're under it. Yeah, that's better. Once we climb up, then we'll be in the center of town."

Now Nick popped off the manhole, and pulled himself into the street. He turned to help Andrew up after. Andrew climbed up with the help of his new friend, and saw Sunsetville for the first time.

Before his eyes could adjust to the light, he took in a gulp of fresh, crisp air that Nick had described earlier. It was a relief compared to the sewer. It was also a relief compared to the air in New Jersey. There the air was filled with 'global warming', something his mother talked about despairingly at the dinner table. Here, the boy figured, there could be no cars in this world. If it had no guns, how could there be cars?

The center of Sunsetville took Andrew' breath away. Behind him he heard Nick say:

"Right? Makes my jaw drop everytime."

The buildings were one or two stories high, built of wood that shimmered homely in the twilight. Amidst the markets that congregated around the cobblestone town square towered an incredible structure: a clock tower, built of stone. Instantly, Andrew thought of Big Ben, the clock tower he'd seen in the picture books his mother had once read him. At last, a pang of homesickness rattled his bones. He managed to dismiss it in wonder, however, as only as a child can do, gazing in awe at the city around him. And the city had begun to light up.

The only way he could describe it was how Disneyworld looked at night, with the illuminated towers and magic that hung in the air. There were no electric lights to illuminate the buildings here, but the sunset (which was not halfway finished) cast a beautiful radiance on the tower and the buildings below. Torches lit some of the houses and streets. Staring at the gigantic face of the clock Andrew saw strange markings that looked like graffiti radiating. They were symbols and designs and obscure markings of purple and pink and magnificent fuchsia that illuminated the clock face. Andrew had only been to Disney when he was four, and though he loved the atmosphere, he resented the crying children, many of whom were older than he. Also, he resented that he couldn't ride the rides because of his height.

Here, though, was a new world, a world without crying children and height restrictions. The boy gazed at Sunsetville, his face illuminated by the falling sun. Here he didn't have to be Andrew Tollson; here he didn't have to be small. Here he was a man of the gun; he could be big as he wanted to be.

III

One watched the two climb into the dusty street. Tom Treeson sat astride a young horse, caramel in color with a rich mane. He recognized Nick, but not the other. The other wore strange clothing, shorts and a t-shirt with a collar, and a mess of dirty blonde hair on his head. In the light of the sunset the boy's eyes burned. He had an unsightly bulge beneath his shirt at the belt, and had Tom known what lay under the boy's shirt his jaw would have dropped to the dusty street.

Tom Treeson rode up to the two slowly. He was an older boy, dressed similarly to Nick, except for the brown top hat he wore. Nick heard him coming and turned to meet him.

"Hey Nick," Tom said, tipping his hat.

"Hullo Tom," Nick said.

"You missed work today, my friend."

After a moment's pause, Nick said "Yeah," and said no more.

Tom Treeson looked up at the clock tower and was silent for a moment. "You missed one hell of a day, Nick. John's laid up in the infirmary."

Nick started. "Johnny? What's happened? Is he all right?"

Tom shook his head. "Crawlies got him. Down below. He was fixing a leak, broke off from the group, and got lost a bit. The next thing we heard was his screams."

Tom shuddered visibly, remembering that morning. The

men had followed John's screams through the sewers, heading northeast through the stone tunnels. You always had to remember which direction you were headed down there or you could end up in a lot of shit.

They had John face down in the muck, spiders crawling over his limp body. Fortunately some of the workers had matches, and they struck a light to scare the beasts away. Tom had never seen spiders like this in his life. They had been bigger than his fist, and fast too. When they saw the light of the match they quit crawling on Johnny and turned to face the intruders. Tom had seen their red eyes, and that's when he'd lost it. He screamed and sprinted at them, waving his match and swinging the wrench he'd brought with him. The other boys tried to stop him, but he was too far gone. He hit one crawlie with his wrench. It flew and splattered against the wall. Splattered wasn't the right word; exploded was better, Tom decided.

He had continued his rage until a spider began to climb his pants leg. He let out a yelp and swung his body, trying to throw it off. As he turned, he saw the black mass behind John's body; hundreds of crawlies recoiling at the light, fleeing toward the sewer wall. Tom Treeson watched the crawlies in wonder as the mass retreated, and then finally remembered the spider climbing up his leg. He looked down and gasped as he saw the beast climbing his thigh in a direct line for his crotch. He swatted at his thigh with the wrench, oblivious to the damage he was doing to his muscle. The wrench tore apart the spider, which finally fell from his pants into the dark water below.

They carried John's body into the streets above, and Tom had to wipe the shit off of John's face to see if his eyes were open.

There was shit in his eyes, thought Tom as he told the two boys his story. Things could've been worse, though. John was alive, just 'not responsive,' as the nurses had said. As for Tom Treeson, he was just glad he'd worn pants that day. Otherwise, the spider would've bitten a chunk out of his calf or worse, slipped into his shorts. Either way, Tom Treeson would've ended up in the infirmary besides John if not for his jeans.

IV

Andrew saw the shadow pass over Nick's face as he heard the story. The part about the crawlies especially terrified Andrew (he assumed the 'crawlies' were spiders, but didn't ask.)

When Tom finished speaking, Nick was silent. No one made a sound, and the bustle of the markets closing for the day seemed far away. Nick finally said:

"Will he be all right then?"

Tom looked at Andrew for a moment. Then he looked down. "There's no telling. The nurses say he's breathin' and such, but that he's gone 'comatoes' and 'non-responsive'. Sounded like a bunch of squabble to me, but I don't know much about doctoring," said Tom, with mystery in his eyes. "But as far as I'm concerned, they've no cure for the bites. The nurses said that the poison is long-lasting, and that not all patients wake up from their sleep. Sometimes they just don't snap out of it, you know it?" Tom shook his head. "And ye know whose fault this all is, dont ya?"

Nick looked up slowly at the grand clock tower. "The lord of spiders," he whispered, and now Andrew knew Nick wasn't telling him something.

Tom Treeson nodded. "Old St. Gerardo. That luney's sent his crawlies down through the sewers to feed," he said, spitting while saying feed. He straightened up on his horse, and looked off into the distance.

"I'll take my leave of ye, and give ye something to chew on: don't be lurkin' round here tomorrow afternoon," he said. "Every maintenance man in town has had it with the old 'saint', or whatever he calls himself. Joe Freeman from the tavern downtown ain't so fond of him neither, and we're all gonna have a word with him."

Andrew knew what that meant. Whoever 'Old St. Gerardo' was, his head was likely to end up on a pole, like in those westerns where the Indians got out of hand.

"But the door to the tower's sealed! Oh Tom, you'll never get into the Clock Tower." Nick cried. All three boys looked over to the door. It was round and wooden, like something out a fairy tale. Nick and Tom continued to squabble, but Andrew kept his eyes on the door.

Am I meant to go through that door? His heart jumped at the thought.

"We know it," Tom answered. "The wizard's sealed it shut, sure. Keep us out. But we've got a way around his tricks. Stop by the tavern on the way home and maybe you'll see what we've got up our sleeves."

Tom rode off soon after. Nick, though in shock from this news, jumped when he read the time on the clock. "Oh! Andrew, we've got to get home real quick. My aunt and uncle don' like me out past sunset, you know." Andrew wanted to comment that he didn't blame them, considering the spiders and all. He chose to hold his tongue instead. Before they left the town square, however, Andrew shot one last glance at the wooden door at the foot of the tower. He had a feeling he was going to open that door.

God help me when I do, he thought.

V

The sun had set, and the city lit up. As Andrew and Nick walked to Nick's aunt and uncle's house, Andrew saw the walls around him come to life. It was the same graffiti which had stained the face of the clock tower. The city walls were covered with these strange drawings and words. The words were indiscernible to Andrew, and Nick had no idea what language it was. Andrew thought it was German or something.

The colors of the graffiti lit up the town in the place of electrical light. Shades of fluorescent green and orange and pink radiated from the walls to light the boys' way. Andrew had never seen such a colorful place in his whole life. His neighborhood in Nayreton got very dark at night, surrounded by the thick darkness of the forest. Here, however, the night was electric. Nick claimed the graffiti was written by oddly dressed people in the town.

"You don't see them much 'cept when they write on the walls," the boy explained. "It's a weird thing, but they talk like little kids and wear new clothing that only little kids wear. My aunt calls them 'kid adults' cause they never grow up, or at least they don't want to." Nick added that all of this was beyond him.

"They sound a bit like hipsters," Andrew said. Nick didn't know what those were, and before Andrew could explain he spotted a few hipsters. Except, they weren't quite hipsters. They were certainly outstanding and strange looking though. They congregated outside of Joe Freedman's tavern, looking up at a man standing upon wooden scaffolding. The hipster-looking people wore high multicolored socks and tunics that were as fluorescent as the graffiti on the walls. The men wore tight clothing that looked like it belonged to women. The women had their hair short and wore hats to look like men. Either gender wore large glasses without lenses in them. Andrew had seen oddly dressed individuals like these in TV commercials back home, advertising the new iPhone or something along those lines. Here were something like those people, except they looked like they'd come from a different century.

The man on the scaffolding was a tall lanky fellow with a patchy beard and sullen grey complexion. He wore an old patched suit, and Andrew thought the hipsters must have picked it out for him: it was bright yellow. Nick informed him this was Joe Freeman.

"Let's watch from a distance," Nick advised. He and Andrew stuck on their side of the street. "I don't want my friends from work to see me, they'd want me to join up." Andrew saw Tom Treeson gathered around some men who were not dressed as extravagantly as the hipsters, and knew them to be the maintenance men.

So Nick's only just met me, and he'd rather stick with me than his friends? Andrew thought. It was a comforting and concerning thought. The two boys listened in to Freeman's sermon:

"He has terrorized this city. He has made a mess of what Sunsetville truly is," Freeman proclaimed. His eyes shone eagerly. His voice was high-pitched and nasally, cracking at every other word. "And what is Sunsetville?"

"Our home!" came the response from the crowd. Freeman surveyed them with a stern glance. He looked as though he had neither shaved nor slept in days.

"Let me tell you all a story, friends and neighbors," Freeman said. He straightened. "My bar always brings in good business. I used to be a little fool, like all of you, thinking things were good here and all. Thinking that I could make it in this city. Well, I was wrong. Dead wrong! We're all fools, don't you know it? Well I didn't, not til that saint came into the bar and played up a scene.

"He told me that night that he was tired of my 'sin' and 'inhumanity.' Said alcohol and the 'harlots' upstairs were turning the town into a mess. So I tell's him, my bar's just fine- it's what this town needs, considering the drought and all. The dry and thirsty men can come to the bar to quench their thirst and such. So he looks me in the eye, and he's tells me he'd show me a dry spell. So he waves his hand, and laughs real eerily. Real creepy, that laugh." The listeners murmured in silent agreement.

"I told him to get the hell out of my bar, and he tips me a wink and tells me things will be real dry round here for a while. Then he leaves, and next thing I know all my beer's gone!" The crowd raised an uproar at this. "All seventy barrels in the cellar, and not a drop of alcohol in 'em! As if all the beer just vanished in midair!"

"Don't forget the ladies, Joe!" a hipster cried. Joe looked down upon the listener and stared. But others affirmed this call, so Joe continued.

"And the ladies. I didn't want to say anythin', but if you insist I'll say a word or two. Well that same night he came in and the beer vanished, the men upstairs with the girls come flyin' out of the rooms all at once, screamin' the damn same thing."

"What'd they scream Joe?" the crowd cried.

Joe leaned in, his eyes bloodshot. "That there were crawlies in the ladies' privates."

The crowd was silent in shock. "All the ladies fled town!" Joe continued. "They don't want to stick around with that kind of sorcery about. So the town's dry now!" He lifted his arms in the air. "No ladies, no booze! What does it say then?" The crowd erupted in anger, but Joe lifted a finger in the air to silence them. After a moment all was quiet.

"We can jibber and flam about this all we went, but I's been saying this past week somethin' needs to be done about it. It's time the wizard pays for it all, yeah?" The crowd began to shake their heads and stomp their feet. It was a scary sight to see, dozens of men and women thundering about.

"Then there's one way to do it then!" Joe cried. He gestured to the scaffolding he stood on. "The door's to the clock tower's locked with his magic, sure. So build this fucking tower and let's rise up to meet him! At the top of the clock tower! What do you say we burn 'im down!?" Joe threw his arms in the air, his voice cracking with the words 'burn 'im down.' The response from the crowd was tremendous.

"Burn it down! Burn it down! Burn it down!" they chanted. Now the maintenance men moved to the base of the scaffolding where construction tools lay. They began to work. Andrew watched and said:

"They're building it up. They're making it into a tower."

"With wheels," Nick added, observing the tower's base. "Come on Andrew. Let's get out of 'ere." The two boys turned to leave. As they rounded the corner around a tall brick house, another hipster-looking fellow nearly crashed into them. The newcomer skidded by the two boys and called to them:

"Be here by two tomorrow boys! That's when the wheels start turning and we burn 'im down!"

VI

The two boys sat on Margaret Smith's front porch, observing the street. It was nightfall at last; the sunset had dragged on for over an hour. Margaret Smith, a bumbling woman plumper than her nephew, treated Andrew with cordiality and kindness. Andrew had asked Nick to keep his guns a secret from his relatives. He also hid his gun in a small purse Nick had lent him once they entered the house. Part of Andrew, after seeing the riot today, wanted to break the entire gun charade, but he knew better.

There's work to do here, he thought to himself as he sat down at the dinner table. *I've never fired a gun aside from my dad's rifle, but there's work to do here. I've got to play this part, to myself and others.*

So he played along and kept it all a secret, thanking Margaret Smith graciously for the food, which was delicious. Her husband, Theodor, was the town postman and apparently still working. At one point during dinner, Margaret brought up Joee Freeman and the riot.

"You'd be best to stay away from all that, Nickolas," she advised. "I know they're your friends and all, but what they're doing is bound to make a bad mess. And the mayor won't stop 'em neither. I always thought Joe Freeman ought to be locked away, what with the awful things that go on in his bar. And now look what he's doing!" She banged her fist on the table for emphasis. Andrew jumped a little, and Nick cracked a grin. "Say, Andrew, where'd you say you're from again?"

"From town, Aunt Margaret," Nick answered in Andrew's place. "From the north quarter, on Begrimble Street."

"Oh, quaint area," Margaret said, though her eyes said differently.

"I don't want to intrude-" Andrew began. His mother had taught him this much politeness.

"Nonsense!" cried Margaret Smith, banging her hand on the table again. Andrew didn't jump this time. "You're welcome to stay the night, or as many as you'd like! Our home's yours', don't you know it?"

Andrew hoped the same could be said of this new world. As he sat on the porch with Nick, hearing the torches crackle on the city streets and gazing up at the stars that belonged to a universe that wasn't his, he sank deep into his thoughts.

There'd been a drought back home, and there was a drought here. Andrew began to wonder if these two worlds were connected by more than a door; maybe they were tied through fate, or something. Andrew didn't have the faintest clue what fate was, but it sounded right.

Nickolas' aunt had used the word at dinner. She'd started lamenting about the fate of the city, claiming the man in the clock tower would be the doom of them all. She said "that St. Gerardo fella" was responsible for the drought. After all, the townspeople had often seen him atop the tower at dawn, his hands outstretched to the sky, mumbling strange words in a foreign tongue.

"He's from the west too," she said with distaste. "He may be a sage and all, but I never liked folks from the desert and I never will."

Andrew had lost all motivation to find him. Even with his six-shooter, what could he do against someone like St. Gerardo? He'd felt ten feet tall earlier; now he just felt small.

Nick looked over at him from his seat on the porch. "Andrew," he said in a low voice. "What's your world like? It's just that, I didn't get to see much of it, you see."

Andrew grinned. "It's sort of like this one, Nick, except…" Andrew looked up at the sky, with stars that burned eagerly and clearly above. He could see thousands of them. "Except you can't see the stars like you can here. Cause of electric light, and pollution, I guess."

"Hm," Nick said. "How can you see your path without the light of the stars?"

For a moment, Andrew was silent. He thought about it. Then he stood up from his chair and stepped up on top of it, to get a better view of the street.

"You make your own path, that's how!" he proclaimed. Nick watched him with wide eyes. "The stars don't have to tell you where to go- you can make your own decisions." He paused for a moment, thinking it over. "Yeah, that's it. Nobody tells you who to be, you make your own path. Simple as that."

"I dunno about that," Nick said. "I was told I'd never be very smart, just cause I was born into farming folk. That doesn't seem very fair. I'd like to go to school but I guess it wasn't in the cards."

They were silent for a moment. Andrew sat back down. "I guess that's true," he offered.

"And your gun!" Nick said, then covered his mouth with his hands. He looked around to make sure no one watched. No one did. He continued.

"Didn't yer da hand your guns down to you? That's the way of the gunfolk, yeah?" Nick's eyes shone. The light of the fluorescent graffiti cast a multicolored shade upon the porch.

"Yes…" Andrew said, nodding his head slowly, playing the part.

"See? We're the same! My parents gave me the farmin' tools, yer's gave you the shootin' tools. I'd always heard stories about the ways of the gun-people, but there's none in this world so I never knew it for sure. But I know *somethin'* for sure: I was born to help, you were born to lead."

Andrew peered off into the street. Suddenly, there was a

pop and bang! that made Andrew jump a little.

"Ah!" Nick said, his face lighting up. "Somebody's settin' off sparkers." Andrew heard the ensuing crackle of childhood a few blocks away. It reminded him of summer. At his own house, sitting on the back porch with his dad at night, admiring his mother's garden in the moonlight. His dad would tip him a wink and pull out a firecracker from his work-bag along with a few matches.

"Want to see a bang, Andy?" David Tollson would ask, a big grin on his face. Firecrackers were illegal in New Jersey, so Andrew supposed this was his family's best kept secret. He felt something ungraspable now thinking about it. If he were older or gone to school more he might have known it as nostalgia, but for now he decided no word could truly describe the pangs inside. He could smell the summer air, feel the grin on his own face as his father had lit the firecracker.

"Nick?" he said, his eyes still glued to the street.

"Yes?" came the reply beside him.

"Do you miss home?"

"Yeah." Nick said. He paused for a moment. "Sunsetville's good and all, but I'm no city-boy. If you think the sky is clear here, you should see down south of the city in the farmin' lands. There you can you see other worlds as clear as the sun."

With that Nick got up. "May I have your leave sir? I'm tired."

Andrew smiled. "Go ahead, Nick. You have my leave." Nick bowed, and walked through the front door. Andrew sat a little while longer, admiring the stars, soaking in the stillness of the night.

chapter three
in the morning

Andrew awoke to brilliant streaks of sunlight. He
looked about him in confusion. Long splashes of yellow and
gold illuminated the pale blue walls around him. The boy
remembered all of the previous day's events.

Thoughts of his mother, his home, and his world that he
left behind all raced through his mind. Andrew could hardly
believe it all happened, and that it had all happened so fast. His
father always reminded him that things that happen quickly are
either beautiful, or beautifully dangerous. Andrew supposed this
whole experience was one or the other; but either way it was
beautiful, and by God it was beautiful. Dreams of independence
danced about the boy's head, intoxicating him with wonder.
Taking in a breath of the fresh spring breeze that rustled past the
shades, the boy stood up.

He heard Nick's snores beside him and nearly jumped.
Nick lay upon his bed, the sheets thrown carelessly over his small
chest. His brown hair curled loosely over his neck and his eyes.
Andrew laughed as he saw the hair over his eyes jump up with
each snore, and then softly fall back over his eyes. Andrew stared
at his friend for a moment, and then remarked:

"I think I'll go back to sleep." He lay down on the couch,
his hands behind his head. Within a minute his snores joined
Nick's.

I

The two boys made their way down to breakfast an hour later, following the smell in a way only young boys can. They headed down the narrow wooden staircase and entered the small kitchen area to find the source of the scent: Aunt Margaret's bacon and eggs steaming on the metal stove. Andrew's mouth watered at the sight of the meal. This beat the hell out of breakfast back home, which usually consisted of Raisin Bran and warm pulpy orange juice.

The orange juice here was warm, but Andrew didn't mind; he and Nick wolfed down their meals with an unnatural speed. Margaret came back into the kitchen to find their plates empty and both boys leaning back in their chairs, and she sighed. "You boys are somethin' else," she said.

Nick had no work or chores to do, so the two decided to go play around in town. A day without school always looked good to Andrew, and today he didn't even have to play truant. There's no such thing as hooky if you're in a universe without school, so the boy reasoned his hands were clean. Not even Aunt Margaret's warning as they walked down the stoop could diminish Andrew's wonder.

"Now you boys be careful," she said, wiping her greasy hands on a kitchen towel. Both boys turned to face her.

"Aw, what's to worry 'bout, Auntie?" Nick asked. He was practically dancing at the prospect of hanging out with his new friend. "Ye know I've been up, under, and around the town more times than I can count." He took a look at his fingers as if to prove the fact.

"I know ye have, but still somethin' seems the matter around Sunsetville recently." She lifted her eyes, surveying the street she lived on. "A funny smell, you could say. And it's not just the sewers giving up that smell, if you know it. But listen here boys, *stay out of the sewers.* Yer both too young to be down there in the dark."

"Yes'm," both boys said in unison. Andrew looked strangely at Nick. *He hasn't told her he works down there some days,* he realized. *Looks like I'm not the only one keeping secrets from my family.* And then he thought, *maybe everyone does.*

"Good," Aunt Margaret said, her eyes still on the street. The neighborhood was out and about at this hour, she knew, and yet things were calm and quiet. "Now scram you too, and don't let me catch ye till sunset! But don't ye be late neither!" And the boys set off, chasing each other down the street through the hot morning air.

"Boys'll be boys," said Aunt Margaret. But there was something about that Andrew boy… she couldn't quite put her finger on it. Sure, there was something odd about him. Maybe it was the way he spoke. Margaret had a different way of talking than most of the city folk around Sunsetville, but she'd *never* heard anyone talk the way he did. Where exactly did the boy say he was from? She couldn't remember. She couldn't put her finger on it.

II

Andrew would remember that morning for the rest of his life. He wasn't sure why; he was too young to really understand the beauty and wonder that filled his soul and emblazoned his spirit. Children have a way loving what's new and fresh, embracing the day with wonder and naiveté. Andrew was too young to grasp this, however; he just couldn't put his finger on it.

The boys sprinted to the center of the town, filled with the hustle-and-bustle of merchants, workers, and tourists. Strange people moved here and there around the boys, who jumped around the crates and boxes around the market. Occasionally a merchant would scold them for jumping on his stuff and the two boys would scurry away from the boxes, hiding behind some more. They chased a furry brown dog around the town square for an hour, and the dog chased them around for an hour more. At one point Andrew, not looking where he was going, ran straight into a man carrying several boxes. Andrew spun away from the man, who tottered and wavered, nearly dropping the boxes. The man was about to regain his balance when Nick, sprinting from the yipping dog, tripped and took out the man's legs, who cried out in dismay as he collapsed onto the pavement. His boxes rained down around Nick and him, the former looking embarrassed and little dazed. Then the dog leapt into the arms of the man and began licking his face, who laughed uncontrollably at the rambunctious mongrel's antics.

Exhausted from the morning's escapades, Andrew collapsed upon the scaffolding of a tower in the center of town. The scaffolding faced the Time-Table Clock Tower. Andrew sat about five feet off the ground, dangling his feet over the edge, bathing in the morning sunshine. Behind him the clock face on the Time-Table ticked away. Andrew paid it no attention. He was lost in pure ecstasy, engulfed in one of those rare moments of childhood when independence and a lack of responsibility coincide perfectly. An adult would've felt the pressures of the day beating around his skull; a child would normally grow bored of sitting around. In that moment of time Andrew lived forever. The people below hustled and cried out, but they could not disturb the boy. They moved in fast-forward; he didn't move at all. Time had stopped for Andrew Tollson. He felt free; free of responsibility, free of worry, free of doubt.

Nick napped below in the shade of the wall. Andrew thought he looked comfortable in the grass, but his own mind was too alive to sleep. In his head he saw visions of glory and freedom in this world. The boy gazed beyond the walls of Sunsetville. He saw tall castles on steep green hillsides, with hordes of horsed men riding across a bridge over a sparkling blue moat around the courtyard. He saw country people out in the fields, working for themselves and their family. He saw great ships upon vast blue oceans, setting out to discover new land, new people, new *worlds*. He saw freedom and independence, and he saw a beauty in his mind and felt it in his soul. It was a fleeting beauty, the kind that only lasts for a few minutes before it becomes a memory that will only be recalled for a moment for the rest of time. He'd remember that beauty when he felt his hands dry and dirty from a long day; he'd remember that beauty when he felt the morning breeze rush through his hair. He'd never feel it again, but the memory remains.

The bells within the Time-Table rang out eleven times. Andrew looked up at the great face of the tower. He felt the time ticking away.

What happened to that feeling? He wondered, looking around frantically. Nick stirred at the sound of the great bells ringing out through the square. The people in the square continued their frantic dance through the stifling noon heat. Andrew realized he'd spent the morning in a daze.

"It's the clock," the boy murmured, looking up at the great tower. But it *wasn't* the clock; not quite, he realized. It was *time*. For a kid who played truant as often as he did, he really wasn't used to feeling like he was wasting time. Now he did. He felt some responsibility, some longing to get moving. He didn't exactly *love* the feeling, but he couldn't deny it.

"But where?" he wondered, and Nick, who had lumbered over to him, gave Andrew a confused look.

"Where's what?" Nick asked, as he rubbed his eyes and yawned.

"Where do we go?" Andrew asked. "Where?"

Nick shrugged. "I usually hang around 'ere on my days off, see if any of my friends show up." Andrew shook his head.

"I mean, what now? What's next?" Nick, who really had no idea what Andrew was asking, came up with a suitable answer.

"I'm getting hungry. Shall we go home? Hopefully my aunt's made some lunch." Andrew sighed. He supposed Nick wasn't cut out for a mission like his. He was a gunfighter. Nick was just a boy.

"Let's head back," Andrew said. Nick began to walk up the street.

"That's good," Nick said. "My aunt makes great lunches, you see. They put you right to sleep. An afternoon nap it is!"

III

Andrew feigned sleep for a few minutes until Nick began to snore. Then he slid out of bed and began to put his things together. He tucked the gun in his waistband of his shorts. He took a look in the mirror on Nicks' wall and stifled laughter at his new clothing.

I look like an elf, Andrew thought with a smile, admiring his new garb. He ditched the kilt and put on his khaki shorts and t-shirt. Then he pulled the grey jacket Margaret had lent him over his chest. In his reflection he saw his gun protruding from his pants.

"The world's youngest gunfighter," Andrew thought as he pulled his shirt over the gun. He jumped as Nick murmured something in his sleep, which sounded like 'pancake'. Yet Nick's breathing steadily continued, and Andrew relaxed. He grabbed the purse Margaret had left for him and slung it over his shoulder. He supposed in this world it was fashionable for a man to wear a purse. This one slung over his shoulder like a small backpack.

Andrew looked over at Nick, and felt a pang of sadness. "Goodbye, Nick," he whispered, and snuck out of the room.

IV

Andrew walked through the streets of Sunsetville, which sat still in the midday heat. Not a soul walked on the streets; it was quiet time, as Nick had informed him. Andrew's Spanish teacher, Senorita Katrina, would've called it a siesta. Andrew wandered past Joe Freeman's bar, and saw the scaffolding-tower that just yesterday had been two levels high. Now it climbed higher than the buildings on the street. Andrew figured the men must have added six or seven floors since yesterday. It was a shoddy structure. The wood that pieced it together was old and splintered, and the tower leaned and swayed in the wind. Yet the gigantic wheels attached to the ground floor promised that it would roll, and roll soon. Andrew didn't want to be around when it did. He headed for the square.

The Clock Tower loomed high above Andrew, peering down like an ancient stone giant. Andrew felt fear knot up in his stomach. He suddenly wanted to run from these great towers, as he had run from school, and his mother. His gun kept him from running. The ancient revolver weighed heavily on his shorts, reminding him he was in for the long haul. With that thought he was hungry again. He sat down on a wooden crate and pulled out some dried meat.

"A boy without some food in his bag might as well be no boy at all!" Nick's aunt had insisted at lunch. Andrew had declined, but Margaret Smith would not have it. She'd packed enough 'dry meat' in Andrew's bag for him to eat for a week. Andrew hadn't wanted it, but Margaret Smith was a persistent woman. After all, she had claimed, she had no use for it.

He chewed on a piece of the dry meat, which Andrew figured was just beef jerky with some spicy seasoning, and threw his bag over his shoulder. He got up out of the shade and walked slowly over toward the foot of the tower. It was good, Andrew figured, that the mob hadn't shown up yet, with their great tower. They had promised to arrive at 2, and it was nearly 1:30. Andrew sighed, and muttered:

"No time to waste." He grasped the handle of the wooden door. "Whatever's up there, I'm coming. Get ready."

"Not without me, you're not!" cried a gruff voice behind him, and Andrew knew it was Nick before he turned around.

V

Nick figured Andrew must've known he was following him. Gunfighters like Andrew were keen to the land around them, Nick knew. Plus, they just had a way of knowing sometimes. Just like his ma had a way of knowing he'd snuck bread from the pantry, Andrew had a way of knowing.

Andrew didn't bother acting surprised. Instead, he shook his head. "Nick, you can't go up there," he said.

"Mr. Andrew," Nick returned. "I ain't afraid of nothing. And I'm still in your services, so I can't let you go up there alone." Nick held a fire-poker in his hands, sharp at one end, and Andrew nearly laughed at the boy's attempt to arm himself.

"In that case," Andrew said, "if you're in my service, I forbid you from following me."

"All right," Nick said. "I won't follow. I'll lead." He stepped boldly past Andrew and tried to open the door. It didn't budge. Nick scratched his head. "How are you trying to get in?" he said.

Andrew approached his friend and looked him squarely in the eyes, placing his hand on the boy's shoulder. "Nick," he said, and Nick immediately straightened. Andrew had a way about him, Nick knew, that could freeze the meanest winds in a dust storm. Now Nick hung his head, sure Andrew would turn him away. This time, he wouldn't be able to argue. Andrew continued.

"Whatever's at the top of the tower is dangerous. If you go up with me, you must promise me you'll let me face it. Remember, I've got the gun. I don't think your fire poker's going to do the trick."

Nick reddened a bit in the face. "Well, of course sir. I was just improvisin', you see." Andrew grinned, and patted his friend on the back.

"Come on, follow me." Andrew said. With that, Andrew turned to the door. Nick watched silently. Andrew grasped the door handle, took a deep breath, and turned it. It did not budge.

"Oh," Andrew said. It was silent for another moment. He tried turning it the other way, but to no avail. The door was sealed after all.

"I told you it was sealed!" Nick cried behind him. Andrew stood by the door a minute, concentrating. Then he let go.

"I figured it would open," he said. "The door in the grove did."

"Maybe this one's not meant to be opened," Nick offered. Andrew didn't buy it.

"There's got to be a way into the tower," Andrew said.

"Well, sure there is," Nick said. "Through the sewers. There's a basement entrance." Andrew turned sharply to look at his friend. Nick raised his eyebrows.

"I found it a couple of weeks ago, it's sort of hidden and secret. But the tower basement's real creepy, and the sewer smells... I didn't stay down there too long." Andrew looked around and found a manhole. He walked over to it, then looked back at Nick.

"We're going down there?" Nick said. Andrew said nothing, but began to lift off the manhole cover. Nick sighed. "Yes, yes we are."

VI

The stench was bad at sunset the previous day. It was absolutely horrid at midday. The choking waft of dry feces was nearly enough to send them back. They pressed on instead. The dark, sticky passageway was illuminated by light streaming in through the sewer grates, but as the two boys wandered deeper into the sewers it grew darker.

"How far to go, Nick?" asked Andrew at one point, his voice cracking a bit. Nick did his best to sound brave.

"Not too far, I don't think. The tunnels are just sort of turney down 'ere in the center of town, like a maze."

They were in the midst of making a right turn when Nick froze. Thankfully there was faint light behind them so Andrew could see Nick stop, otherwise they would have ended up falling over one another. Immediately Andrew saw why Nick had stopped; voices were audible up ahead. Or, rather, one voice was audible. Andrew put a finger to his lips and listened in.

At first Andrew couldn't quite make out what the voice was, but eventually, as the voice approached them he heard words. A shadow drew near to them, the shadow of the person talking, projected onto the wall in front of them. A hunched shadow danced on the wall in the fleeting light. Andrew tensed up as the voice approached, and it was an eerie one: high and wavering, as if it were floating on an icy wind.

"Race now, *race* through these dark corridors just as fast as you can! Find the door, for I know it's here! The door, the door, the door, the door! Find the door, the door to the new place, the new world, I know it's here! Somewhere in the dark…" And the rustle of tiny ol' legs through the dark brought chills down Andrew's back.

"Hurry, no time to lose. Go now, through the dark, find the door. Speed to all of you!" Suddenly the voice rose in pitch. "And don't let me catch you crawling around til you've found it! There's not a second to waste! I need the door! I need to know what's on the other side. Behind the door, there's something that won't let me *sleep!* Find the door, crawl through the dark to find the light! Now scram, all of you miserable creatures, don't come back til you have the answer!" The rustle of tiny legs once again filled the chamber.

"*Spiders,*" whispered Andrew. "Don't make a sound."
But his racing heart was too loud to quiet. The boys huddled

together as the tiny black beasts approached. Andrew felt the sweat on Nick's face, pressed against his shoulder.

"Somebody'll come, don't worry," he whispered to Nick. The terror was rising now; Andrew had begun to tremble and shake in fear. *Some good I'm doing him*, thought Andrew. *I can't help from shaking too.*

In his head Nick heard his mother's words: *They say everyone eats eights spiders in a lifetime, Nick.* She hadn't meant to scare him; she had just tried to comfort him one night when Nick had woken screaming with a spider in his mouth. The screams had come out gargled, as if his mouth was full of taters. But these weren't taters; taters didn't *wriggle* and *squirm* when you ate them. After a moment Nick had coughed up the beast, which lay twisted and mangled on the floor, dragging its crippled mass away to safety. He'd never done well with spiders since-- the feeling of wriggling taters in his mouth was simply too much to bear.

"Nick," Andrew said beside him. "Nick, grab my hand." They joined hands, a huddling mass of fright, awaiting the dark terror in the sewers. The spiders came round the corner, and they came in droves. They drowned the fleeting light on the walls and ceiling, bringing utter darkness to the boys.

"Don't let go!" screamed Andrew. He didn't think holding hands would do much, but his instinct told him to do it. Something about it felt right, too; in some weird way he felt safe with Nick's hands in his. He closed his eyes.

"We're going to be all right," he said, as the spiders swarmed by. Beside him, Nick was saying it in unison with him. A sea of green-silver eyes peered ahead at the tunnel, yet missed the boys entirely. In the dark the spiders lit up, with a similar fluorescent writing upon their bodies as the hipster writing on the walls of Sunsetville. The rustling of legs stopped as the black mass swarmed away from the children. Light gradually returned to the tunnel, and the boys stood up slowly. Nick cried out in joy.

"Ha-ha! Take that, and that, and that-" Nick stopped dead silent. The projection of the figure on the wall was no longer a projection. A long dark shadow stood before them.

VII

The figure waited silently at the end of the hallway. Nick walked beside Andrew, peering at the strange man-shadow.

"Who comes to the hall of spiders?" asked a powerful voice. Andrew felt the voice in his head, echoing around. Before he could answer Nick had stepped in front of him.

"You'll not lay a hand on Andrew!" the boy cried down the corridor. Nick held the fire poker in his hands, ready to strike out.

Nick, you fool, Andrew thought, reaching out for his friend. The shadow's laughter echoed through the hallway. It was a deep and powerful laugh. Nick cried out in pain and dropped the fire poker. It fell on the stone floor, and as Andrew watched it, it began to melt. Nick began to blow on his hands, red in the dim light from the melting fire poker.

"So quick to rise after your fall, boy?" came the voice again. Nick quit blowing and looked up. "How would you like to fall again?" Andrew heard something ugly in that voice. He'd heard the same ugliness the day before, as he fled through his mother's garden. The boy took a deep breath, his hand on the gun in his waistband, and stepped forward.

Stand tall, he thought.

"Who's this?" the voice asked. In the dark he was only a shadow, but Andrew thought he could hit him.

Andrew drew the gun, and the voice shut up. The tide had turned.

"Fuck you, old man," Andrew said, and fired. The gun jerked backwards in his hand—the boy nearly dropped it. The crash of thunder from the gun echoed in Andrew's head. The shadow cringed as the wall beside him exploded in plaster and dust. He'd missed.

Andrew didn't have time to think. He turned the cylinder, thumbed the trigger back and aimed. He looked up and the figure was right in front of him.

Andrew saw the grimace on St. Gerardo's face. He was short, squat, and ugly. He wore robes with a gold cross across his chest. He was balding, yet thick, black sweaty hair lay across the back of his head. A thick beard ran under his chin, an Abe Lincoln beard if Andrew had ever seen one. The rest of his face was bare, except for his twisted snarl and fat nose. Andrew saw the yellow eyes.

They're the color of dust, Andrew knew.

"Give me the gun, boy," St. Gerardo spat. His voice had lost its power. It was thin and hateful. St. Gerardo reached out and grabbed the barrel of the revolver. Andrew felt a bolt of electricity travel up his arm. He didn't let go, both hands on the handle of the gun.

"Shoot 'im!" he heard Nick cry behind him. He tried to pull back the hammer, and St. Gerardo cawed out. He began to shake the gun fervently back and forth. Andrew held on for dear life. Then a new voice filled his head and silenced his racing heart.

VIII

Come to me, gunslinger. There is safety in the Southern Woods.

Both Andrew and St. Gerardo quit struggling for the gun. The voice spoke again.

Come quickly. There is hope yet for this world. Make haste to the Southern Woods.

After a moment of silence, St. Gerardo made a move. He cried out and pulled away, retreating quickly. Andrew raised the gun to shoot him in the back, but the man was too fast. He retreated down the corridor into the shadows. In a moment he was gone. Andrew took a step forward after him. Nick cried out behind him:

"Sir! The crawlies!"

Andrew heard it now. The tiny rustle of legs approached. *Like tiny snapping*, Andrew thought with a shudder. They'd heard the crash of the gunshot. He turned and saw Nick beckoning him toward the side of the sewer. High on the wall was another manhole.

"Go!" Andrew exclaimed. "Grab the ladder!" Nick jumped up but missed it. He was too short. Andrew hurried over and grabbed the boy, giving him a boost up. Nick reached the ladder and pulled himself up, pressing all his weight against the plate above.

Andrew saw their green-silver eyes first. Thousands of silvery lights filled the darkness ahead, moving at a steady pace. The wave approached at a high speed. Light blinded Andrew as Nick popped open the cover and pulled himself into daylight. When Andrew looked up, he saw Nick's hand.

"Jump, Andrew! Grab hold!" Nick cried. Andrew jumped. He missed the ladder by a few inches, but grabbed Nick's hand. For a moment he felt Nick's weight drop and his arm sag, but

Nick's other arm reached down and grabbed beneath Andrew's outstretched arm. Nick would not let him go. With his free arm Andrew grabbed the last ladder rung and began to pull himself up as Nick heaved upwards with all his strength. Andrew flew out of the sewer and into the street, falling onto Nick in the process.

Andrew jumped to his feet. *"Where's the cover?"*

Nick was ahead of him. He slammed the cover down on top of the manhole and leapt backwards. Andrew heard soft thuds coming from the manhole, just tiny pangs of spider-bodies banging against the cover. One spider, however, had escaped the manhole and wandered dizzily around the dusty street. It was about the size of Andrew's fist. Nick yelled and stomped on the flailing creature.

"That's for Johnny!" the boy screamed. His words echoed around the square.

Johnny, Andrew thought, panting heavily. *Who's Johnny?* Then he remembered Tom Treeson's story. *The mob,* he thought, staring up at the clock tower above them. It was 1:55. *They're coming.*

"Nick," Andrew called to the boy, busy scraping the guts off his shoe onto the pavement. Nick looked up. "We can't stay here."

"Should we go to my aunt's?"

Andrew shook his head. "You can," he said, "but I can't. St. Gerardo's after me—you saw him! I've got to get out of town."

"To the Southern Woods?" Nick asked. Andrew looked sharply at him. Nick shrugged. "I heard the voice too, you know." Andrew nodded.

"I've got a colt," Nick continued. "Rode it 'ere. Trust her with my life."

"Take me to the stable," Andrew said. Nick nodded.

"All right. But Mr. Andrew?"

"Yeah?"

"I'm coming with you. To the Southwoods, I mean."

Andrew nodded. Nick led the way up the cobblestone street, and Andrew followed close behind, his left hand still trembling from the thunder of the gun.

chapter four
what lies beneath

I

Nick led the way to the stable. In the distance they heard yelling and heavy machinery. The time had come. Joe Freeman had brought war to Sunsetville.

The boys headed north into the city, up a tall winding street. They passed a street-side banker who cried out for them to stop and invest. Next came a few sleeping drunks, whose naps had lasted the entire day. The road did not seem as though it would end. When it did, they reached the top of Sunsetville. Andrew peered back and saw a great wooden tower creeping steadily toward the Clock Tower.

"That's just crazy," Andrew muttered.

"Here!" Nick cried. "The stable's in here."

Nick led him inside to a wide barn, filled with horses housed by stable walls. Sunlight streamed into the stable. Andrew decided this was the first rural thing he had seen in Sunsetville. Nick beckoned him over to the last horse in the barn. The horse was brown and young, but strong. It was a fine horse, with a thick chestnut mane. Nick began to untether it after he'd opened the gate.

"No time to lose," Andrew said. Nick nodded.

Andrew led Home Sweet Home out of the barn while Nick put a saddle on his back. Home Sweet Home warmed up to Andrew, and nuzzled the side of his face. Andrew jumped, and Nick laughed.

"I think he likes you!" Nick said. "I'm nearly as old as 'im, you know. We grew up together."

The boys led the horse out of the barn. To their left, a fat old man with a grey beard stood gawking at the side of the barn. There were the strange colorful markings on the wall.

"It's a crime!" the man cried. His arms were crossed over his thick chest. "As if they haven't got enough walls to draw on, now they mark up my stable!"

"I think it looks nice," Andrew said. He liked the hipster-writing. The man didn't even turn to look at the boy.

"Nice?!" the old man cried. He covered his eyes with one hand. "Nice, he says!" At last he turned to look at the boys. "Do you boys know what this says?" They shook their heads.

"It's hate speech," the man said, and narrowed his eyes at the boys. "The youngsters, they wrote it. The cross-dressing folk. Hate-speech, for the people of the desert. Of the east." Andrew raised his eyebrows.

"Oh," he said. Nick, sitting on the front of the horse, lent him a hand. Andrew climbed up and sat behind Nick. "You'd think the youngsters'd be a little more forward-thinking, but some things never change." The old man turned back to the wall. "When you get to to be my age, boys, you learn hate's a universal tongue. Don't matter how you dress it up, with colors or however you like it."

Andrew nodded. The two boys rode off.

II

By the time the boys reached the square, the wooden tower had arrived. The creaking and groaning of the gigantic wheels was deafening as the 'youngsters' inside rowed away. There were dozens of them inside, helping turn the wheels of the tower. Andrew thought it was all absurd. Joe Freeman sat at the top of the tower, wearing a pair of ridiculous orange goggles to match his fluorescent and flowing orange suit. Had the boys been closer they would have seen his skinny legs pedaling away on the stirrups he'd designed himself. Nick laughed at the sight.

Andrew hadn't wanted to stop, but they did anyway. The two boys sat on their horse by the walls of Sunsetville, not far from the foot of the Clock Tower. As the leaning wooden tower rolled by, Andrew heard the heaves and ho's from the young men and women inside, operating the great wheels. Up at the top, Joe Freeman shouted commands and encouragement to the people below.

Nick started. "Tom," he said. "Tom's in there!"

"Who?" Andrew asked.

"Tom Treeson!" Nick cried. "My friend!"

"Oh," Andrew said. He remembered now. *All* of Nick's friends were in there. As the tower came to a halt at the foot of the tower, Andrew groaned. Things were going to get ugly. Joe Freeman's caws pierced the air.

"*St. Gerardo!*" Joe screamed from the top of the wooden tower. "*Come out! Face justice, by my hand!*"

"*Stop this!*" came a new cry. It was so close to Andrew that he started and nearly fell of the horse. Beside him a plump young woman with red hair and a redder face had both her hands upraised to the sky.

"Is that the mayor's daughter?" Nick asked. Andrew shrugged. This was too ridiculous.

"*Stop this, Joe!*" she screamed.

"No" replied Joe, in a small voice.

She groaned and stomped her large legs on the ground. "*What are you doing? This isn't your job!*"

"Go away" was the next reply. The woman began to mutter.

"Why I ought to kill him! He's going to make a horrible mess! Who the flying hell does he-" she went silent. St. Gerardo stood atop the Clock Tower now, facing his audience.

III

"Did you need me?" St. Gerardo asked. No one said anything. The square was quiet. Then Gerardo continued, in a deep and powerful voice.

"Did you need something? From me?"

Joe at last spoke up, having prepared himself. "Yes! Yes we do. The game's up, you wizardly fuck!"

St. Gerardo threw his head back in laughter. To Andrew and Nick he was only a speck standing atop the great tower. Still, his voice carried. It was thin and hateful, as it had been when the old man had tried to take the gun from Andrew in the sewer.

"You have led your friends to an unfortunate end, Joe Freeman," St. Gerardo said. He stood at least twenty feet above the wooden tower, which was only tall enough to reach the clock face. Nick gasped, and jumped off his horse. The plump redheaded woman stepped in his way.

"Let me get through there!" Nick cried. "My friends are in there!"

"No way," said the woman. "No way you're going near that tower."

"It's time to pay, old man," Joe Freeman said. Andrew squinted and saw a butcher knife in the man's hand.

"For your bar?" St. Gerardo asked.

"Yes!" Joe replied.

"I suppose I should pay for that," Gerardo said, unable to hide his laughter. "All right! Come up here and make me pay."

"You better pay!" Joe returned.

"I said I would," the wizard returned.

"Well good," Joe replied. "You've got to pay—that's house rules."

"I see. And you're the house?"

"Yes," Joe said. He began to shout. "*Boys! Roll it forward! Heave!*" The wheels creaked into motion, and the wooden tower began to roll forward on the downhill slope to the Time-Table Clock Tower.

"You're the house," Gerardo said to himself, though his voice was still audible through the square. "*And the house is sin.*" His yellow eyes burned in the afternoon light. The wooden tower closed in.

"No!" Nick cried, and ran around the plump woman. She couldn't stop him. Andrew leapt off the horse and sprinted after his friend.

"*Consider this your penance, Joe!*" cried St. Gerardo. He threw both hands into the air, reaching for the hazy sky above. Nick stopped short, watching silently. Andrew nearly ran into him. Then the manhole beside them exploded.

If Andrew hadn't acted quickly, the spiders would have gotten Nick. He grabbed his friend and pulled him away, back toward the horse as the humming of a thousand subterranean beasts approached the surface. Around the square every manhole cover had popped into the air. The spiders emerged from the holes, free at last from the dark sewers. Andrew had thought there were a great many when he was in the sewers; now he saw there were *thousands* of them. They made their way to the wooden tower as it crashed against the clock tower.

"Come on Nick," Andrew said, breathing heavily. "We've got to go. We've got to go now." Nick didn't move. He watched paralyzed as the black mass enveloped the Joe Freeman's tower from all directions. The beasts flew through the cracks of the old wood and swarmed the inside of the tower. In a matter of seconds the base of the wooden tower was black. Andrew saw the fluorescent and colorful markings on the spider's bodies were invisible in the daylight; like the hipster graffiti, these only showed in the dark. Now the spiders were pure black, no longer hiding what lay beneath their colorful markings. Screams began to rise from inside the wooden tower. The image of the dozens of young people inside the tower, prey to the spiders, made Andrew's head spin.

"They're trapped!" the plump woman said. "Oh god, they're trapped!"

"Let's get out of here Nick!" Andrew said, directly into Nick's ear. Nick did not respond. He was watching Joe Freeman. The man in the orange suit had not said a word. At first he had looked down at the feast below him, but presently he burst into action. He took a running start and leapt for the Clock Tower.

He missed. Joe smashed into the side of the clock tower and bounced off an arch beneath the clock face. He landed on a ledge a few feet below, his body bruised and beaten. Andrew saw him try to move, but all he could do was twitch. Then Andrew saw the wizard.

Where did he come from, the boy wondered. In all the commotion, Andrew had quit watching him. Now St. Gerardo danced on the same ledge Joe Freeman lay mangled on. As Gerardo leapt over to Freeman, Andrew grabbed Nick once more.

"Nick," Andrew said. "Look at me!" It was no use. Nick was transfixed by the horror enveloping his friends. *He could've been in that tower with them,* Andrew knew. *Prey to the spiders.*

"Observe carefully, boy!" came the thin voice again. Andrew looked up and saw St. Gerardo, standing over Joe Freeman. "Took a real close look at what you've gotten yourself into!"

"*Nick, look at me.*" Andrew said. Nick blinked and met his gaze. The two boys stared at each for a moment, and Nick nodded.

"You'd be smart to *run away,*" Gerardo called, throwing his hands in the air like a circus clown. "Both of you boys! Before things get ugly." Andrew couldn't see his face, but he could picture the ugly grin Gerardo was wearing. "But leave your gun here. *Give it to me, it's mine.*"

"Let's go," Nick said. He made his way for the horse. Andrew followed.

"Where are you two going?" the plump woman asked.

"To safety," Andrew said, without turning. He mounted the horse, and sat behind Nick. "You'd be smart to leave town, lady."

"Maybe I will," the woman muttered. She saw the gun protruding from his shirt. "You've got a gun?"

Andrew nodded. The woman nodded nervously. "Kill him," she said. "I don't know who you are or where you're from, but when you get the chance you should kill him."

Andrew said nothing as Nick turned Home Sweet Home toward the gates of Sunsetville. Yet Gerardo wasn't done. He called again:

"Running's no use boys! You'll just end up like old Joe here!" The wizard gave Joe a hard kick to the abdomen, hard enough to send him off the ledge. His body fell into the black mass below, landing with a sickening *thud.* As the boys rode off, St. Gerardo's laughter filled the square.

IV

Nick said little as the two boys flew across the wide fields. The boy knew this land well, having grown up in the south. He led Home Sweet Home through miles of green, though the green was faded already, past its prime. Andrew asked Nick if his farm was nearby. Nick just shook his head.

"Further south," the boy yelled over the rushing wind. "Down by the kingdom of Brymino."

They rode for what seemed like an hour. Nick stopped after a while to give Home Sweet Home a rest. They camped in the shade of a small thicket of trees. As far as Andrew's eye could see, they were surrounded by plain. Andrew lay down beneath a tree, and took a deep breath. He could nap, he knew. Today had been long. Still, the afternoon sun burned in the sky; Andrew didn't think it was any later than three. Nick sat silently on a tree trunk, watching Home Sweet Home graze. Andrew was dozing off when he heard the sound of horse-hoof beats. He opened eyes to see a great purple carriage hurtle by them at breakneck speed. Suddenly, Nick ran after it, shouting and yelling.

"What are you doing?" Andrew asked, climbing to his feet. Nick didn't look back, as he hailed down the runaway carriage. At last the carriage began to make a wide-arc around the field, turning back toward them. Andrew caught up to Nick.

"Who is that?" Andrew asked.

"Magnet Salesmen," Nick answered. Andrew raised an

eyebrow, but Nick didn't see. At last Nick's face brightened, at least a little bit. The carriage slowed down as it approached the two boys. Driving it was a fat man, with a tall skinny man beside him. The fat man wore a purple suit and hat.

"G'afternoon, boys!" roared the fat purple one. He pulled hard on the reins, and the horses driving the cart stopped. "Fine day for a ride!"

Nick said nothing. He bowed slightly. Andrew followed suit. The fat man leapt out of his seat and landed awkwardly in the grass. He rolled forward and sprawled into the dirt. He jumped up to his feet and began to dust his suit off, which was now stained green. Andrew laughed out loud at the sight of it.

"Er... don't mind me boys... So!" The man straightened. "How can we help you today? Is it water you're looking for?" 'For' sounded like 'fahr'. "On this hot and dry afternoon, it'd do you boys nicely to have a drink. Or some juice instead?" the salesman leaned in as he said this.

"Do you have a compass?" Nick asked.

"A compass?" the fat man asked, raising one bushy eyebrow.

"Yes?" Nick returned, raising his own.

The fat man straightened and took off his hat, running his hair through the mess of black-grey hairs on his head. "Well, of all the things... of course we've got a compass! It's been acting strangely as of late though..." He turned to the tall skinny man. "Lucio! Have we got a compass in there?"

The tall skinny man began to rummage through the back of the carriage, which Andrew found to be more like a painted wagon. "Ev'ry compass we've got's been acting strangely these past few days, you see," the fat man informed the boys. "Don't know what it is. Strangest thing, right Lucio?" Lucio returned from the wagon and tossed a metallic object to the fat man, who caught it without looking at his partner. The fat man stared down at the compass and shook his head. "See? It's all backwards. Give it a look boy." He tossed it to Andrew.

Andrew looked at it. The compass pointed north. He looked up at the salesman. "What's so weird about it?" The fat salesman raised both eyebrows this time.

"What's so weird? What's so weird, he asks?" The fat man looked back to Lucio. "Did you hear it, Lucio?" Lucio said nothing. The fat man turned back to Andrew to Nick. "What's so weird? I'll tell you what! It points north. I've never seen something like it, not in all my years!"

"How does it usually point?" Andrew asked. Now Nick looked at him strangely.

"South," Nick said, as if this was common knowledge. Andrew shook his head. The fat salesman scratched his head again.

"Look boys," he said. He was sweating profusely in his purple-green suit. "I'm not here to debate which way's north, or which way's south, or which way a compass is s'posed to point. If you'll be wanting that, it'll be three in bronze. And if yer still wanting some juice, it'll be four!"

Nick reddened. "We don't have any money," he said. The fat man nearly jumped.

"No money! Why'd you stop us then?"

"Look!" Nick returned. "The compass is broken."

"We'd be doing you a favor," Andrew said.

"Why a favor? Boys with no money, and you can call it a favor? That's a nice compass, I tell ye! Good metal in that one, no matter which way it points!"

"Isn't there somethin' we can do for it?" Nick asked. The fat salesman took off his hat for the third team and scratched his head. Suddenly, he brightened.

"Sure there is. I could use some entertainment. I'll make ye a deal," he leaned in again, and this time Andrew and Nick leaned in too. "Tell ye what, here's what ye can do. If ye can knock the hat off my partner's head from where ye stand, it's yours. Use this piece here." The salesman dug in his pocket and flipped a silver coin to Andrew. Lucio had said nothing, but his eyes were wide now.

Andrew nodded. "Ye only get one try though, boys," the fat one said. "So don't-"

Andrew moved so quickly the fat salesman hardly saw him throw the piece. When he looked over to Lucio the man's hat was nowhere to be found. Lucio's long red hair stood on end, and his eyes were wider than ever. The fat salesman looked back at Andrew.

"Yer a weird one, ye know." The fat salesman began to walk back to the wagon. "Keep the compass. It's broken, anyhow. Lucio! Get your damn hat, and the silver too. We'll be going." The fat man leapt back up onto the seat while Lucio scrambled around in the grass. Without waiting for his partner the fat man whipped the horses, which began to trot forward. Lucio jumped and leapt onto the back of the carriage, his hat in his mouth. As the carriage flew away, Andrew could hear the fat man yelling at Lucio to get back on his seat.

The boy looked down at the compass in his hand. There appeared to be nothing wrong with it. He turned in all directions, yet the compass continued to point north. He looked up at Nick.

"Where I come from, compasses point north," he said. Nick shuffled his feet.

"That's kind of weird," Nick muttered.

"Why'd we want a compass, anyway?" Andrew asked.

"It'd be nice to know where we're going," Nick returned.

V

Nick warmed up after the affair with the Magnet Salesman. Andrew showed him how to find south when the compass pointed north, and Nick thought that was pretty cool. The two boys mounted Home Sweet Home.

"Now I know where we're going," Nick informed Andrew. They rode off, the sun still high in the sky. They crossed through an endless green plain, flat and serene. Eventually, the terrain changed; leaves and ferns littered the ground. Andrew spotted the gigantic forest ahead. They approached it at full speed, and the Southwoods rose to meet them.

Nick told Andrew that there were no paths through the forest as they drew near. They dismounted and led Home Sweet Home toward the line of trees that marked the entrance to Southwoods.

After about a quarter-mile in, Nick turned to Andrew.

"I ain't so sure about this, Andrew," Nick said.

"What's wrong?"

Nick shook his head. "It's just… as a kid, I heard stories about this forest. You ever hear stories, Andrew? Real scary ones, that your brother tells you to keep you up at night?"

Andrew nodded. He had no siblings, but he followed Nick's drift. His father had told him a scary story or two (much to the dismay of his mother) about ghouls in the River Warren. Plus his friends at school always told the same stories. They never really scared Andrew; they intrigued him. As a young boy he often wandered down to the River Warren, searching for his father's ghouls. He never found any. Nick and he continued into the deep forest, which hung over them in thick green.

"Well," Nick whispered, "my oldest brother, Jons, he told me these 'ere woods were haunted. He said an old sorcerer lives 'ere, one who hates when people look around his forest. Lots of kids get lost in these woods, my brother said, and he said anyone who does gets turned into a tree!" Andrew laughed. Nick shushed him. He continued after a moment's pause.

"The sorcerer does it to them, of course. He turns them into trees. That way the kids will be lost forever. And what's more," Nick lowered to a whisper again, "he says if you listen closely, you can hear the trees crying out for their parents."

Andrew offered Nick a smile. "Don't worry so much Nick," he said, though he wasn't so sure himself. "The only sorcerer we've got to worry about is far behind us, remember?"

They continued southward, following Nick's compass. After what felt like an hour of walking however, they found nothing. No sunlight streamed in through the canopy, and thick mists settled on the forest floor. Hunger and weariness welled up in the boys. They searched desperately for signs of humanity. Still they wandered south.

The mist grew thick and cool. Andrew could only see the outline of Nick and the horse he led beside him. To take his mind off the wandering, Andrew asked Nick to tell him a story.

"There's plenty to tell," thought Nick. "I do remember one about this place, I think my ma' told me. Once upon a time, before this forest had grown so large, there was a fair princess named Ellamina. She lived in the fine kingdom of Brymino, down south of these woods. Ellamina's parents wanted her to get married and all, but she wouldn't have it. She thought she was too young. Her da' wouldn't listen to her, so she snuck out of the kingdom one night."

"She snuck out of the kingdom?" Andrew asked, his eyebrows raised.

"Snuck right out," Nick replied.

"I see," Andrew said. "Do go on."

"She came north to this old forest. The forest was young and small back then, and in its center Ellamina found a bright grove. She stayed there and cried for a while. For a year or two, she cried, and then one day a deer found her.

"'Ellamina!' the deer cried. 'Ellamina, men of the north have learned of your beauty and have come to find you! They wish to bring you north and marry you!' But Ellamina would have none of it. So instead she sang, and her voice was so pretty that flowers bloomed around her. Everything in the forest stopped to listen to her, even the men from the north, you see. Her song went like this:

> I am but a maiden, young and fair
> But no cares that I am so scared
> Let me live forever, never to prime
> Let me marry never, never to prime."

Nick paused. Andrew opened his eyes. He had drifted off to Nick's gentle voice. As they climbed over a fallen tree, Nick continued.

"The forest heard her, and wanted to protect her. So suddenly, trees began to grow! Great tall oaks, Andrew, like the ones we see today. Like the one we just stepped over! The forest grew ten times, as you see, and heavenly mist from Ellamina's tears fell on the forest floor. The men from the north were so close to finding the grove. But now they were lost in the mist.

They wandered forever, but nev'r found Ellamina.

"And then the forest turned Ellamina into an evergreen tree in the center of the grove, the prettiest tree. It was a good tree, and it never lost its leaves. It lives forever there in the grove. My ma' says if you listen closely you can still hear the hunters calling out for Ellamina, and you can hear her song:

> I am a maiden, young and fair
> But no one cares that I am so scared.
> Let me live forever, never to prime
> Let me never marry, never to prime."

Nick's story ended, and Andrew looked up. Ahead there was sunlight streaming in from the trees. His eyes grew wide, as Nick cried out at the sight of it. Up ahead lay a forest path bathed in bright sunlight.

"The grove must be ahead," Andrew laughed, and ran toward the light. Nick cried out for joy and tried to catch up, the horse behind trotting at a steady pace.

VI

The boys reached the sunlit path. Andrew felt relieved; they had been in the dark for too long. Here he could see the blue sky above the canopy. He was hungry, but didn't stop to eat; there was no time for hunger here. Instead, he and Nick followed the sunny path that led steeply down the forest hill. Andrew tried to see ahead, but the mist obscured his view.

The path led downhill for what seemed like miles, but finally began to level. Andrew thought of the path he had followed yesterday in his own world after he had found the gun.

There was no strange figure to follow here, but he still felt as
though he was headed in the right direction.

They spotted the grove. It lay directly ahead, with trees
encircling a large patch of grass. Sunlight poured into it. Nick
stopped.

"Somethin' feels wrong, Andrew," Nick said. He shook his
head. "I dunno about this." Andrew drew his gun.

"Don't worry, Nick," he said. "I'm a gunfighter, remember?"
Yet Andrew worried as well.

Could this be one of St. Gerardo's traps? He wondered.

"Only one way to find out," Andrew muttered, and walked
into the grove. Nick followed, leading Home Sweet Home
behind him. As soon as they passed through the ring of trees, the
light became blinding.

"You've come a long way, Andrew Tollson, and proven
braver than I thought," said a deep voice ahead. *Sounds a lot like
St. Gerardo's voice,* Andrew thought, and thumbed the trigger
on his revolver. *Only five shots left.* And in the blinding light he
couldn't see a thing.

"This is a meeting of great fate, boy. I have watched you
closely since you entered this land. You must now answer one
question."

"Who are you?" Nick cried out, shielding his eyes from the
light.

"The gunfighter is said to be of legend, one who will restore
the order of light to this world. Is that what you have come to
do?"

"Yes!" Andrew cried. He stepped forward into the light.

"*So be it!*" the voice cried. "I am Warren, sage of the West,
servant of the winds! A beacon of light for those who live in the
darkness!"

Nick stepped beside Andrew. "Then come forward! Show us!"

The light dimmed, and both Andrew and Nick looked around. The grove was empty, save a few stones and a great white fir tree in the center.

"Where'd he go?" Nick asked.

"Up here," came a small voice. The boys looked up. Sitting on one of the branches of the fir tree was a young boy, bearing a long bamboo staff.

VII

"Hello," Andrew said. The boy nodded. He swung his feet to and fro as he watched Andrew and Nick.

"You're a kid?" Nick asked.

The boy said nothing. He was skinny, Andrew saw, and his hair was thick and pure blonde.

Very skinny, Andrew thought. *He's hardly a twig.*

"Are you Warren?" Andrew asked. "Did you say all of that before?"

"Yes," the boy answered. He didn't move.

"Well, come down here and we'll talk," Andrew said.

"I'm not leaving."

Andrew raised his eyebrows. "What?"

"I said I'm not leaving," the boy said. He stopped dangling his feet. "I'm not leaving this grove."

"Okay," Andrew said. He looked at Nick. Nick shook his head. Andrew looked back at the boy.

"We can just talk then," Andrew said. "Come on, Nick." They walked over to the stones that encircled the fit tree and sat down. Andrew looked up at the boy on the tree.

"What now?" Andrew asked.

"We tell our stories," the boy said, and finally began to descend the tree in one deft movement. "I'll go first."

THREE

Interlude

chapter five
warren the wise

I

"Will you sit?" Andrew asked.

"Yes," Warren said. He walked over to a tree stump beside the rock Andrew sat on. Once Warren sat down he looked up at Andrew and Nick.

"The world is drying up," he said.

"Is it?" Nick asked. He looked around for proof.

"Oh yes," Warren said, staring at the forest around him. "I'm afraid there's no hope for it. This land's cursed. There's no way around it, not for us."

"Are you sure?" Andrew asked. He ran his hand absentmindedly over his gun.

"Quite sure," Warren replied. "My brother's just the start of it."

"Your brother?" Nick asked. "Who's your brother?"

"You didn't know?" Warren asked. He crossed his legs. "Why, it's Gerard." Nick and Andrew looked at each other in confusion. "St. Gerardo, as you know him, I assume. That's what he calls himself now."

"He's your brother?" Nick cried. "Does that make you a wizard too?"

"No," Warren responded, and crossed his arms. Andrew thought he looked all tangled up. "We're not wizards. That term is silly."

"Then what are you?" Andrew asked.

"I wish the people wouldn't call us that," Warren continued. "We're sages, quite different from wizards." He looked at Andrew and Nick for reinforcement, but the boys stared blankly at him. "Sages are wise, boys. They know the land and how it works, as well as the creatures that dwell on it."

"So magic?" Nick asked, wide-eyed. Warren shook his head.

"No, although it looks like it. Just an aptitude for the elements. A sage is a friend to the natural."

Nick considered this. "St. Gerardo isn't much of a friend."

Warren sighed. "No, although he was once my friend. He's lost now."

"What happened?" Andrew asked.

"It doesn't matter much anymore," Warren responded. "He went east, to the deserts, and came back different. I'd been gone so long, across the ocean-"

"The western sea?" Nick cut in. Warren shook his head.

"No," Warren said. "The southern ocean, below Brymino. I was searching for the fountain of youth."

"Well, you found it?" Andrew declared.

"No," Warren said, shaking his head again. "I found nothing there. Nothing at all." Andrew and Nick said nothing. The grove was quiet for a moment.

"What happened next?" Nick asked. Warren blinked.

"I haven't been tellin' a story!" Warren said. "Just giving facts, Nickolas."

"I thought you were tellin' a story," Nick muttered.

"You should tell it," Andrew added.

Warren sighed again. He was full of sighs. "It began a few days ago, when I began to dream. All good stories are but a dream, you see…

II

*Rain splattered against the stone walls of the Clock Tower,
and within Warren heard the heavy splash of the downpour against
the clock face. Still he heard the ticking. Inside the tower he could
always hear the ticking. His old-man knees popped as he stood
up from his desk. He grabbed the staff, the one he'd found in the
bamboo thickets of his youth, and left Gerard's chambers.*

*He couldn't concentrate tonight. Certainly no maps were going
to be drawn this evening, Warren thought as he climbed the long
spiral stairs that led up the clock tower. Not after what he'd heard
this afternoon. The staff felt heavy in his hands and with each step,
each tick of the clock, he thought:*

*He'd returned to Sunsetville at the news of his father's death,
old Hirayln. The Old Sage, as the people of this land knew him
(although too many referred to him as a wizard, Warren thought),
had lived a great many years, yet his time had come. Gerard had
given him the news upon his return: a pack of bandits from the
east had raided Hiralyn's tower and murdered him. Gerard had
lamented how their father had always tried to civilize the men of the
desert, and how it had been his downfall. Gerard had always been
so critical of their father's efforts.*

*Gerard had changed too, Warren knew, since he'd been gone.
Not only had Warren left Romini to explore south, but Gerard had
gone off into the endless desert east of their father's tower. Why he
went Gerard never disclosed to anyone, but the trip had changed
him.*

*"Made him darker," Warren grumbled as he climbed the stairs.
In his old age this climb was difficult. Still his mind was awake,
and aching, urged by the ticking of the clock.*

*Warren had gone to visit Hiralyn's tower after Gerard told
him the news. The magical fortress of Warren's youth was empty*

and quiet. Yet it was not entirely empty; Warren felt the ugliness. Something unnatural lurked within the walls of the tower. He dared not enter it, for what had killed his father would likely kill him too. As Warren left his father's tower, he began to wonder about his brother.

Warren had reentered Sunsetville dressed as a beggar. He headed into the western quadrant, where the youngsters dwelled like idiot bohemians. The cross-dressing and extravagant colors always left Warren with a bad taste in his mouth, but he had needed answers. These youngsters knew all the gossip. He had gotten all the answers he needed: Gerard had been terrorizing Sunsetville, dresssed up as a saint who bestowed punishment upon sinners. And they had whispered about one dark secret, about something most unnatural that Gerard had come across.

Gerard certainly was different, *Warren thought as he reached the top of the stairs. The rain had stopped, he could hear. The clock had not stopped ticking. Gerard had always had a fascination with crawlies, Warren knew, ever since he was a boy. But now the beasts were all over the place. Warren had killed a few of them in Gerard's study, much to Gerard's fury.*

And there was the yellow walk-man, *Warren thought grimly. Warren had never seen anything like it. Gerard said he'd found in 'some ruins out east', which confirmed Warren's fear that Gerard had been crawling around dark places in the desert. The 'walk-man' was strange, and came with a band Gerard would wear over his head.*

"It speaks to me," *Gerard had told him, sitting on his bed in the clock tower study.* "Whispers wisdom into my ears."

It had spoken to Warren too, and said nice things. About salvation, Jesus Christ, and penance. This religion Warren knew; a few people down south followed it. Gerard had twisted it strangely, though—he heard that the world was ugly, and it bothered him. He told Warren he wanted "to fix it." The way he said it was wrong, though. Twisted, somehow.

"What have you done, Gerard?" Warren wondered as he approached the door to the roof of the clock tower. Outside he could hear the wind, but no rain. The rain had stopped. Still the clock ticked on. With the endless ticks echoing around his old head, Warren opened the door.

III

Gerard's back faced him. The wayward sage, as their father had once called him, wore a dark cloak over his purple robes. His hair was wet and matted against the back of his neck. He was short and squat, Warren saw, and that was the way it had always been. For a pair of brothers they were opposites. Warren had always been tall and gangly, even since his youth. Gerard and he had always been at odds.

"It's too wet, brother," Gerard called to him. His voice was flat in the wind. Warren watched his brother, who gazed over the town of Sunsetville from atop the roof of the clock tower.

"Is it?" Warren asked.

"Far too wet. This world is not suited to such relief."

Warren said nothing. Gerard did not turn.

"Things changed, you know. Since we lived in the desert."

"All that has changed is you, Gerard," Warren said, grasping his bamboo staff with both hands and stepping toward his brother.

"Not I, brother. I always knew I wasn't meant for this world. But now… this world isn't fit to continue on."

"Is that so?" Warren asked, his brow darkening in the rain.

"Quite so. The walk-man told me. 'When sin has taken

this world, the dead shall rise and take back what is theirs.' I'm paraphrasing, of course."

"Then it's true, Gerard?" Warren asked. He braced himself. Gerard said nothing. "Brother… what have you done?"

"They just don't rise…My minions," Gerard said. "Only when it's dry. The rain—it ruins everything, right brother?" Gerard turned at last, to face Warren. His eyes burned in the light cast by the youngster's graffiti.

Then came the fighting. Lightning rained down upon the town. Gerard had learned many dark things in the endless desert, and his wrath was terrible. Most of the bolts fell upon Sunsetville. Smoke began to rise from the fires. Warren saw all this as he struggled with his brother. He put his mind to stopping the fires, and that was when a bolt struck him. Red flashed over his eyes, as he fell to his knees. He coughed up something that tasted like blood. Gerard stood over him.

"Nothing but a child," Gerard snarled. "You and this whole world! Children, all of you!" Warren managed to look up through the pain into his brother's yellow eyes.

"Look," Warren said through gritted teeth. "See how it pours." Gerard looked about him. The rain had begun to fall again. It came in droves now. The fires down below were no match to this tempest. Gerard cried out, watching the town below him in the rain. Warren attempted to crawl forward, to reach his staff. Gerard turned to face him.

"I'll give you penance," Gerard said. He walked slowly over to Warren. "Worse penance than you know. To live as a child… that is a sin." Gerard touched Warren's staff, and Warren knew what he had done. The staff was useless now. The staff he'd carried for a hundred years was powerless. Gerard crossed to him and thrust his hand against Warren's forehead. Warren grew weak, and he leaned

against his brother's legs for support. Gerard laughed. Warren felt
his limbs and muscles tighten and grew numb, and groaned aloud.
Second childhood, then, had come at last.

"You're just like this world, brother. You'll dry up too." Then
everything was black, and Warren could no longer hear the clock
ticking.

IV

"What's all this got to do with a dream?" Nick asked.
Warren, whose eyes had been closed shut as he told the story,
snapped to attention.

"Everything's got to do with a dream, Nickolas," Warren
said. "We could be dreaming now, for all we know." Andrew
looked around.

"I'm not so sure that's true," Andrew said. Warren looked at
him. "I mean, I dreamed last night. But that was different. I'm
awake now."

"Are you, though?" Warren asked, narrowing his eyes.

"Yes," Andrew replied.

"Suit yourself," Warren said.

"If your staff is broken, why are you still carryin' it?" Nick
asked.

Warren reddened. "Well, I—I don't want to let it go, you
see. It's from my childhood, and-"

"How did you get here?" Andrew asked.

"I woke up here," Warren said. "Or perhaps I didn't wake—
perhaps I'm still dreaming. And you two are part of that dream."

"I don't think so," Andrew said. "I feel pretty real."

"I have had strange dreams as of late," Warren thought. "Is

it possible to dream while you're already dreaming?"

"I doubt it," Andrew said. "What are your dreams?"

"I'm in a great forest," Warren said, thinking deeply. "Not as deep as this one, but very large. There is a river too, but the river is nearly dry." Andrew sat straight up.

"The River Warren!" he said. Warren and Nick both shot him a look. "The River Warren… you're dreaming about my world."

"I thought so," Warren said. "For you were in my last dream, the one yesterday."

"I followed you!" Andrew cried. He thought of the cloaked figure in the forest. "You led me here!"

"I remember. And it was I who called for you to come here earlier today, when you were in the sewers with St. Gerardo. I dreamed then too, as I dream now."

"Was I in any of your dreams, Mr. Warren?" Nick asked. Warren thought a moment.

"Ah yes, yes you were, Nickolas. Two nights ago, I fancied you fell a long way from a tall height. As you approached the ground, I thought to myself: what if brought him to the dreamworld, the forest with the river?" Warren smiled. "So I simply blinked and thought of you there, and there you were." The boys were silent for a moment. Warren looked at the two of them from his tree-trunk.

"So you see, boys, it is true. You have been a part of my dreams all along. It all makes sense! Our lives are simply a dream." Warren announced this, and threw his hands wildly in the air as if he had figured it all out.

V

Andrew shifted uncomfortably on his rock. The entire time Warren had been talking Andrew had thought of his dad's roommate from college. Andrew had never met David Tollson's roommate, but his mom and dad (who met at Monmouth) would sometimes joke about Jake Renson. Jake was an English Major. David Tollson was an engineer. They did not see eye to eye. Andrew's dad said once that 'Jake was so convinced he was living in a dream that he saw no reason to wake up and go to class.'

Andrew, only nine at the time, asked his dad why Jake thought he lived in a dream-world. David Tollson laughed, and said he'd live in a dream world too if he never did any of his work. Andrew knew this meant that Jake spent a lot of time lying around doing nothing.

Maybe all Warren needs is something to do, he thought. *He spends a lot of time doing nothing.*

"Come with us," Andrew said. "We'll fight your brother. End the drought!"

"Don't be silly!" cried Warren. "I have no intention of leaving this grove. I told you this!"

"Why do you want to stay here?" asked Andrew. "There's nothing to do!"

"Here I am safe," Warren said. "I can live forever. The world dries up all around us, but I have found immortality here in this wood."

Andrew shook his head. Warren continued.

"I know what you'd have me do. You'd have me follow you north, to help your friends who were bitten by the spiders. The ones in the wooden tower. I saw all of it, you know. But North's no good. That way lies death.

"The compass used to point south, toward warmth, toward youth, toward dreams, toward immortality. But now it points north, toward death, toward the cold. What kind of world is this, that draws you north?"

Andrew said nothing. Nick cut in.

"Do you mean the folks in the wooden tower… are they eaten? By the crawlies?"

"No," Warren said, annoyed by Nick's interruption of his monologue. "No, they're not. Gerard's spiders bite and paralyze, and in some cases even put people into a deep sleep, but they do not kill. Your friends, Nick, are all laid up in Sunsetville. They don't wake, but they are not dead. *And there is a cure.*"

"What is it?" Andrew asked. Warren shifted uncomfortably again.

"It's a certain plant, the "*Crawlie Curaenus,*" Warren said.

"Is it like Spider Grass?" Andrew asked. He envisioned the weeds growing in his garden.

Warren shrugged. "Not many know of it. It grows deep within the forest of Eldenwood, in a grove similar to this one."

"Eldenwood to the north?" Nick asked.

"Yes," Warren said in a hushed voice. "To the north."

"Then what are we waitin' for?" Nick asked. He climbed off the rock, and Andrew followed. "Let's go!"

"You ought to be careful, Andrew Tollson," Warren warned. He did not move from his tree-stump. "My brother wants what you have. Your gun."

"I'll put a bullet in his head," Andrew returned. He and Warren locked eyes.

"Then it is murder you seek," Warren said.

"He'd do the same to us," Andrew returned.

"No surprise that you follow the compass north," Warren

said with a sigh. "For death is your path, boy."

"You'll die here too, you know," Andrew said. He had not moved. He put his hands into his pockets. "You won't live forever, even if your brother did this to you. Everything dies, don't you know? That's the way it is here. The clock is always ticking."

"Go." Warren closed his eyes. "Go, now. I'll hear no more. But know this—if you kill Gerard, any doors in this world will be shut against you. If you ever hope to return home, you should seek these doors—not close them!"

"What are you talking about?"

"Do not as, for I do not know. I just know that as long as Gerard and I are alive, the doors to this world remain open. The bond between us, and the gun you carry have opened them. If that bond should break…"

Andrew stared at the boy with the broken staff on the tree-stump for a few more seconds. Then he turned to Nick.

"Let's go," he said. "Come on." The two boys turned and left the way they came.

VI

"Do you think it's true?" Nick asked. Andrew stepped over a fallen tree and looked over at Nick.

"What's that?"

"That we're part of his dream?"

Andrew smiled. "That's stupid. We can't be."

"But he brought you 'ere! And he saved me from my fall…" Nick's voice trailed off. He looked back at Home Sweet Home, whom he led with one hand through the forest. In the other he followed the compass, leading the two boys north.

"Well, how did you fall?" Andrew asked. "You can tell me, you know."

Nick was quiet for a moment. Then he said, "St. Gerardo, Gerard...whatever you want to call him, he did it to me." I got up early yesterday and went to the town square. I saw some ravens sittin' on top of the clock tower, so I began to throw some stones at 'em. I didn't think I'd hit 'em, they were so far up there. But I did. The raven dropped fast, and hit the ground. It was real ugly, you see, and I didn't want to watch nummore. So I turned to run and there he was..."

"Gerard?" Andrew asked. Nick looked down at the ground and continued.

"He was real mad. About the bird. He grabbed my hand and asked me if I wanted to fall. I was real scared, and din't say anything at all. Then I was fallin', just like that." Nick snapped his fingers. "From real high. One second I was standin' on the ground, but the next I was fallin' from the clock tower. I was scared, you know?"

"But then you woke up in the grove?" Andrew asked. "My world?"

"That's right."

Andrew thought for a moment. Then he snapped his fingers. "If Warren is Gerard's brother, no wonder he could save you! They know the same tricks."

"What tricks?" Nick asked. Andrew shrugged.

"Gerard used a trick to make you fall, but Warren knew a trick to save you. They both probably learned it in wizard school or something."

"Yeah," Nick thought. "That sounds about right. How'd you ever get so smart, Andrew?"

"You have to be this smart to be a gunfighter, Nick," Andrew said. "It's just part of the rules, you know?" Nick nodded.

"We don't need him anyhow," Andrew went on. "That Warren is no help. He'd probably just complain the whole way."

"Yeah!" Nick added. "But what about them dead people?"

"What dead people?" Andrew asked. Up ahead he could see the end of the forest.

"The dead people Warren talked about," Nick said, lowering his voice. "The ones Gerard is raising."

"We'll have to keep our eyes peeled," Andrew said. "I've only got so many bullets left, you see. We can't be wasting them on every dead person we see."

"Okay, good." They reached the end of the trees and reemerged into daylight. It was late afternoon now; the sun threw shadows over the field ahead.

"What now?" Nick asked. Andrew looked down at the compass in the boy's hand.

"We go north."

FOUR

Magnetic North

chapter six
the villages by the sea

Another rode north through the forest that afternoon.
Saramina Bellsgrove whipped through the trees upon a grey
stallion, having left Brymino earlier that day. She knew the
Southwoods well, and led her horse upon paths littered by leaves
and branches. Had she not found the grove and discovered
Warren the Wise, she would have passed the two boys walking
north through the forest. Instead, she was interrupted as she
tode through the grove.

I

Home Sweet Home led the boys west toward the Villages
by the Sea, as Nick called them. Nick figured they could stop
at the villages for the night, and then head to Eldenwood
tomorrow. Andrew agreed that this was the best course. He
wanted to see the ocean, too. Nick described it to him:

"It's very big, you see," Nick told him as they rode through
fields of green and gold. "Everythin' west of the villages is sand,
and then blue water. The bluest you've ever seen. I went there
when I was real little, and it was somethin' nice. All that water,
blue as the sky."

They rode onward. After an hour of riding, the forest
behind them receded into the horizon and again they rode
through endless fields. The farms they passed through visibly
suffered from the drought. Fields normally in full bloom were

brown and yellow in their thirst. Crops reached toward the sky, begging God for water, before collapsing and rotting, never to see the harvest. Andrew finally saw what a drought could do.

"Gerard did this," he murmured. "All of this."

They rode on along some streams. The streams were low and wanting. Little vegetation grew along the side. Up ahead Nick spotted something.

"Looks like that backpack's walkin' itself!" he called to Andrew. Andrew looked up and saw a large pack ahead with two feet treading forward.

"That's no backpack, Nick!" Andrew called back. "That's a backpacker!"

They closed in on the fellow in a moment. As they did the traveler threw an arm up to wave them down. Nick slowed the horse to a trot and pulled alongside the man.

"Hello boys!" the backpacker called. "Little late to be out riding!" He had his hood pulled over his pale head to shade his eyes. He wore a multicolored tunic and sunk low to the ground. Andrew thought his backpack was about three times his size. The bag was covered with pots and pans and masks. Andrew thought he spotted a cross-necklace under one of the flaps of the bag.

"Sun's not down yet," Nick said. "We've got a little ways to go, anyhow."

"Are ye headed toward the sea villages?" the backpacker asked. Nick nodded. The backpacker let out a boisterous laugh. His teeth were rotting, Andrew saw. "I'm headed there myself!"

"How much farther?" Andrew asked.

"Shouldn't be too long til you smell the ocean," the backpacker said. He stared straight at Andrew.

"Nick," Andrew said. "Nick, let's go."

"Yep!" cried the backpacker. His eyes were bright yellow.

He reached out a hand, that Andrew thought was nearly a claw, and grabbed Andrew's leg. *"Just follow the salty smell, boys. But you can't run! Not for long!"*

"Nick!" Andrew cried, grabbing hold of his friend. The backpacker stepped beside the horse, but Nick was faster. He dug his feet hard into Home Sweet Home's sides, and the horse whinnied and started forward. Andrew swatted away the backpacker's other hand as he and Nick lurched forward. He felt the claw on his leg slip away, and he closed his eyes and prayed for it all to be over. He felt the wind rush against his face as Home Sweet Home sprinted forward, and did not open his eyes for a few seconds. He could hear his heart pounding in his ears. The sound mingled with the panicked sound of Home Sweet Home's horse hoof beats. When he did open his eyes, he saw Nick in front of him, leaning over Home Sweet Home's neck, whispering words into the horse's ear. The world flew by them. Andrew turned his head.

Behind them the field was empty.

II

"Is he followin'?" Nick asked. His breath was heavy.

"He's gone!" Andrew said. "There's no one there!"

Nick slowed Home Sweet Home down to a trot and turned to Andrew.

"What was that?" he asked. His eyes were wide. "I didn't see much... but I *heard* him."

"That had to be Gerard," Andrew said. "His eyes..." he shivered. "It's too much. I should have shot him." Andrew cursed. "I could've done it right there! And now he knows where we're headed!"

Nick nodded. "Yes, but we'll get there faster. We've got a horse, you see. It's another two hours to the village I think, but on foot it could take him all night!"

Andrew exhaled. His heart was still racing. "Okay." Still, he slid his hand along his gun. *Should I have been faster?* he wondered. In his mind he could imagine the flash of the gun, the report of the fifth bullet, those yellow eyes widening as they faced their doom… he had been so close.

"Let's go," Nick said. He looked around. "I don't like this place. Andrew?"

"Yeah, Nick?"

"Can we… can we forget what just 'appened? I don't like to think on it."

Andrew shrugged. "Sure. Let's get going then."

They set off again, headed due west. The sun began drop in the sky as they pressed onward through the fields and rolling plains. Gerard couldn't dry up the ocean, and soon the boys could smell the sea breeze, gently lifting their spirits. Seagulls soared on the wind above them, guiding Home Sweet Home toward the water ahead. The boys rounded a large ridge and suddenly they descended upon a great cliff overlooking the Western Sea. The tide broke down below upon beaches of dark red sand. Andrew loved the sight of the ocean; it reminded him of his family's day-trips to Point Pleasant. The boys turned northward as the sun prepared for its final descent below the horizon. Nick and Andrew approached the Villages by the Sea.

The sun over the ocean cast golden streaks of fire on the wooden buildings ahead. The cliff rose before Andrew and Nick steeply, finally rounding off evenly where the village was built. The city sat upon a plateau. As Andrew and Nick climbed the steep road, Andrew saw all of Romini laid out before him. Far off east he spotted the grand walls of Sunsetville. Behind that the land dried and became sand—Andrew figured this was the eastern desert. To the north he spotted great patches of green.

"Eldenwood," he murmured. "Hey Nick, what are those mountains beyond the forest up there?"

"Kirondacks, I think," came Nick's reply. "They're big." Andrew had figured as much.

"If I remember right," Nick continued, "there's a whole series of villages 'ere. Maybe five or six of 'em".

The villages stretched northward toward the cliffs. As they passed into the first village, Andrew took in a deep breath and smiled. The air was dry, but salty. The boys and their horse trotted past an old library to their right, and Andrew figured he ought to look for maps there to lead them to Eldenwood.

"That's where my uncle sometimes rides out to when he's workin'," Nick said, pointing out the post office next to the library. "Let's hope he doesn't come out now. I'd be in loads of trouble, for sure."

Andrew dismounted and turned to Nick. "I'll be right back Nick," he said and stepped toward the library. "Watch the horse, and… that." Andrew motioned toward his pack, slung over Home Sweet Home's pack. Nick knew well enough what was in that bag.

"With my life!" Nick called to Andrew. Andrew nodded, and headed inside the library.

III

Nick didn't like Andrew being gone. He couldn't get the voice of Gerard out of his head. *Just follow the salty smell boys!*

Just the thought of it made Nick shiver. He remembered all too well Andrew's panicked yells for him to get moving as the backpacker had closed in on them. Being separated from Andrew now, on this strange rocky street, made Nick uneasy.

People rushed about him in the dark. Many had their cloaks pulled up to protect themselves from the salty wind that blew in from the sea.

I wish I could see their faces, Nick thought. *Any one of them could be Gerard!* He saw one tall skinny fellow gliding through the dusty street, and tensed up. Nick didn't take his eyes off the specter until the man had turned off onto one of the side streets.

"I'm scarin' myself, s'all," Nick muttered. "The old saint's miles away, he can't get 'ere." In mentioning Gerard's name Nick looked around wildly. The street was quiet. He got up and took Home Sweet Home to an outdoor market across the street to buy some feed. Still, he felt the hair on his hands and arms standing on end.

Andrew emerged after that, carrying a large scroll in his hand. "I've got it!" he called to Nick. "A map of Romini! Let's check it out." Nick followed him over to the edge of the cliff that overlooked the water and sat down. Home Sweet Home stood silently behind the two boys as they admired the map.

"The librarian inside was real nice," Andrew said, unrolling the map. "He told me all about the map. Romini is just like a compass, he said—there's something for each direction."

"Well I coulda told you that, Andrew!" cried Nick. Andrew looked up at him. "Well, maybe. I forget my directions somedays. But my pa' told me the only compass I need is the one in my head, so that's about all I need."

Andrew looked down at the map. "See here, there's something for each direction. South you have the Kingdom of

Brymino." He pointed to the drawing of the great castles below Southwoods on the map.

"That's where I'm from! Or at least to close to it," Nick said. Then Nick pointed out a section not far northwest of Brymino. "See those farms? Smithire! That's where I'm from, Andrew!"

Andrew nodded. "And out to the east, that's the desert. Where Warren and Gerard are from." At the mention of their names both boys looked up. The street around them was empty, illuminated in the pale moonlight.

Nick showed him the great mountains to the north, and then the House of Dundain to the west, directly north of the Eldenwoods.

"That's where we're headed," Andrew said. "The Eldenwoods. I figure we can just follow this map when we head over there tomorrow. What do you say?" Nick nodded. Andrew looked down at the map and saw in the center the great walled city. "Then it's over to Sunsetville, to heal all the spider bites." Andrew smiled. "We'll be the healers, Nick. Everyone will be all right, thanks to us."

"I hope so," Nick said. He was looking out on the water. "And then what?"

"Then, we kill him. Gerard. We'll put a bullet in between his eyes!"

The two boys looked up at the ocean. They were quiet for a moment.

"Nick?" Andrew said.

"Yeah?"

"The water's greenish-grey."

"What?"

"The ocean," Andrew said. "It's not blue. You said it was blue."

"That's true," Nick said. In the dark the water was violet,

but Nick had seen it when the sun was up. Andrew was right; it had been a murky color. "I guess things change when you get older. Not like outside things. Inside things. The way you see the world. It looked so dreamy when I was a kid... but now it's lookin' pretty real."

"That's all right," Andrew said. "It's kind of pretty that way. It's like that in New Jersey too. The ocean, I mean." The two boys were quiet for a long time.

IV

Nick didn't want to eat at the Pub of Mirrors, an ancient wooden building in the third village. Andrew had convinced him it would be all right: the tavern was full of people, he insisted. The boys wouldn't stick out at all. Besides, there were plenty of inns in the different villages; how would anyone looking for them know which tavern they were in?

Nick relented, and tied his horse to a post outside the inn. As he made his way for the door, Andrew stopped, thinking it might be smart to bring his gun inside. He was thinking of a scene from the end of *Unforigven* when Clint Eastwood shot up a bar full of armed men who had killed his friend, played by Morgan Freeman. Andrew wanted his gun in his belt in case there was any danger like that. He tucked the gun into his waistband and draped his shirt over it.

The inn was as Andrew had imagined it, loud and hectic. Yet mirrors of all shapes and sizes hung from the ceiling, reflecting the conversations and exchanges of the bar. One large antique piece with a gold frame hung above Andrew and Nick's table. When the waiter came, a skinny man with dark hair tied back and sharp blue eyes, Andrew ordered black ale with his Slip Fish. There was no drinking age in the villages, so Andrew figured he would give it a try. At first the waiter couldn't hear him over the singing of the sailors at the bar, who chanted dirty limericks. At last the order was communicated.

"Haven't seen your faces before," the waiter said. "New in town?" He leaned in, revealing fair skin. His blue eyes focused in on Andrew.

"That's no business of yours!" Nick cried out. The waiter straightened and bowed his head.

"Sorry about it," the waiter said, though he hadn't taken his eyes off Andrew. "Your food will be out in no time, no time at all." Then he turned and strode into the kitchen. Andrew gave Nick a look.

"What was that for?" Andrew asked.

"We've got to keep quiet 'round 'ere," Nick said, and put a finger to his lips. "People talk in a town like this. They run their mouths, that's what my da says."

Andrew looked over and saw the waiter by the door of the kitchen. Blue eyes burned as they met Andrew's green. The waiter turned quickly and headed into the kitchen.

"I suppose you're right," Andrew said. Another waiter stopped by the table and delivered the boys' drinks.

V

Saramina stepped into the kitchen and cursed silently under her breath. She caught one waiter on the way out and asked him to bring the boys their drinks. The fellow nodded, too busy to realize that Saramina didn't work there. Her disguise had worked flawlessly thus far; she played the part of the man well. She always did.

Yet the curly-headed one was on to her. She had let it slip at the table with her question. *Stupid,* she thought. There was no doubt these were the two boys Warren told her about. She had ridden hard toward the sea and seen the two of them outside the first village, overlooking the ocean. It was clear which boy carried the gun; it was the green-eyed boy, the one she'd locked eyes with. She knew that glare well.

"Play the role," she muttered under the breath. "Just play it well, don't let them figure you out." The boys had unnerved her. Andrew, his name was Andrew, according to Warren. She couldn't remember the name of the other boy. It wasn't him she had to worry about anyway.

She reemerged into the inn and looked around in disgust. This entire village made her feel vile. *So weak,* she thought, looking around at the scores of men and women around her. *The city on a plateau. Democracy. What a sham.*

She had been to the villages before, but today it all seemed wrong. This was what was wrong with the world. No greatness. Everyone the same. Here on the plateau, Saramina knew, there was no great ambition. No great castles, princes, or kings to look up to.

"Or princesses," Saramina muttered to herself as she looked over to the boys' table, using the mirrors this time. She felt for the long knives beneath her white pants, both blades pressing against her long bare legs. The royal steel felt cold against her thighs. It wouldn't be long now; as soon as the boys left the tavern she'd surprise them. Then the green-eyed boy would have to hand over the gun. But for now, she would keep her eyes on them. She looked up and jumped as she saw the deformed man sitting down at the boys' table.

VI

For Andrew, it all happened so fast.

Nick and he had been so lazy, blind to everything but their drinks. The ale was hard to swallow at first; it was thick and sour. Soon it went down smooth. Nick, who was drinking a lighter ale, came to the same conclusion. The commotion and noise around Andrew blended in with the kick of his drink, and the world became a blur. Andrew finally put down his empty glass, and found himself face to face with the ugliest man he'd ever seen.

The man gazed intently at Andrew, and offered him a twisted smile. The teeth were missing, with lips cut and chapped. Scars and burns made a map of the man's weathered face. The skin peeled and flaked, especially atop his bald head. His eyes were a bloodshot hazel.

"Don't mind if I take a seat, do ya boys?" Andrew said nothing. The man was already sitting. He leaned in close over the table, and Andrew smelled his breath. It was rank. It was the smell of a man who had spent far too long at sea.

Nick's left hand reached slowly for his butter knife. The old man saw it. A man like this didn't miss much. "Watch that hand, boy," he said, though his eyes never left Andrew. "Be a shame for you to lose yer right hand, yes it would." Nick dropped his left hand to his side, but with it he brought the knife. The old man knew it. Andrew dropped his hand to his gun. There was no doubt in his mind this man was dangerous; there was something fundamentally wrong with him.

The old man showed his teeth, or lack thereof, in a sneer. "Name's Stricker, boys." Then his eyes flashed. At last he looked at Nick, and Andrew saw the man's hand drop. The boy looked up at the mirror above. It gave a perfect view of the old man's back. Andrew saw what the old man had on his belt, what he was reaching for. Andrew drew his gun a split second before Stricker pulled out a long knife, the kind Andrew thought of as a bowie knife. It shimmered in the dim light. Someone screamed at the table next to them, but no one took notice. The waiter with the blue eyes began to step forward.

Andrew saw all of this. Still he focused in on Stricker's right hand, which held the handle of the knife. As the old man raised the weapon above his head he cried:

"*Teach ye to respect yer elders, boy!*" Stricker lifted the knife high above his head and rose from his chair. Nick fell backwards from his chair in fear, clenching his butter knife with a shaking fist. Andrew's gun thundered and Stricker's right hand disappeared, gone in a flash of blood. The bowie knife dropped onto the floor with a clang as everything above Stricker's right wrist disintegrated.

Stricker brought down his arm to smite the boy, and his blood splattered onto Nick's cloak. Nick stifled a scream, struggling to sit up. Then Stricker screamed as he saw his stub of a hand. He held up his wrist in front of his face, watching the blood fountain from where his hand once was.

Amidst his screams of terror others began to scream, but no one moved. Andrew tucked his gun into his waistband and ran behind Nick. He grabbed under Nick's arms and hoisted him up, away from the bleeding monster.

"Come on!" Andrew cried. "Let's go!" Nick and he ran for the door. Stricker, meanwhile, stumbled backward and fell over another table, collapsing in a puddle of his own blood. At the bar, no one moved nor noticed the strange waiter who moved swiftly out the back door.

"Hell!" cried a man with wily orange hair and a thick grey beard. "That were a gun in that boy's hand, Jenkins!"

The bartender looked over to him. "There ain't no such things as guns, fool," he said. "You had one too many drinks, that's all!"

"It ain't true! I've only had four, I swear it!"

"I know it!" exclaimed the bartender, pouring the man another beer.

Stricker climbed to his feet. His eyes bulged from his head. He let out another screech, and ran for the front door. He ripped through and emerged into the warm salty night air. He saw to his left the two boys leading their horse off into the darkness. He turned to follow, he stopped when he felt a sharp sting in his upper back. He froze, the pain running deep. Then he turned, stifling a scream, searching the darkness behind him. Another arrow flew, burying itself into his abdomen. Stricker bent forward. Blood spilled out of his open mouth. Stricker dropped to his knees as the world became a blur. He looked up. A woman clad in a waiter's outfit stood before him, holding a bow. Stricker tried to scream again, but only a gurgle of blood escaped. He vomited into the grass.

The woman loaded another arrow. She began to hear voices, however. One voice she knew all too well.

"He's here," Saramina muttered. "Gerard." She knew why, as well. The boys. The gun. She cursed and ran past Stricker toward the boys. Stricker knelt on the grass, wondering how he could have ever confused that woman to be a man.

VII

Andrew and Nick ran through the dark village, leading Home Sweet Home. Stricker was right on their heels, Andrew knew. The loss of a limb wouldn't stop that man. Nick led the horse into a dark alley, and turned to Andrew.

"Are you hearin' that voice?" he asked. Andrew shook his head. Then he heard it. It was a whisper.

"*The dead do rise,*" it said. The whisper echoed through his head. Andrew knew that voice all too well. Nick did too. His eyes grew wide.

"Gerard," Nick said. Andrew nodded.

"We've got to leave the village," Andrew said. "Now."

Nick was way ahead of him. The boy mounted the horse in a clumsy struggle and offered his hand to Andrew. Andrew climbed up behind Nick, who dug his feet hard into Home Sweet Home's sides. The horse whinnied, and reared up. He was not ready for the excitement.

"Hold on!" Nick screamed as the horse kicked forward and rushed through the night. The beast whisked the boys uncontrollably through the village streets.

"To the right!" Andrew screamed. "To the right!" Nick leaned over to the right, and the horse began to turn. They ran straight into the bodies as they turned.

Home Sweet Home stopped short and reared again. This time Andrew fell from the horse, and onto the dirt. Nick landed on top of him. The boys' heads bumped, and they both rolled over in pain. When Andrew looked up he saw something that was not human.

"*The dead do rise... they walk,*" came the whisper again. Four sets of dead eyes peered at Andrew in the dark as the figures approached the two boys.

VIII

Andrew sat up. The figures lumbered toward him, closing in. They were quicker than Andrew expected. As they emerged into the light, Andrew saw their weathered skin, dried and brown like raisins. Andrew couldn't tell whether they were men or women. They were too withered and dry. The two in front towered over Andrew and Nick. Behind him Andrew could hear Home Sweet Home whinnying and running around in circles.

Andrew sat up and tried to crawl backward, but the creature above him was too fast. It swooped down upon him, reaching out with long grey arms. As it drew close, Andrew saw it's twisted mouth open to reveal sharp teeth, and knew that this zombie longed for blood. He thought he could hear Gerard's laughter in the darkness as he drew his gun.

Four bullets left, Andrew thought, batting the wrinkled arm away from him. *One for each of them.* The one reaching for Nick was nearly upon the boy, who was dazed from his collision with Andrew. Andrew thumbed back the trigger. Then the zombie behind him recoiled sharply, falling back into the darkness. It stumbled and fell flat on its back. Andrew looked at the twitching monstrosity in surprise, then remembered Nick. He turned and saw the zombie above Nick fall back as well. A green arrow protruded from the creature's head.

"What in the—" Nick cried. He tried to get up again. Andrew turned and saw the other two dead figures closing in. He managed to stand and raise his gun. He did not hear the approaching horse-hoof beats behind him, but he did feel the horse and its lady rush past him, close enough to knock him over. The horse glided between the two creatures. Both shadows fell to the ground. Andrew rushed forward.

"Who are you?" he called. As he drew beside the pair

of fallen zombies, he saw a long hunting knife stuck in each creature's torso. Andrew took one close look at the monstrosities. They were like the old folks in the rest home he'd visited once, where he visited his grandmother. The same wrinkled skin that had made Andrew feel sick at the Yamington Rest Home covered the reanimated dead. Andrew felt thankful the dead fellows were wearing pants, even if they were tattered.

"No time, boys!" came a call from the darkness. The horse reemerged in front of him. Andrew saw the rider. It was their waiter from the restaurant! His hair was no longer tied back—it flew wildly over his forehead and neck.

"What's he doing 'ere?" asked Nick, who had finally managed to stand up. Their waiter paid no attention, but rode by the two boys. With one deft movement he pulled his two hunting knives from the fallen corpses (who twitched and gargled strange noises). As the horse passed Andrew, the boy took another look in his blue eyes.

"You're a girl," Andrew said a wonder. The lady on the horse said nothing, but dismounted and hurried over to Home Sweet Home, who ran in circles around the thicket of grass they'd stopped in. She reached out and grabbed the horse, drawing herself close to the wild colt and whispering softly in its ear. Beside Andrew the woman's horse neighed softly.

Home Sweet Home stopped her whimpering, and rubbed against the lady's forearm. She led the colt over to Nick and Andrew, and mounted her own horse.

"Hurry," she said. Andrew spotted a rich green bow upon her back. "There isn't much time. There may be more of them."

"Who are you?" Nick asked.

"Follow me," she said. She turned her mare directly east, and kicked off into the night. Nick turned to Andrew. Before

Nick could ask, Andrew put a hand upon Home Sweet Home's side.

"There's no time, Nick!" Andrew said, climbing up the horse's side. "Come on!" Nick nodded, muttering to himself, and mounted once Andrew was safely atop the horse. He gave Home Sweet Home a pat, and the horse began to trot. After a second they picked up the pace, following the strange lady into the night.

the door opens

I

Home Sweet Home carried the two boys away from the Villages by the Sea down a steep grassy slope. Sitting at the bottom of the hill in the dim moonlight, they spotted the lady and her horse. She did not turn to see them. She let out a "whoop!" and her horse set off, away from the boys.

"Speed up, Nick!" Andrew called.

"Yeah, let's catch up," Nick said, and he pressed his boots against Home Sweet Home's sides. The boys flew down the hill and came upon the horse ahead of them. They nearly pulled ahead of her, but her mare was fast. She led the way east, toward the dawn.

They rode this way for nearly an hour. The lady never turned around to see if the boys followed. Andrew could see the side of her face, as the wind blew her long dark hair back. In the moonlight she was breathtaking. Andrew thought she looked a little like his mother had in the pictures of his parents' wedding. Blue eyes, sharp and determined, peered through the darkness as she leaned out over her horse. She was young too; Andrew guessed maybe twenty years old, though he couldn't be sure. He didn't know many girls, anyhow. This girl, however, was the most beautiful girl he had ever seen. Her mouth was moving— she was singing. Andrew watched silently. He caught a few of her words, carried on the wind that blew his brown-blonde hair back from his eyes:

Take me to the light
And open my eyes
Take me to the light
For I have ridden long to-night

The lady and her horse changed course after an hour
of riding, turning northeast. Nick followed the turn with
occasional glances at his compass. Soon they were headed
directly north. Andrew could no longer smell the sea.

"How far are we from Sunsetville?" Andrew shouted to
Nick over the wind.

"Beats me," Nick called back. "It's a little while that way!"
He pointed over to his right, to the east. Andrew nodded. His
eyes began to grow heavy as they rode north through the fields.
He had been awake for hours, and spent more time on a horse
than most spend in a lifetime. He thought back to the sewers
earlier that day, when he'd faced Gerard. The thought jolted him
awake. He turned his head to look behind him, and saw a single
horseman far behind them. In the darkness he couldn't make out
who it was.

"There's someone behind us!" he cried. Nick nodded.

"I think she knows," he called back. Andrew nodded, but
let his hand slip down to the butt of his gun. He still didn't have
an idea who this beautiful lady was either. He wasn't ready to
trust her.

After a few minutes, the lady slowed her horse down. Nick
caught on and pulled beside her as she led her mare toward a
small patch of trees ahead. It wasn't the Eldenwoods, Andrew
knew. It was far too small. He turned to the lady.

"Who's that behind us?" he called. She continued to stare
forward, leading the horse into the trees.

"He'll catch up," she said.

When the rider did catch up, Andrew, Nick, and the lady had already dismounted. The lady took her bow off of her back and stored it on her saddle. Andrew figured she knew the rider. Still, he kept his hand on his gun. Nick stood beside him, watching the rider approach.

The horse was tall and dark, and the rider matched the look. He was a young fellow, with thick, dark hair that was tossed back by the wind. He had a scrub beard to cover his small mouth. Sharp cobalt eyes, darker than the lady's blue, peered at the three of him. He wore a beaten jacket and what appeared to be jeans. Andrew guessed him to be no older than the lady.

"Hullo," he remarked. "Fancy seeing you here, Saramina."

"Did you follow us?" she returned. Andrew noticed she had not taken her knives off her waist. They crisscrossed neatly over her thighs.

"Not at all," he returned, dismounting. His eyes widened. He had the biggest eyes Andrew had ever seen. "It's... good to see you again, Saramina. It's... been too long."

Saramina looked away, and Andrew thought she blushed. The rider looked over to the boys. "And who are these strapping young gentlemen?"

"There's no time for introductions!" The lady called back. "If Gerard spotted you, we're not safe here, Luke. Were you spotted?"

Luke raised his eyebrows. "No, don't think so. I haven't seen anyone for miles, Sara. Nobody except you." He narrowed his eyes again on Sara, who stepped in front of him.

"How did you find us?" she asked again. She was close enough to kiss him, or kill him.

Luke scratched his head and grinned. "Just spotted you guys riding!" Sara didn't back off. "Look, I'll explain myself! But can we sit down? I've been out all day!"

Sara turned and walked away toward her bag. Luke gave the two boys a small smile.

"I'll take that as a yes, Saramina!"

II

Saramina sat quietly on top of her pack as the boys began to munch on some dry meat. Hunger had begun to well up in Andrew since they left the tavern without their meals, and he could ignore it no longer. Luke sat quietly, staring at the ground. Neither boy paid any mind to his companions' silence. After a few minutes of this, Luke spoke up:

"Boys, I ought to introduce myself. I'm Lukemir, from the Northfleet."

"Northfleet?" Nick asked, his mouth full. "Up by the Sarna ranges?" Luke shook his head.

"A little bit east of those ranges. The Northfleet spreads all over the Kirondack range." Nick nodded, though he hadn't paid much mind to the geography lesson. "And this is Saramina Bellsgrove, boys. She's the princess of Brymino." Saramina said nothing.

"Thank you for savin' us!" Nick said, through his chewing. "Those dead things were scary."

"Dead things?" Luke asked, looking up at Saramina. She didn't look back.

"Zombies!" Andrew cried, food spewing out of his mouth. Luke raised an eyebrow.

"The dead," Sara said. "Gerard raised the dead in the villages by the sea."

"I see," Luke said. He looked down at the ground and was silent for a moment. "It is a sad fate that awaits our world."

"No way!" Andrew cried. "I'm gonna shoot him in the face! Gerard, you'll see!" Then his eyes widened, and he covered his mouth.

"So you're the boy with the gun," Luke said. Saramina looked up.

"How did you know?" she asked Luke. Her eyes narrowed. "How did you find us?"

"A dove told me," Luke said. "One of Warren's doves." Saramina sighed and looked away again. "I left Dundain this afternoon when I heard what happened in Sunsetville, but Warren's dove caught me first. Warren wrote this to me," Luke pulled a wrinkled piece of paper from his jacket pocket.

"What's it say?" Nick asked.

"Says Saramina here would be coming through the Villages by the Sea, chasing after two boys— one with a gun."

"How did Warren know you were following us?" Andrew asked Saramina.

"I ran into him this afternoon," she said. "Headed toward Sunsetville through the Eldenwood, I found the grove." She looked away again. "What I found there was just sad."

Nick nodded. "I know! Can you believe he's a kid now?"

"He put that in the letter too," Luke added.

"He's become a helpless child," Saramina said. "There's nothing to him now. Just his little grove and his useless staff." She sighed. She had not spoken this much the entire night. "I ought to start with this afternoon. I heard word that Joe Freeman, from Sunsetville, was planning on killing St. Gerardo."

"It's true," Andrew said. "We saw it all happen today." Saramina's eyes flashed.

"Did he do it?" she asked. "Did Freeman kill Gerard?" Luke chimed in.

"No," Luke said. "We were told by Rosalind—Mayor's Suneri's daughter—that Freeman is dead, and all the people in his tower were bitten by Gerard's spiders." Saramina sat back.

"You ran into the mayor's daughter?" Nick asked. "Why, she was 'ere with us when it all happened! The crawlies, that is."

"Yes," Luke said. "She crossed the Fords of Dundain before five with the news. I was about to cross the fords when I ran into her."

"Do you live in the Dundain?" Nick asked, his eyes shining.

"No!" Luke laughed. "I don't really have a home, boys. But look, I'll get to my story in a minute. Sara, you were saying you found Warren on your way to Sunsetville."

"Yes," Saramina said. "And I gave him a piece of my mind too. He kept scolding me for chasing after St. Gerardo, said 'death was my path' and that vengeance wasn't mine to decide."

"He said the same thing to us!" Andrew said. "He tried to convince us this was all just a dream."

"It made me sick," Saramina spat. "Real pathetic, to see him spewing out that sentimental crap. So I told him what I thought." She lowered her voice. "I told him I was going to kill his brother."

"Sara…" Luke said. Saramina spoke right over him.

"I told Warren he was a fool to sit in that grove, and grope for immortality. I told him to look at the tree stump he sat on. Told him that was proof enough that everything dies."

No one said anything. In the distance, Andrew heard a deep ringing. The bells rang twelve times.

"We're not too far from Sunsetville, yeah?" Nick asked

Luke. Luke nodded. It was midnight.

"Well, Warren didn't say much after that," Sara said. "He just sat there. Eventually he told me about you two boys, and said I'd be better off keeping you two out of trouble than chasing after his brother. So that's what I did, and it's a good thing I did." She crossed her arms. Andrew saw she was staring at the gun in his pants, and wondered if keeping him and Nick out of trouble was Saramina's only reason in following them.

"What happened to your brother?" Andrew asked. She looked from his gun to his eyes. That's when Andrew knew.

She is a gunfighter too, he knew. *She just doesn't have a gun. And she wants mine.*

"He died of the dry cough," she said. "Made him real sick, real fast."

"Tuberculosis?" Andrew asked. In his mind flashed a picture of Doc Holliday from *Tombstone,* coughing up blood into a handkerchief. Saramina didn't answer.

"I was sorry to hear that," Luke said. "I was just on my way home when I heard, two months ago—"

"I remember," Saramina snapped. "Didn't bother showing up for the wake either, did you?"

Luke said nothing, just hung his head and ran his boot against the dirt. Andrew thought he looked like a little kid. The camp was silent again. Andrew caught Saramina looking at his gun again. She noticed this time. Blue and green eyes met, and locked in on one another.

"Well Luke," Saramina said, without taking her eyes off Andrew's. "Why don't you tell us what you were doing in the Dundain in the first place?"

"All right," Luke said, and looked up at last. Andrew broke away from Saramina's eyes and looked over to Luke. "Last night,

I was headed down from Ilglesas. You know, just north of the mountains. As we passed through the Sarna ranges, I caught a glance of something strange atop the peak—a bright, blinding light."

"Which mountain?" Nick asked. "Sarna Dias?"

"No," Luke said. "Sarna Mensis. It was a light from the top of Sarna Mensis."

III

He knew the mountain well. He had been living off the land since he was thirteen. Luke remembered well the day he'd left the belligerence of the Northfleet behind, only thirteen years old. He had seen so much since then; Romini had become his home. Yet he had done so little.

The boys were captivated by his story. Kids loved the romantic and melancholic, Luke knew, and he was both. Yet the boy on the right, with the green eyes, watched cautiously. It was the same look Saramina gave him. *He's much older than his years,* Luke knew at once. *His eyes give away everything.*

"I made my way up a path I'd discovered two years ago, along the side of Sarna Rauros, over the falls. Sarna Rauros and Sarna Mensis connect at Rauros' peak by a long, narrow ridge." Luke held his arm up and laid it straight across. "The path is so narrow that only one person can cross it at a time. Fortunately, it was just me crossing yesterday evening."

"Was it hard to see in the dark?" Nick asked.

"It would have been, if not for the moonlight and the light radiating on top of the mountain," Luke said.

"I see," Nick said in wonder.

"I reached the top of Sarna Mensis soon after," Luke said. "And what I found there I did not expect to find." He had been crazy to climb the peak at night, he knew; he'd always heard stories that the top of the mountain was haunted.

"There's no such thing as ghosts," Saramina interrupted. "Quit trying to scare the kids, Luke. When you die, you die."

Luke shook his head. "Don't be so sure. On top of this mountain, the restless dead wander."

"Kind of like the zombies, Sara," Andrew said. Saramina raised her eyebrows.

"Sort of," Luke said. "Only these are ghosts from the stories I've heard. And they linger there, forever."

"So what was the light?" Nick asked. "Ghosts didn't faze him much tonight, considering his encounter with the zombies."

"I climbed up to the top of the mountain, which is a sort of plateau, I guess. A very small plateau on top of it all. There the light was blinding, and I had to shield my eyes from the glare." Luke put a hand in front of his eyes, and in his head he saw it all so visibly. The light had been so bright, so blinding. Yet there was something in the center of the light, some beacon that he couldn't quite make out... He had crept forward, shielding his eyes, ready to reach that beacon and wed his melancholy forever to this object of wonder. Seven slow years of wandering seemed like a passing moment in time as he crept closer into the light.

"What was it?" Nick whispered. The two boys were leaned in toward Luke. Even Saramina locked her eyes on Luke. Luke looked up at the stars and took in a deep breath.

"It was a door," he said. "A door stood alone atop Sarna Mensis."

IV

Andrew lay on the cold ground, stretched on a hide Saramina had brought in her bag. Nick lay a few feet away, apparently asleep. Saramina slept on the edge of the camp, curled up among the blankets. Her long legs protruded from the bottom of her hides. Andrew thought she looked peaceful, but knew better.

A girl like that doesn't sleep peacefully, he knew. He kept his eye on her for a moment longer, not sure what to think. Then he saw Luke, sitting on a rock in the center of the camp. He was keeping watch. Andrew pulled himself off the ground, and wrapped the hide around him. The night air was chilly and dry. Above them the stars shone clearly.

"It's going to be a clear day tomorrow," Luke said, without looking up. He moved a short knife over a piece of wood, something he called 'whittling.' He was making a door, Andrew saw. Luke at last looked up at the boy.

"They say those who sleep often are lonely," Luke said. He glanced back down at the wood in his hands and smiled. "And those who can't sleep wish they were."

"That doesn't make any sense," Andrew said. Luke looked up at him.

"You'll understand once you've seen the world. It is a lonely place, you see." Andrew shrugged. He didn't get Luke. Andrew thought leaving home and seeing the world was exciting; he didn't get what was so damn sad about it.

"We'll be leaving for the Eldenwoods tomorrow morning," Luke said. "If Warren's right, we'll find the berries there to help the people in Sunsetville."

"Plants," Andrew said. "It's plants we're looking for, in some grove there." Luke nodded.

"I'm not sure which grove he's talking about, but there's a great many I know in that woods. We'll figure it out, I suppose. Who knows? We may even run into Ryundain the Proud, while we're there."

"Who's that?" Andrew asked. "You and Sara mentioned his name earlier."

"He's a lord of the House of Dundain," Luke said. "Heir to his father's throne, you see. He's a stout fellow—let's just say he makes Sara look modest."

"I see," Andrew said, without much of a clue as to what that meant.

"I'm not even sure Sara will want to come with us," Luke said. "She has no interest in helping the victims of the spiders. She just—" He cut off, and looked down at his hands again.

"She just wants to kill St. Gerardo," Andrew finished for him. Luke nodded. "I don't blame her. If she doesn't, I will." Luke looked up at him.

"Don't be sure," Luke said. "That's murder, Andrew. I'm not sure a kid your age can really understand what that means. In fact, I think you'd be better off heading to the door."

"The one on top of the mountain?" Andrew asked. Luke nodded. "I don't think so. It might not even lead home, and if it did I wouldn't go. I like it here. Here I can do what I want." Luke sighed.

"You should get some sleep kid," he said, and Andrew saw that same sad look come over his face. "Tomorrow's a big day."

"Yeah, whatever," Andrew said, and got up. He lay down. Before he shut his eyes, he thought he saw two blue eyes peering at him from the other side of the camp. Saramina shut her eyes after a moment, and the boy wondered what those blue eyes were searching for.

V

The boy awoke to blue eyes less than a foot away from his face.

"Where is it?" Saramina hissed. Behind her the dawn sky brightened to a royal blue.

"What are you talking about?" Andrew asked. He knew exactly what she was talking about.

"Where is it?" she hissed again. "Your gun! Give it to me, quickly."

"No," Andrew said. He hadn't moved.

"What's going on?" Andrew heard Luke behind him. "It's so damn early—is it time to leave already?"

"Stay out of this," Saramina said. She didn't look away from Andrew. "I've searched everywhere, kid—your bag, the ground, everywhere around this grove. It's got to be on you, or under your little bed!"

Andrew stared calmly into her eyes. "It's not," he said. "You're not going to find it."

"Get up." Andrew got up slowly. Saramina tore apart his makeshift bed, throwing the blanket and hide around the camp. Andrew saw his bag and all its contents spilled out into the dirt.

"Sara, you were supposed to be on the watch—what's all this about?" Luke asked.

Saramina finished ransacking Andrew's stuff, and turned to the boy. Her eyes blazed. Andrew knew she hadn't slept a wink, not during Luke's watch or her own.

"*Where is it?*" she hissed. She stepped in front of the boy. Andrew didn't back down.

"Sara, look at yourself!" Luke cried from the other end of camp.

"Stay out of this!" she cawed. She looked over at Luke at

last. "This is a man's job I'm doing—no place for a boy like you."

Nick suddenly sprang from under his blankets. "Get away from Andrew!" he cried. He took a step toward her, but Saramina put her hand on one of the hunting knives below her belt. Nick froze.

Saramina turned back to Andrew. Her dark hair fell wildly over her eyes. She bent down to Andrew's level, so their faces were nearly touching. Andrew felt the tickle of her hair against his ear.

"Tell me where it is," she said. "I'll finish the work. Just give it to me." Andrew said nothing. They stared at each other for a moment longer.

"Oh!" Saramina cried. She broke away, straightening as she walked backward. "So you *have* hidden it. I see!" A wide smile broke out on her face. Her blue eyes welled up. "Some good you'll do with it. Some good it'll do for us when Gerard takes it from you!" She stooped down and picked up her bag. Behind her, her horse was already saddled.

"Sara, don't go—" Luke said.

"You *boys* have fun with your plants and your doors." She turned and leapt on her horse in one fierce movement. "I'll go do the real work you're all too scared to do." As she turned the horse she caught Luke's eye. "Coward," she spat. "That's all you are! Pacifist coward!" She dug her heels into her mare's side, which sprang forward into the clear dawn air. The lady and her horse raced off into the morning, headed north. The camp was silent as she left.

VI

"She's just having an off day," Luke said as he began to untether the horses.

"I dunno," Nick said. "She seemed pretty angry to me."

"No, no, women are just like that," Luke said. "They just have days like this, you see."

"Wait!" Nick cried. "Andrew, where's your gun?"

"Check your hide."

Nick walked over to his makeshift bed, and lifted up the hide. He looked up in the wonder.

"'ere it is!" he cried. Andrew flashed him a smile as he began to clean up the mess by his bag. "How did you ever get it 'ere?"

"While you were sleeping last night," Andrew said, "I snuck under your bed. For safe-keeping."

Nick's smile stretched from ear to ear. "Well, that was sure smart of you! I'm real glad it worked." He picked up the gun by the handle and ran over to Andrew. "Take it! I don't like holding it much."

Andrew took it and tucked it into his bag. Luke walked over to the boys and spotted something in the grass. "Looks like Sara forgot something," he said, as he picked up a thick hunting knife. Nick recognized it immediately.

"That's Stricker's!" he cried. "That's his knife!"

"I'd nearly forgotten about him," Andrew muttered.

"She must have picked it up when you blew it off 'is hand!" Nick exclaimed. "Like pow!" He mimicked the gunshot with his forefinger and thumb.

"Perhaps you should hang onto this, Nick," Luke said. "Just in case. I have no use for it." He handed the knife over to Nick. The boy's eyes widened as he held the knife in his hand.

"I've nowhere to put it!" Nick said. Luke showed him a convenient place to store it on his saddle.

"Are we heading out?" Andrew asked as he slung his bag over his shoulder.

"Not yet," Luke said. Behind him, to the east, the sky was a blinding blue-yellow. "You boys go back to sleep. We'll have all day to ride. And Andrew," he said, as Nick turned back to his makeshift bed. "I'm sorry. About Sara."

"Don't be," Andrew said. "It wasn't your fault, it was hers." Luke nodded, though Andrew knew he didn't agree.

"Sure," Luke said. "She'll be back. I'm sure she will." Andrew didn't think that was true either, but didn't say anything. Luke stood looking out at the north, as the light from the sun illuminated the fields before him.

chapter eight
lovers meet

I

Andrew woke to breakfast. He moved uncomfortably in his makeshift bed. Above him Luke held out his hand. In it were half a dozen berries, each colored differently.

"Choose carefully," Luke said. "The multicolored ones are poisonous."

Andrew grabbed two pink berries and looked up at Luke, who smiled and nodded. As he ate the berries he felt a sharp rush of sugar on his tongue. His eyes welled up, and Luke laughed.

"There's a lot of energy to be found in those!" he called as he packed up his bed.

"Do you 'ave any meat?" Nick asked. "I'm starved."

"No meat," Luke said. "I don't hunt animals."

"Well," Nick responded, "just 'ow are you not hungry all day?"

"This," Luke said, and showed him a few mushrooms on the ground. "Cheese too, if I can buy it. Would you like one?" Nick wrinkled his nose.

"Mushrooms are the worst," he said. Luke raised his eyebrows. "It's like eating spiders, Luke."

Andrew and Nick chowed down on some dry meat while Luke cleaned up camp. Luke had found a spring nearby, and filled up two canteens with fresh water. Andrew drank a little, though Luke warned him not to indulge himself.

"We'll need it for today," Luke said. "It's not quite dry where we'll ride today, but with the drought you never know if you will find any other springs." Andrew nodded, and took only a few sips.

They set off after breakfast. Three riders on two horses headed due north, over majestic open fields. The sky was clear and bright, and the few trees they saw that day swayed in a dark green haze with the breeze. Andrew thought the sky looked taller than ever before. The sun was bright and hot, but the breeze made it bearable. Luckily, they found several springs along the way. They stopped at one spring in the early afternoon that sat between two grand hills of boulders.

"I ought to tell you boys about myself," Luke said, as he bent down and began to fill the canteens. "I'm the son of a farming family up north, in one of the Northfleet villages." He stood up and tightened the cap around the canteen. "I had four brothers, but lost all of them one day. They fought in the Third War, you see."

"The Northfleet's always at war with itself," Nick said to Andrew. Andrew nodded, and turned back to Luke. The boys sat in the shade beneath a tall rocky ridge.

"That's right, Nickolas," Luke said. Nick grinned to hear his full name. "My brothers were all older than I was, you see. Another year and I would have been there with them, likely would have died as well." He looked to the north again longingly, as if he wished this were true. "It was a terrible mess, that day. I remember the captain who rode up to our old house—it was real cold, you see, and he was bundled up to deliver the terrible news.

"Most of the young men in the village died that day.

It was a mistake, putting them all in the same regiment like that. Whole villages could disappear at a time that way. I walked through my own, and heard a young woman—recently widowed, I'm sure—sing a song before a dying willow behind the general store. I still the remember the song, I hear it in my dreams sometimes."

Much to the boys' surprise, Luke began to sing. His voice was light and lovely, and it floated over the spring water and into the clear air:

"The last of my friends have climbed over the horizon
Leaving me cold and alone
Tomorrow may come but the sun won't be rising
When home is no longer home

First went Tom, son of Frank,
Never in life did he draw a blank
Next went Andrew, the musician friend
Playing his fiddle to the bitter end
Kind and wise was my old friend Lenny,
His green eyes were dimes in a sea of pennies
Followed by Joe, the cool and the blue
In the end not even he stayed true
Next went Sean, by the break of dawn
The morning seems so bleak now that he's gone
Last left Seth, and by his hand
I had first learned to love this land

The last of my friends have climbed over the horizon,
And now I stand as the last
Thought tomorrow the sun won't be rising,
I won't be stuck in the past

Come tomorrow let me rise
Seek the road with grey-green eyes
And I too will climb over the horizon
To find a place where the sun will be rising."

The boys were silent as he finished. Andrew thought it sounded like something out of the Civil War documentaries he'd watched in history class. Luke turned back to them.

"I knew I could never fight again," he said. "I was trained, sure; since I could walk I'd been given a sword. But it was no use to me. I brought one with me as I ran away of course, but I knew I would never use it." he motioned to his saddle. A thick sword hung in a blue-gray sheath on the horse's side.

"You ran away?" Nick asked. Luke nodded.

"I made my way south," he said. "I wandered these lands for a few years, but found it all the same. More fighting, more hate. There was one I met," he said. "Warren of the Winds. He became a good friend of mine, and we wandered together for a little while. He was headed south, you see, and suggested I follow him. He told me there was a rich kingdom down there, where my destiny might be," Luke paused, "easier to find." He walked over to his horse, and hopped on.

"We should be headed north," he said. "We're losing daylight. Come on!" He turned his horse and began to trot off from the spring. Nick and Andrew hurried after the wanderer.

II

The man who approached the company of the west looked nothing like a woman. Saramina had been practicing cross-dressing her entire life. Though she had met Ryundain several times, he was entirely fooled by the disguise. She'd tracked the company throughout the day, listening to the ground for the sounds of their horse-hoof beats. When she caught up to them in the late afternoon, she wasn't surprised to find they were headed in the opposite direction: due south.

She informed them she had come from the Villages by The Sea, and this caught their interest. Ryundain informed the strange young man that their company was headed toward the Villages, to investigate strange tidings they were hearing. He wondered if this young man (Robin was the name Saramina used) had seen anything odd in the villages. As soon as Ryundain asked this, Saramina knew she had her chance to reel him in.

"There was a man with a gun there," she said. "Shot a thief. The village is running wild about it."

"Why, that's exactly what we've come down to investigate," Ryundain said. "Although a scout told our court that it was a boy with the gun, not a man."

"This man looks like a boy," Saramina returned. She had her dark hair tied back, and wore loose fitting clothing. "He is Lukemir of the Northfleet." Ryundain raised his eyebrows, and though he didn't say it, Saramina saw recognition. She continued.

"Lukemir left the village with two young companions this morning," she said. "I know where they are headed." Ryun leaned in, and his eyes blazed.

"Can you take me there, Robin?"

Saramina smiled. This was too easy. "Oh yes," she said. "Yes, I can."

Saramina set off with them, but the company did not stick around long. After a few minutes of riding, one of the men pulled alongside Ryundain's horse and asked to speak with him. They halted, much to Saramina's dismay; she wanted to reach the Eldenwoods before nightfall. Otherwise Luke and the boys might slip into the woods, and make the search much more difficult.

Frederick, one of the lords under Ryundain's command, spoke feverishly with Ryundain while the company rested. They made no attempt to conceal their conversation, and Saramina heard every word:

"You're breaking the laws of our people—of your father!"

"You need not remind me of my father's laws," Ryundain responded. He straightened. "We are still investigating the incident, only the incident has changed. The gun has moved, you see—"

"Our orders," Frederick returned, "were to head to the Sea and investigate there. Not follow some non-westerner stranger into the woods!"

"Then you'd let the gun slip away so easily?"

"I would," Frederick returned. He was a head shorter than Ryundain, but his red hair matched his temper. "The gun's not all we're looking for. I will not let this stranger lead The company of the West into who knows what. And if you would, then you break every law we hold dear, by the honor of the House of Dundain."

"I am lord and master of this company," Ryundain said slowly. "You'd do well to remember that." Frederick stormed away, and the company turned to follow. Ryundain watched in surprise as his men rode off, to the north. He and Saramina stood quietly in the shade of a tall chestnut tree.

"Fools!" Ryundain called after them. "You are servants! I am your lord! Your master!" He watched them go, shaking a large fist at them. Saramina had to bite her tongue. Soon this man would be her servant, once she held the gun.

He turned to her. "How far are we?" he asked. Saramina paused before she answered, taking him in. He was a large man, towering over her with a brown-bearded magnificence. Poets had written epics about this man, she knew. She was not afraid of him, but she knew how to play the part.

"Just an hour or so," she said, letting her voice tremble. "We'll be there before nightfall, if we make haste."

"Let's go,'" Ryundain said. He hopped onto his horse. She looked up at him.

"Are you sure you still want to go?" she asked. She knew exactly what the answer was.

"Yes. Quit wasting my time, let's be off." She bowed and nodded, turning toward her horse. Ryundain could not see the smile on the Sara's face as he mounted his horse.

III

Luke and the boys reached the woods as the sun began to dip into the horizon. The warm air turned crisp and cool as they dismounted. Luke led the two horses toward the edge of the trees, and they walked ways through the edge of forest. Andrew thought this forest looked somewhat ordinary. Luke put it differently:

"These woods are very old," he said. "When we find an opening, we'll camp there."

"We won't look for the plants tonight?" Andrew asked, following Luke.

"Oh no," Luke said. "There is darkness in these woods. Dark things sleep in the forest, and we'd do well not to wake them."

Nick, who had a sullen and tired look on his face, looked up.

"What kind of strange things?" he whispered.

"Not many know," Luke answered. "But I think you ought to get some sleep tonight. You look ill. At least in your sleep you will find peace."

Something had occurred to Andrew during their ride that afternoon. It was just an idea that hit him while they rode, and now he couldn't shake it. He hurried his pace so he walked beside Luke.

"So Luke," he said, not sure how to begin. "When you went south, what happened?"

"Lots of things" was Luke's reply. Luke didn't look over at Andrew.

Andrew figured he'd just ask. "Did you," he started, "and Sara…" he trailed off, not sure how to say it. "Did you guys… were you in love?"

Luke said nothing for a moment. Then he smiled for what seemed like the first time in a long time. He looked over at Andrew.

"You're a sharp kid," he said. "I suppose I ought to tell you another story." Andrew nodded. Luke looked back. "This grove up here will be a suitable place, I think. Let's set up camp." He began to tether the horses to a tree as the boys entered an opening in the woods.

IV

"If we had a car," Andrew said, "we would have been here in two hours. Tops."

"What's a car?" Nick asked. He stared sullenly into the fire.

Andrew sat down next to the boy.

"It's like a horse," Andrew said, "but not really. It's got four wheels, and runs like a machine."

"Like a clock?" Nick asked. Andrew nodded.

"Exactly, like a clock."

"So it moves on its own?" Nick asked. "Nobody needs to move it?" Andrew shook his head.

"Maybe it's not like a clock," Andrew said. "But a car is ten times faster than the fastest horse." Luke finished setting up his bed, and walked over to the fire pit they had dug.

"I think it'll be a long time before this world catches up to yours," he said as tossed a few sticks into the fire. Smoke burst upward as the sticks exploded. Nick jumped and let out a little yell. Andrew looked at him, and marveled at the dark rings under his friend's eyes.

"You all right?" he asked.

"Oh yeah," Nick said. "Don' go worrying about me."

"I promised you boys another story," Luke said, as he sat down on a stone across from where Andrew sat.

"Does it begin where your last one left off?" Andrew asked.

"Sort of," Luke said. He absentmindedly ran a hand through his dark hair, wind-tossed from the day's ride. "It took me a little while to actually take up Warren's suggestion. To go south, I mean."

"Why?" Andrew asked.

Luke shrugged. "I was waiting for the wind to turn," he said. Andrew raised an eyebrow, but didn't say anything. "It did though, about two months ago. It had been a dry winter, but when March came, it was so warm…" He closed his eyes and took a deep breath. He inhaled a mouthful of smoke and nearly coughed. Nick stood up.

"I'm headed to bed," he said. "Beggin' your pardon. I need some sleep."

"All right," Luke said. "Go right ahead." Nick went right to his makeshift bed on the forest floor and lay down. Luke turned back to Andrew.

"I went south. It was a few days' ride—I had to ride around the Southwoods. I don't know the trail through, like Sara does. I was excited though—going to a new kingdom meant a new start. I made my way down there with some friends too—a few other wanderers I'd met along the way. They're still in Brymino, you see. They didn't leave.

"We all took on new names. Said we were lords of the Northfleet, rich and young. I never thought it would work, but it did—the royal family in Brymino was very kind. They took us to the castle," Luke said. He closed his eyes again and looked up at the canopy. "It was the most magnificent thing you ever saw. The turrets and the towers were so tall, it was hard to believe!" Luke opened his eyes. "You wanted to climb each one, all the way to the top, see what you could find."

"Saramina?" Andrew whispered. Luke shook his head.

"No," he said. "She came later. I never did climb those towers. But someday." He spread his hands out in front of him.

"I went out on a hunting expedition the next day, with the prince and his men. All the royals of Brymino rode out with us. There was one," Luke smiled, "Robin, was his name. I knew he was a woman the moment I met him. The others were fooled, but her disguise didn't fool me for a second."

"Saramina!" Andrew cried.

"Yes," Luke said. "It was she. She was the finest hunter among them—that first day I saw her kill a doe a hundred yards out with her bow. It was on the run too. One of the men had scared it, but she stood tall and dropped it." Luke smiled. "There's something enchanting about a woman like that, Andrew. You're too young to understand."

Until a few months ago Andrew hadn't even liked girls. He nodded now. He thought he saw what made her so alluring.

"After the hunt was over, I followed her. She rode out to an old way station a few miles outside of the kingdom, and waited for me there. I dismounted, and walked around to the entrance of the cabin..."

V

He was sharp, but she was sharper. As he opened the door she stepped out from behind under the stoop and pressed a long hunting knife against the back of his head.

"Who are you?" she asked. She still wore the hunting clothes, though her hair was no longer tied back. Luke didn't turn to see her.

"Someone who's not who they seem," Luke said. "Someone like you." He turned slowly to face her. She didn't drop her knife. "Who are you?"

She stared at him for a moment. Clear blue eyes looked him over. They were sharp, but they were a woman's eyes; that was how Luke had known.

She sheathed her knife. "You're not a lord, are you?" Luke shook his head.

She turned away and began to walk through the field behind the cabin. The grass was long and thick, and she strode confidently through its long grasp. Luke followed her as she took the bow off of her back.

"What are you—" Luke asked.

"Showing you what it means to be a man." She leveled her

bow at a tree in the forest. Luke guessed it to be a hundred-fifty feet away. She let go of the arrow in the bow, and the twang *was all Luke heard as the arrow buried itself into the tree. As he approached the lady he saw a target painted on the tree. The arrow had landed on the innermost rung.*

She turned to him. He didn't say anything, but took the bow from her hands.

"Give me an arrow," he said. Her hands were long and soft. Her eyes never left his until he turned to face the tree. He raised the bow and aimed. He saw the widow singing before the willow, saw the look on the officer's face as he told his mother that his brothers weren't coming home. Then he decided it didn't matter, and let go of the arrow. He didn't watch it, but turned to the woman standing beside him.

He took her. They lay in the tall grass for a long time, and watched the day pass into night. At first, he could forget it all. His entire past was lost in the tall grass. Then, as the stars began to light up in the sky, memory flooded through his naked body. He turned to her and tried to speak, tried to tell her, but she put a finger to his lips.

VI

"I always tried to tell her," Luke said. "But I couldn't."

"What happened?" Andrew asked. He'd been watching the fire in front of him, imagining the dancing sparks to be Luke and Sara. Now he sat up and looked at the young man sitting across from him.

"We continued this way for a few days," Luke said. "Each time I saw her, I fell for her a little more. Even on the hunting trips, when she was dressed as a man. Her brother led the trips, so he knew about her too. But he kept it a secret, because he knew his sister wanted to hunt and fight. She was, after all, the best with a bow among them.

"We would lie in the tall grass at night, or in the day, and she would tell me how she dreamed of glory and war. How she hated that Brymino was a nation sworn to peace. She dreamed of the day she could leave home and fight. I heard all of this," Luke said, "and it tore me apart. I wanted to tell her who I was, how I really felt about war and all the fighting, but whenever I tried she would put her finger to my lips." Luke was silent for a moment.

"So I never told her. I showed her instead. I didn't want to, but…" Luke trailed off. "But sometimes you don't have a choice. It had only been a week since I'd met her, and we were hunting that morning. Her brother wasn't there—he'd just come down with the dry cough two days before. I had just been thinking about how lucky I'd been that I hadn't had to kill anything during those expeditions when we came across a wild turkey.

"The leader of the expedition, Jakes, turned to me and he said, 'Kill it.' So I lifted my bow and took aim. All the thoughts, all the memories—they flooded me again. The widow and the willow. That was all I could think of. And this time I couldn't shake it off. It was a part of me, and I couldn't forget it." Luke bowed his head. "I missed the turkey, and I meant to. With every bone in my body, I meant to miss that animal."

Luke sat silent for a moment. Somewhere an owl hooted. Nick mumbled incoherently in his sleep.

"The men of the expedition made fun of me for missing such an easy shot, but they eventually forgot it. But Saramina," Luke shook his head. "She saw it all. And she knew I meant it."

"She got mad?" Andrew asked. Luke nodded.

"Yes. And when I pulled her aside afterward, I told her who I really was," Luke said. "She called me a coward. I think she couldn't believe that she had lain with someone she didn't really know. These are all very adult matters, you see—"

"You two didn't really act like adults," Andrew interrupted.

Luke sighed. "I know it. I wish we had taken our time. But time was against us, and after that day we didn't lie together. I never saw the way station and its tall grass again. Her brother's condition worsened, and I—" Luke paused, not sure what to say. "I felt I was running away from who I was. That I was losing myself."

"So you ran away?" Andrew asked.

"It's not so simple," Luke said. Andrew shook his head. He had heard enough. Luke was acting like a *sap,* as the older boys at school would say when somebody got all mushy over a girl.

"I'm going to bed," Andrew said. He rose from his stone.

"All right," Luke said. "Tomorrow we'll find the spider grass and bring it to Sunsetville. It's only an two hour ride from here. And then, it's off to Sarna Mensis and the door back to your world."

"I don't think so," Andrew returned. "About Sarna Mensis. I'm not going anywhere til I've killed Gerard. I'm going to put a bullet in his head."

"I don't think you have a choice," Luke said. He looked up at Andrew from across the fire.

"You always have a choice," Andrew said. He turned toward his makeshift bed.

"You know that gun doesn't make you God, kid."

Andrew stopped. He balled up his fist. Without turning he said,

"What's God got to do with it?"

"You, Sara, you're no different," Luke said. "You think killing's going to make things better. It's not your choice to make."

"I don't see where God comes into it," Andrew said as he turned around. "Where was God the day your brothers died?" He stopped, realizing what he'd said. Luke looked up at him sharply.

"How about the day you found your gun on the forest floor?" Luke asked. "You think that was just luck?"

"Look," Andrew said. "In this world, you can either run away or turn and fight. I guess I'm the only one wants to make a stand."

"From what I've heard," Luke said, looking down at his hands, "you've been running away this whole time."

Andrew shook his head. "I'm going to bed," he said. "You can stay up and think about the stars and all that. I've got things to do tomorrow." He turned and left Luke, who stared into the fire.

VII

Saramina and Ryundain came upon the boys in their sleep. Even Luke, who sat on a stone beside the dead fire, seemed to be nodding off. Saramina knew that made sense; he was too weak to even keep a watch. She felt the long blade on her hips, ready to strike.

"We kill none," Ryundain whispered. He crouched beside her, peering through the dark leaves of the thick green trees in front of them. Sara nodded. Ryundain turned to her.

"I'll take on the man, Robin," he said. Sara wanted to tell him Luke was far from a man, but held her tongue. "Luke. He will have the gun." His confidence was high. He didn't care if Saramina wanted the gun; it was his for the taking. Such was Ryun's nature, Sara knew. She had needed to trick him, otherwise he would have taken the gun from the boy.

"Sure. I'll stop the two boys from interfering while you do," she said. Ryundain smiled. Then he pressed his finger to his lips. Saramina froze; the gesture awakened something in her. She turned and watched the company through the leaves, and suddenly she felt the entire forest bearing down on her. She closed her eyes, but she couldn't escape it. Her memory awakened.

"You're leaving," her father had said. She didn't turn her horse. She knew that voice well. She heard his soft tread and the tap of his staff in the grassy courtyard. She knew it all too well.

"I am," she said. "I... have to."

"I wish..." her father said, "I wish I could go with you. I do."

She turned her horse and offered him a weak smile. His ancient face looked warmly up at her in the afternoon light. A light beard of grey matched his long hair, beneath the crown. Now he reached up and took the crown off.

"What's happened to this world is sad, Sara. It is a faithless land we live in. Yet, it is sadder that old men like me sit around and watch it all fall to pieces. We cling to our fleeting youth. I see now how futile it all has been. And burying my child... I—" Geromino stopped himself. He clung onto his staff. "I would have ridden out with you, Sara. Your brother would have as well."

Sara looked down at her horse. It always hurt her throat when tears welled up in her eyes. "I've got to go," she said. "I've got to make things right."

"*I know you do,*" he said. "*And you will. For him, you will.*"
Sara *said nothing. The pain was dull in her throat. She wondered if everyone felt this way when they cried. Her father walked over to her horse.*

"*Remember,*" he said softly, touching her hand. "*Sometimes the pain reminds us we're alive. That we don't dream.*" He smiled. "*And you must promise me one thing, Sara.*"

"*Yes?*" she asked, biting her lip as a single tear ran down her smooth cheek.

"*You must forgive Luke, if you ever see him again.*" Geromino said. "*And you must forgive yourself.*"

Saramina saw this in a fleeting moment. It was as fleeting as the leaves on the trees. She saw the leaves in front of her blowing on the breeze and she knew all the hate she had in her, all the grievances against the world and Gerard and her brother could be as light and fleeting as those leaves on the wind. She closed her eyes, and felt the pain in her throat again. She smiled and felt all the heaviness leave her bones.

Then the boy woke up screaming.

chapter nine
the night in the forest

I

Nickolas Smithson did not sleep that night. He lay awake
on the deerskin mat he had laid out, hearing the voices of
Andrew and Luke by the campfire. He hadn't slept the last night
either.

He supposed he was sick, though he wasn't even sure that
was right. He had been plenty sick before, and knew the feeling.
No— he decided *see-through* was the right word. As if everything
he thought was suddenly visible. It all started when he had lost
the compass. Nick worried Sara had kicked it away when she
had searched for Andrew's gun this morning. Still, he didn't
mention he'd lost the piece. Since he had lost it, the night before
and that day had become a blur of emptiness. Lying down beside
the campfire, Nick thought of the last few days with Andrew,
and thought of home. Then he drifted somewhere between
waking and dreaming.

He woke in a dark long corridor. Andrew lay beside him,
and Luke sat a few feet away. They were no longer in the grove,
however. Nick recognized where he was at once. The sewers
beneath Sunsetville stretched out before him, winding in filth
and patchy darkness. Nick remembered the spiders flying
through these sewers and felt his stomach clench. He sat up
and tried to wake Andrew, but he couldn't speak. He opened
his mouth, and no words came out. He looked ahead and

heard footsteps. They were slow and echoed through the sewer hallways.

Nick looked around in desperation. Andrew slept soundly beside him, his small chest rising and falling peacefully. Nick wished he had that enviable peace. *He's always so calm,* Nick thought.

Suddenly, he wished he had Andrew's gun. He wanted the power and title that came with it. He took a step toward Andrew, but stopped, his eyes on Luke.

Luke sat in the darkness, staring off into the distance. Nick tried to shout out, "someone's coming" but he made no noise. The only noises in the sewer were dripping water and those slow footsteps that grew louder with each passing moment.

Luke's eyes were closed. Nick figured he was sleeping and cursed him. "Wake up!" Nick yelled again. "Somethin's coming! The spiders!" It was no use—he was silent. His own rushing heart drowned out the words in his head. Then he heard a new voice.

Not the spiders, boy, the voice purred. *Something much worse than the spiders.*

Nick shook his head. He began to reach for the gun. *I've got to use it,* he thought. *The others will thank me!*

The others don't even notice you, the new voice said in his head. It sounded like his own, he thought. *They don't care about you.*

No! Nick screamed silently. Now a figure appeared in the darkness ahead. Nick spotted the tall silhouette in the darkness, bearing pale eyes that burned through the night.

You know it's true, the voice in his head whispered. Nick blinked and shook his head. These weren't his thoughts! *Why does it sound like my voice?* He wondered. *Get out of my head!* He tried to scream.

You're nothing to them Nick, the voice suggested. *Why not just shoot him? The boy. He's the real monster. He'll just throw you to the wayside when he's done with you.*

That's not true! Nick mouthed, though his hands reached for the gun.

"Oh, but it is," the figure in the darkness said. "I hear you, Nick. You're silent to them, but I hear you. Oh, how I hear you!" Nick grabbed the gun from Andrew's hide and raised it.

Kill the boy, Nick.

"Fuck you!" Nick screamed, and his voice cracked. He screamed and fired the weapon.

II

Ryundain didn't say a word. He watched the curly-headed boy sit up from his bed with the gun, pointed into the forest darkness. He saw the fire in the boy's eyes as he screamed and pulled the trigger. He saw the gun explode in the boy's hand with a crash that threw the youngster backward. He was silent for a few seconds longer as Luke and the other boy woke and hurried over to their companion. The curly-haired boy, who had shouted as he woke, Ryundain knew, was the gunfighter of legend.

Ryundain had come a long way. He thought of the days of his youth, dreaming of having a gun. His father, King of the Dundain, would scold him.

"Quit pretending," his father would tell him, sitting up on his high throne in the Hall of the Falling Sun. Thick locks of grey fell over the man's face. "There's no such thing. The Dundain do not recognize the law of the gun. Grow up."

Ryun had felt the dark presence in the wood with him, but the boy had been faster—whatever had been lurking the darkness must be dead now, Ryun figured. He reached into his purse and felt for the grip of the magnificent object there. *The boy-gunfighter will have some interest in this,* Ryun thought. *I'll have to show him.*

Beside him, Robin looked over to him. His eyes shined a bright blue, and Ryundain saw something strange there. Something feminine, he decided. Robin hadn't looked this way before. Ryundain had seen the confidence in him since the moment he had met Robin. Now, he looked different.

"Do you think Nick was shooting at us?" Robin whispered. Ryun raised an eyebrow.

"How do you know his name?" Ryundain asked. Robin blinked and looked away, and said nothing. Ryundain looked back to the grove and saw the boy. *Nick,* Ryundain thought. *Perhaps short for Nicolai? A fitting name for a gunfighter.*

"We must keep silent," Ryundain said. "There is… something strange going on in these woods tonight." He bent low and pressed his ear to the forest floor. "Yes… I can hear tremor. We must be ready to protect the boy-gunfighter, in case danger arises." Robin turned to him.

"What are you talking about?" Robin asked. Ryundain kept his eyes locked on Nick.

"I serve him now," Ryun said. "*Nicolai, bearer of the gun.*"

"What are you talking about?" Robin asked. "The gun doesn't belong to him. And his name's not Nicolai. It's Nick."

Ryun waved a hand at his companion. "Didn't you see his eyes? The curly-haired boy has the instincts of a gunslinger." The moonlight illuminated Ryundain's face in ghastly white as he laid a hand on his giant sword, preparing to jump out in case danger approached. Robin shook her head and turned to watch the company in front of them.

"I shall serve him," Ryundain whispered. "The ancient law of the gun commands it."

III

Andrew jolted awake. He reached for the gun beside him. He found nothing but leaves. He sat up and looked around.

"What was that—" he stopped when he saw Nick lying on his back, eyes wide. He held the smoking gun with both hands. Luke had run over to the boy.

"Oh no, of all the things—" Luke said.

Nick eyes grew wide as he saw the gun in his hands.

"What happened?" Andrew asked. "Luke, weren't you on watch?"

Luke scratched the back of his head. "Well yes, but I might have dozed off." Andrew raised his eyebrows. "It's been a long day, and all—" Andrew shook his head and looked down at Nick, offering him his hand.

"It's all right, guys, we've still got three shells left in the chamber."

"*Don't touch me!*" Nick screamed. Andrew jumped. A silence fell over their camp. Then Nick dropped the gun, and finally broke down. He put his hands to his eyes, sobbing softly.

"Nick…" Andrew said. He sat down and put an arm around his friend. With his other hand he tucked the gun into the waistband of his pants.

"He wanted to kill me, don't you see it!" Nick cried, his head still in his hands. "I… I shouldn't even *be* 'ere with you all! I'm jus' a kid. And since I lost my compass… well…" He sniffled and threw his hands up. "It's been no use! I jus' feel lost."

"You mean this compass?" Luke asked. He ran over to his bag and dug around a little bit. Nick and Andrew raised their eyebrows simultaneously. Luke returned, holding out the compass in his hand.

"Where'd you find it?" Nick asked. He wiped away the tears on his face and reached out for it. Luke tossed it to him.

"This morning," Luke said. "On the forest floor, near last night's camp. I went into the bushes to use the bathroom and saw it lying on the ground there."

Nick reddened. "I… forgot to check there," he said. "I used that spot the night before, I think."

"If I'd known it was yours," Luke said, "I would have given it back right away. It's a great piece, that compass—even if it does point north." Andrew saw his friend fiddling with the compass. *He'll be all right now,* Andrew knew. He looked into the forest darkness. The moonlight was thick tonight, but only their grove was illuminated. Everything else was shrouded in patchy darkness.

"Nick," Andrew asked, getting to his feet. "Nick, what were you shooting at? And who wanted you to kill me?"

"St. Gerardo! Who else?" Nick asked, giving his friend a look. "He's been in my head all day, since I lost it. Now he's 'ere…" Nick looked up. "And I think I missed."

As Nick finished, deep laughter filled the grove. Andrew turned, surveying the darkness around him. He laid his left hand on the gun.

He knew that laughter all too well.

IV

"Oh, you've all come so far."

Luke looked frantically around. The swamp they'd camped beside sat still and stagnant, yet he kept his eyes upon it. It stretched out far into the dark. The water was vibrant in the moonlight. Andrew saw the water begin to ripple and change. Luke turned back to Andrew.

"Something's in the water," he said. Andrew nodded and pulled out his gun. Luke shook his head. "No! Get the horses!"

Andrew gave the water one last look, then relented. He turned and grabbed his makeshift bed, rolling it up in one daft motion. Then he ran over to Nick, who had grabbed Home Sweet Home.

"Follow me!" Luke called. "We've got to find the Spider Grass *now.*"

"Hold the horses, or they'll flee!" Luke screamed. The hair he'd combed back flew over his face now, undone by the wind. "Andrew! Don't use the gun!"

Andrew didn't even think to use it. He grabbed the saddle on Home Sweet Home and ran toward Luke, who led his horse along the eastern edge of the swamp. Nick followed on the other side of the horse with Stricker's blade in hand.

V

"What are those things?"

Andrew turned to look at Nick. He ran behind the horse, his eyes wide. He surveyed the forest with weary eyes.

Luke continued to hurry through the forest. He took a

sharp turn around a fallen tree, and stopped for a moment, listening to the wood.

"We must hurry," he said, and continued on. "There are more of these barbarian types. The forest is awake. Gerard has used this to his advantage."

"What are they?" Nick asked. He rubbed his eyes, and Andrew marveled at the dark circles there "The forest-folk?"

"Descendants of a bohemian race," Luke answered. "Their ancestors once farmed the land of the Dundain, but a great drought hundreds of years ago ravaged their land. The Dundain cast them off their land through great violence. They came here to live in solitude.

"Legends say the gunfighters of old came to this land to solve that violence," Luke said. "Men who used their guns for life, not death. But the ancestors of these farming-folk were too bitter to return to society. Their race has dwelled in these woods for a long time."

"You should have told us they were 'ere!" Nick said. After a moment, Luke said:

"I forgot." He continued to lead them deep through the darkness. The moonlight illuminated the forest, and Andrew thought he saw movement out of the corner of his eye. His eyes darted over to a fallen tree, but saw nothing.

"If I remember right," Luke said, "the grove we're looking for is very close. But we've got to be quick when we get there—there are more forest-folk , and my brother has turned them against us."

The forest had come alive around them. The commotion had woken up all the wildlife—Andrew could hear a chorus of birds chirping against one another. Up ahead a herd of deer scattered through the dark ferns, which waved gently in the breeze. The starlight and moonlight burned through the canopy and threw patchy shades of ghastly white over the forest floor. Andrew saw all of this, following Luke toward the Spider Grass.

They emerged through a clearing in the trees, but Luke stopped before they could emerge into the grove. He turned to his companions. His dark hair fell wildly over his bright blue eyes. He focused all his attention of Andrew.

"Listen," Luke said. "Gerard may know we're here. We've got be quick— here in this grove, we're vulnerable." Andrew looked past and him and saw the entire grove was illuminated by the moonlight. Thick grass, colored a dark green, littered the floor. It tangled and fell over itself, like hundreds of twisted spider legs. Luke looked directly into Andrew's eyes.

"We must be swift," he said. "Nick—you and I will keep guard. Andrew will grab the grass."

"We just pull it?" Nick asked, his voice trembling a bit. Luke nodded.

"Grab as much as you can." Luke said. Then he turned and headed into the grove.

Andrew hurried after Luke, scrambling through the moonlit grove. He could hear Nick behind him. His eyes searched the grove below him, and soon he saw the weeds. Some thistle grew around the trees and ran along the ground, but even in the dark it was easy to distinguish the spider grass. Andrew bent down and ran his hands along the dirt.

"Just pull it as quickly as possible," Luke said as Andrew reached for one weed of spider grass. It grew in throngs around them. His blue eyes scanned the trees around them. "We don't have much—"

The world folded like a hood over Andrew. He was numb suddenly, and his head swam in a pool that shook slowly and silently. Luke and Nick disappeared, and the trees above him receded into the starry sky until they were no longer visible. Andrew took in a huge gulp of air and made a conscious effort to look down.

He still grasped the weed in his hand. Only this weed was longer and skinner in his hand. It felt slippery through the pins and needles that filled his fingers.

What in the world, he wondered.

He looked around and saw a stone wall jutting to his left, running into the darkness. He turned his head and neck without letting go of the weeds and saw the porch behind him, dark and shadowy in the patchiness of the night. He was in the center of a gigantic nighttime garden—the one he had grown up in.

New Jersey, he tried to say, but no sound came out. *I'm home.* He looked down again at the patch of weeds that surrounded him now. His mind swam, pondering what had happened. The gun was still tucked in his pants—he could feel the cold metal gently press against his back. Then the patch below him began to move.

The rest of the flowers in his mother's garden were silent and still, watching the magic unfold. Andrew started violently, but didn't let go of the weed. It slithered in his hand, and he thought *let go of the weed!* He couldn't, though. His hand was closed tight around it, and his hand was asleep. He tried to move backwards from the patch of Spider Grass that was rising around him, but he couldn't move. He felt the strand of grass in his right hand curl up around his wrist. At first, it tickled. Soon, it was tight. His hand woke up, searing in pain. He opened his mouth to yell but no sound came out.

A long strand rose in front of his eyes, lightly touching the side of his neck. Andrew tried to back away, but he was trapped by the weeds wrapped around his arms. He felt one weed tighten around his calf, and he sighed in pain. Still, he kept his eyes on the strand in front of him as it wrapped around his neck.

"*Oh, you've come so far,*" came that wretched voice again. From somewhere in the distance, Andrew thought he could hear shouting and the sound of steel. He kicked and gargled—he couldn't even attempt to scream now the weed was around his neck. He felt one strand moving up his back, and knew what it was going for.

No, he thought. *No, you won't take it. Get away!* Still, he felt the gun shift as the weed wrapped itself around the weapon. He was helpless, and now he was weightless—the weeds picked him up from the ground and pulled him under, covering him in a slithering sea of green. He felt a tight grip on his legs, and a sharp pull. He gargled again, and his vision began to grow fuzzy. Still, the pulling on his legs continued, and he knew this pulling wasn't from the Spider Grass. There were two hands on his legs, pulling him.

"Andrew," Luke said. The boy had gone stone still.

"Andrew!" He gave a sharp call. He reached down to touch him, and the boy was cold. He wasn't moving—he simply lay on the ground, with his hand clutching the strands of grass.

"What's wrong?" Nick asked. He was standing on the other side of the grove, and held a long hunting knife.

"I don't know," Luke said. "Andrew! Hurry!" Andrew didn't flinch. The boy stared unblinkingly at the weeds in his hand.

"Out of my way!" called a boy's voice. Luke jumped as a shadow passed to his right. Before him stood a boy in a silvery robe, carrying a long staff.

"Look at that!" Nick cried. "It's Warren the Wise!"

"No it's not," Luke said, reaching out for the robed boy. "Warren the Wise is an adult. Kid, who are you?" He grabbed the boy's shoulder, and the boy turned. Two brilliant blue eyes gazed at him.

Luke blinked. "Warren…" he said.

"Take your hand off of me, Luke," Warren said. He had light and delicate features, and a mess of light blonde hair sat atop his head. Luke stumbled backwards, thinking of the bearded wrinkled Warren he knew. He recognized that face… it may have been a hundred years younger, but Luke recognized it. Especially the blue eyes.

"This boy needs help." Warren turned back to Andrew, laying still on the forest floor. "But keep a watch of the woods— my brother has awoken something foul tonight."

"What's happened to him, Warren?" Nick asked, hurrying over. Warren gave Andrew a long look.

"This grass," Warren said. "I should have known." He stepped backwards and held his staff in the air. "*Release!*" he cried. "*Release this boy from his memories!*" Warren closed his eyes and began muttering words in a strange tongue. Luke nearly laughed. Warren slammed his staff on the ground again. Nick raised an eyebrow at the boy-sage.

"Damn this useless thing!" Warren cried. He picked the staff up again, and brought it down on his knee. The *snap* echoed through the forest, and Luke watched the staff break clean in half. Warren threw the halves of his staff into the woods.

"Nick," Warren said. "Help me pull!" Warren sat down and grabbed Andrew's legs, and began to pull feverishly. Luke had to stifle laughter at the sight. Then a voice echoed through the trees:

Oh, you've all come so far.

Warren turned to Luke. His eyes burned in the moonlight. "Something's coming!" he cried. "Get out your sword, man!"

VI

The grove was too still. Sara knew it, watching from behind the trees. She assumed Ryun knew it as well—he was sharp. She put one hand on her belt, where the knives crisscrossed. She looked over at Ryun, who hid behind a tree. He put up a finger. *Not yet,* his eyes said. Sara nodded.

The whole affair had been ridiculous. She had been prepared to rush out and help them when Nick had fired the gun, but Ryun stopped her. He wanted to play guardian still, rather than join the company. Sara knew what that meant: Ryun was only going to protect Nick, not the others. She cursed the man's pigheadedness, but followed him to the grove. When Warren showed up—that was the greatest surprise of all. She had written the old sage off, yet here he was, to turn the tide.

Movement in the spider-grass woke her from her trance. The grass was so thick, and yet she saw something move to the left where Andrew lay. Beside her, Ryundain saw it too. There was something rising from the grass. Ryundain moved before she could—he pulled out his sword and sprang forward as the figure emerged over Nick. Sara cursed and followed suit, and saw several black shapes emerge from the trees at the edge of the grove. Three of them hovered toward Nick. She saw them in the moonlight—they were thick, broad forest-folk. They sprang out toward Nick, before Warren or Luke could notice.

Nick looked up and jumped in surprise as the figure beside him lashed out with a spear. He fell back, yet Ryundain arrived first. He caught the wild man's arm, and wrestled him backward toward the edge of the grove. Sara watched, amazed, as Ryundain turned away from his enemy and stepped in front of the three advancing wild men.

"You won't touch him!" Ryundain cried, bringing his sword forward in a might arc over his head. There was a great clash. Sara looked away, and cried out as a dark figure descended upon her from the trees. She tried to draw her knives, but froze as the figure emerged into the moonlight. A wily woman broke toward her, with long stringy brown hair and red eyes. She held a thick silver pike in her hands. Her stomach, Sara saw, was round and full.

Is she... Sara thought. She cried and fell back, unable to pull her knives out. For the first time in her life, she failed to draw. Sara stumbled backward into the thick green weeds, naked in her vulnerability. The woman towered over her, letting out a shrill squeal of delight as she brought the pike down.

VII

Luke glanced around wildly as the shadows descended upon them. He kept his hands out in front of him as the assailants rushed by—he would not draw his sword. He could not use it against them. He refused.

He stepped in front of Warren, but Nick was defenseless. Yet another had rushed out of the trees to defend the boy. In the moonlight Luke thought it was Ryundain the Proud. *That can't be*, Luke thought. *This is all so lunatic!* Then he saw another figure dance by him, and knew it was Saramina.

Luke watched as she spun aimlessly into the center of the grove, watching the commotion unfold around her. Luke wanted to step forward and yell her name, but one wild man caught up with him. The man thrashed wildly with a club, and Luke side-stepped neatly and grabbed him by the back of the hair. He tossed the barbarian aside into the weeds, away from Warren.

Luke looked back to Saramina. A strange round woman jumped on top of her—Sara had fallen back into the weeds. The woman stood over her, a long pike upraised in the clear night air. Luke stepped forward as the woman squealed and brought the pike down. Luke considered stopping, and letting it happen.

In a moment, Luke drew his sword and lashed out.

The grove was silent as Luke stood over the fallen woman. The remaining barbarians fled into the trees. Beside Sara, Ryun had wrestled half a dozen barbarians to submission. Luke let out a long breath, looking at the fallen woman beside Sara. He stood that way a long time, looking at the two of them. Sara looked back at him with eyes like a child. Finally, he extended his hand to her. She took it, and he pulled her to her feet.

"Luke, I—" she stopped herself. Her dark hair fell wildly over her eyes. She didn't bother to push it back. She stared at him, breathing heavily. He stared back. Her hand was still in his.

She looked down at the slain woman beside her. Luke squeezed her hand and she looked back up at him. Her eyes glimmered in the dim light.

"I couldn't do it," Sara said. Her voice cracked a little bit. The others, scattered around the grove, watched in silence. "I saw myself when she came at me, and I just couldn't—"

"Sara," Luke said. "That day I shot the arrow—I never looked. Was it—"

"Right next to mine," she said. Their eyes met, and Luke pulled her in. They kissed for what seemed like minutes. Warren let out a sigh beneath them as he pulled on Andrew's legs again.

VIII

The world began to spin again as the hands on his legs pulled furiously. Andrew's sight became spotty; his house became a blur as the weeds around his body tightened their stranglehold. He tried to kick, but the hands on his legs held fast. Then they pulled again, and the entire sky above him crashed down.

He looked up and saw two blue eyes peering down at him. He reached for his throat and found he could move his arms again. He grabbed his neck, and felt the weeds around it. They were loose now. Andrew let out a long exhale.

"Hello, Andrew," said a voice above him. Andrew looked up as his vision sharpened.

Warren the Wise hovered over him. Andrew stretched out his arms. He was stiff. Then he sat up violently.

"What happened?" he blurted out. "Where's my house?"

"Your house is gone," Warren said. Andrew saw Luke and Sara standing behind Warren, holding each other. He blinked and turned back to Warren.

"What happened?"

"You got really still!" Nick cried. "Like a stone! You scared us all! And then the forest people came..." His eyes gravitated over to Nick and Sara. Andrew saw a large woman laying in the weeds, mangled and bloody. Luke held his sword in his left hand, and Andrew saw the long red streaks on the blade.

"The weeds..." Andrew said. He turned back to Warren, who was climbing to his feet. "They tried to kill me! Did you pull me out?" He narrowed his eyes at Warren. "I thought you weren't coming."

"I changed my mind," Warren said. He wiped the dirt off of his silvery robe. Then he turned to the forest, surveying the darkness with his blue eyes.

"At least you brought the weeds with you!" Sara called. She was trembling a little bit in Luke's arms. Andrew looked down at himself and saw a dozen strands of spider weeds clinging to his torso. They were wrapped around him completely. Andrew remembered the tight pull of the weeds, and shuddered. Then he got to his feet.

As he pulled the weeds off of him and into his bag, Andrew turned to the man beside Luke. Andrew thought he looked at least six and a half feet tall, at least as tall as Joe Freeman. This man, however, was much huskier than Joe Freeman. He had an enormous girth, and a thick brown beard. His hair was combed neatly over two hazel eyes. Nick was staring up at him.

"Who are you?" Nick asked him.

"I," the man said, and stopped himself. "I am your servant." With that he bent to one knee and bowed his head. "My name is Ryundain, lord of the House of Dundain. Yet I am bound to you, Nickolai, man of the gun."

Andrew waited for Nick's response. Nick didn't say anything. Everyone in the grove stared, except Sara and Luke, who were still kissing. In that silence, Andrew looked around him and realized just how similar this grove was to his world. There was nothing magnificent or absurd about this forest. The tall old trees sat silently in the moonlight, watching the scene below. He thought of the days he wandered through the forest by his house, dreaming of adventure and the chance to run away. Now he dreamed of home. He took his hand off the butt of his gun.

Ryundain looked up at Nick. "I will follow you," he said, "and serve your good word, Nickolai. Do you accept me?"

"I think you've got it confused," Nick said, scratching his head.

Warren started. "Enough of this!" he cried. "We have no

time for this tomfoolery. My brother still lurks somewhere in this forest. There may be more forest-folk as well."

"Where should we go, Warren?" Sara asked.

"To the bridge!" Warren cried. "Gather the horses! If we hurry, we can make it there before daybreak."

IX

The company of six rushed through the forest as the black starry sky above brightened to a dark blue. Five horses trailed behind them. Andrew wished the horses weren't with them—the beasts slowed down the company immensely. Still, they would need them as soon as they left the forest.

Andrew felt the wind pick up behind him as they fled. It became torrential, ripping through the trees. He turned and saw Sara's dark hair fly wildly in front of her face. Home Sweet Home whinnied nervously behind him as he rushed past a fallen tree.

"Warren of the Winds," Andrew muttered. "They call him Warren of the Winds." The wind became visible as leaves and twigs whipped past them, to the north. Warren was pushing the wind in their favor.

As they reached the edge of the woods, Warren began to mount his horse. "My brother will follow us," he said, "but if we reach the bridge before he does, we can make a stand."

"He won't have a chance," Ryundain said, fixing the saddle on his horse.

"Don't be so sure," Warren said, turning his horse straight ahead. Laid before them were miles of plains, dark and mellow in the dim light. Still, the light grew with every passing moment.

"The bridge is only a few miles from these woods," Luke said.

"Let's get there as quickly as possible." He looked over to Sara, who was seated on her colt. She nodded, and he nodded back.

"I didn't think you'd come," Andrew said. Warren spared him a glance as he climbed onto his horse.

"The wind changes," Warren said. "And so do I. And perhaps," he looked over at Saramina, who offered the boy a small smile, "the harsh words of one fiery young lady woke me from my dream." He began to lead his horse in front of the company.

"Mr. Warren," Nick said. "What happened to Andrew back there? Why did he go so still?"

"These are all things I can explain when we cross the bridge!"

"I saw my house," Andrew said. "My world."

"The forest is very old," Warren said. He prepared his horse to set off. "It does not surprise me that certain links between our worlds exist within this place. But they are only temporary—they could only bring you there for a little while." Then he clicked his tongue against the roof of his mouth and his horse jumped forward.

Nick climbed on Home Sweet Home's back, and looked back at Andrew. He offered his friend a hand, which Andrew took as he mounted the horse.

"This is all just rotten," Nick said, his head downcast. "I'm sorry I fired your gun, Andrew."

Andrew laughed. "Just get us to the bridge, Nick," he said, adjusting himself behind Nick. "Then we'll call it even!"

Nick pressed his boots into the sides of his horse as the others led their horses forward, away from the Eldenwoods. The six riders rushed off to the north on five horses, as the sun began to climb over the eastern hills.

I

Andrew ran his hand over the gun in his waistband as Home Sweet Home trailed the four horses. *Three shells,* he thought. The gun felt lighter. He shot a look behind him, surveying the fields. No one pursued the company. Dull light sat placidly over the grass as dawn approached. Andrew turned as Nick led the horse up a steep ridge. Before them lay the Saltmine.

The river sat between two gigantic cliffs, the southernmost cliff they rode upon now. Down below the water ran lazily between the cliffs, meandering westward toward the sea. This river was much wider than the river Andrew knew— the River Warren. Andrew turned to Ryundain, who rode beside them.

"Where does the Saltmine lead to?" he shouted over the wind. Ryundain looked over at the two boys on the horse.

"It winds east a little while," he said, "then turns north! All the way up to the House of Dundain!"

"Dundain's surrounded by the ocean and the Saltmine!" Nick said. "Everyone knows that!"

"That's right!" Ryun called. The wind picked up, and drowned out his words. Andrew felt the wind pushing at his back, leading their horses along the edge of the cliffs. *This has got to be Warren's doing,* he thought. *We've got the wind on our side now.*

As they climbed a little higher on the ridge, Andrew spotted the bridge up ahead. Bridge was an exaggeration, Andrew thought. It was the shabbiest thing he'd ever seen. It swung haphazardly in the wind, hung only by a few cables attached to poles on either side.

"There lies Dundain!" Luke called ahead. "Hurry!" Andrew didn't blame him for his haste. Though no one appeared to be following the company, he still felt a thick knot in his stomach.

Warren reached the bridge first, crossing it with surprising dexterity. He didn't dismount at all—his horse was only a small colt, and he floated lightly over the swinging bridge. Luke and Sara reached the bridge next, slowing their horses to a stop. They hopped off.

"The wind, Warren!" Sara cried as they began to walk their horses across the bridge. Just as she called it, the wind began to die. The bridge stopped swaying fiercely as Warren closed his eyes and began muttering to himself. Andrew watched the boy-sage with fascination as Nick slowed Home Sweet Home to a stop. Ryundain had already reached the bridge and followed Luke and Sara across the pass, leading his horse. Andrew jumped off Home Sweet Home's back once they reached the edge of the cliffs.

"Hurry, Nick!" he called. Nick leapt off the horse's back, landing close to the edge of the cliff. He cried out in surprise and grabbed hold of the post that supported the bridge. It let out an audible crack, and Andrew ran forward and grabbed his friend. He pulled Nick away from the edge of the cliff.

"Boys! Cross now!" Luke called. Andrew looked up and saw Luke, Sara and Warren gathered on the cliff opposite to them. Ryundain had nearly reached the end of the bridge, leading his horse onward. Andrew looked doubtfully at the post Nick had nearly snapped with his fall, and turned to his friend.

"Let's go," Andrew said. His voice sounded weak and thin. He grabbed Home Sweet Home and began and crossed onto the wooden planks that supported the bridge. The sun to his right had climbed over the hills and lit up the river below. Andrew didn't look down to see the sight.

He was nearly at the end of the bridge when he heard Nick's gasp. He turned and saw the boy was right behind him. Behind Nick, at the other side of the river, a single horse and a rider sat quietly.

"Nick," Andrew said. "Don't stop. Come on." Still, he gave the rider one more glance before he turned. Gerard watched the boys with a blank stare and sat motionless atop his large black stallion. Several colorful bags were strapped to the horse's saddle. Andrew turned and began to walk toward the end of the bridge.

"Almost there," Warren said from the other side. "Don't stop moving." He didn't take his eyes off his brother. As Andrew reached the end of the bridge, he felt the wind pick up again. The river below them picked up in volume as the water began to race forward. Andrew stepped onto solid ground and led Home Sweet Home off the bridge. Nick followed behind him as the bridge began to sway in the wind again.

"Will you cross?" Warren called out. Gerard didn't answer.

"Go ahead!" Luke cried. "We're not afraid! Go on!" Sara nodded, and slid her hand into his. Andrew looked around at the six of them. They stood together on the cliff, facing the dark rider ahead. The boy slid his hand off the butt of his gun.

"Do you think you've won?" the rider asked. His mouth hardly moved, yet the words boomed through the valley. "All I see is six fools." His mouth twisted into a snarl.

"Will you cross?" Warren asked again.

"The dead do rise," Gerard returned. His thin black hair flapped in the wind, which rose again. Andrew nearly fell over this time; the wind began to blow in both directions. "*The wind,*" Gerard said, "*blows the restless dead from their graves. They walk on the plains of the Dundain.*" Gerard and Warren's winds clashed, and Andrew saw the river below thrashing and turning wildly. The conflicting winds tossed the water violently.

"That may be so," Warren said, "but you shall never walk in these lands." His long silver robe rippled in the wind. "Not while the six of us stand together." He gave Gerard a smile. "I ask you again, brother—will you cross?"

"This isn't over," Gerard said. He dug his boots into his horse, and turned to the east. His voice no longer boomed. It sounded thin and flat. "I know of the door too. You can run wherever you like," he said, his eyes on Andrew, "but I'll be waiting atop Sarna Mensis."

"Enough!" Warren cried, and the wind rose again. Gerard's horse neighed and stood up on his hind legs, but Gerard kept the stallion under control. "Be gone!" Gerard scowled and kicked his heels into his horse's side. The horse and its rider flew off to the east as the wind died down. The six watched him go as the valley calmed and quieted.

II

"That was awesome!" Andrew cried, looking over at Warren. "How'd you do that?"

"I didn't do anything at all," Warren said. He let out a long breath. "It was the six of us, together—Gerard wouldn't cross. He couldn't."

"What do you mean?" Nick asked. "He's nev'r been scared of us, not once! Not even of Andrew's gun!"

"What do you mean, Andrew's gun?" Ryundain cut in. "That's your gun!" He turned to Saramina. "And you—you're a woman?" Sara reddened and smiled.

"All of this needs explaining," Warren said.

"I cross-dressed," Sara explained. "I... I was going to try to steal his gun," she looked down at this. Andrew watched her with interest. "But I couldn't... I just couldn't."

"And I saw through her cross-dress," Luke explained. "I knew she was a woman."

"You always do," Sara said. She offered him a small smile. Then she turned back to Andrew. "I owe you an apology, kid. I've crossed you since the minute I met you. You too, Nick." She shook her head. "I was just angry."

"That's all right!" Nick exclaimed. Everyone looked over to the boy. "There's no need to worry anymore, everyone." He offered a small grin to the company.

"Why's that, Nick?" Luke asked. "Because you found your compass?"

"Nope!" Nick said, with a dumb grin on his tanned face. "I don' need it no more, guys!"

"What?" Andrew asked. "What do you mean?"

"Take a look!" Nick said. He took Stricker's blade out of Home Sweet Home's saddle and crouched down. The company gathered around the boy as he carved the blade into the dusty ground. He drew a large circle, and began to fill it with lines. On the outside of the circle he drew four large x's. He pointed to the x at the bottom of the circle.

"That's you, Sara!" he cried. "You're from south. And that's you Luke! Cause you're from the north, near the mountains."

Nick pointed to the x at the top of the circle, and drew little mountains in the dirt with the blade. "And Warren, you're there—" he pointed to the x on the right side of the circle. "You're from the east, and the deserts. And Ryundain—the gun is Andrew's, not mine—but you're on the left side, to the west. And right 'ere," Nick shifted back to the middle of the circle, and drew the biggest x of all. "That's me! From Sunsetville!"

The boy stood up and admired his handiwork. The others around him stared at the diagram silently. No one said a word. Nick looked around.

"I couldn't figure where you shoul' go, Andrew," Nick said, scratching his head. "Real sorry about that."

"I'm not from this world," Andrew said. He didn't take his eyes off the carving in the dirt. "I don't... belong in this circle." Yet as he stood there, he didn't feel that way. The six travelers stood silently, admiring the carving. Andrew realized at last what Nick had drawn—a compass.

III

Andrew reached into his bag and felt the spider-grass inside of it. Home Sweet Home rode swiftly on the wind, following the company's horses as they flew northward. The Plains of Dundain rushed by them. Andrew felt the weeds in his bag and pondered what lay ahead.

They had eaten breakfast by the bridge—Warren demanded they 'break fast on the field of victory'. Anything involving food was fine by Andrew. They'd eaten some potatoes Warren and Ryundain found growing on a field nearby, which Sara cooked to near perfection. Andrew had never eaten such potatoes in his life. Above the field of victory the morning sun cast a haze of blue and gold over the Saltmine.

Warren explained to them over breakfast his decision to ride north. This was Andrew's favorite story of all. Warren had sat frustrated, he told them, after Saramina had given him a piece of her mind in the grove (Sara laughed at this point in the story, and admitted she had been pretty harsh.) After a while, Warren became uncomfortable sitting on his tree-stump, and got up. He paced around the grove for hours, arguing with himself as to what he should do. Finally, he had gotten so sick of arguing with himself that he left the grove, headed north through the forest. He decided that going northward was better than doing nothing, and that the grove had lost its magic for him. As soon as he left the Southwoods, he whistled for his horse, Immortality.

"Immortality," Warren said, munching over the potatoes "had gotten older since I'd set her free. That's what always happens—we get older when we're free to roam." He clucked over to the horse, a tall silver steed that grazed lazily beside the company. "Still, she rode mightily, and the wind was at our back. I was lucky to have found you in the forest last night."

Sara rode beside Andrew now, her head lowered into the rushing wind. She looked at the open fields before her—she loved the Plains of Dundain—searching for wild horses. She found none. In her mind she kept hearing Gerard's words:

"The wind blows the restless dead from their graves. They walk on the Plains of Dundain." She remembered the dead bodies she'd seen in the Villages by the Sea. The ones with the withered skin and rotting faces. She hadn't shown it then to the boys, but those things unnerved her. There was something unfair about it, she decided. Gerard had no right raising the dead, and using them

for his schemes. She pictured her brother stumbling around, with rotting flesh and groping arms. Moaning and screaming. She shuddered.

Get it together, she thought. *If there's anything you've got to do, just stick by Luke.* She looked up ahead and saw him riding beside Warren. He looked good in the morning light, she decided. When he didn't shave he had a fine little gruff. She thought it suited him well. She smiled and dug her heels into her horse, pulling up beside the two riders.

The hills and plains brightened with the rise of the morning sun. Soon packs of wild horses did appear, much to Sara's delight. Often they would ride alongside the company before branching out to toward the sea to the west. The wind was at their back, and Sara knew Warren was responsible for it. She eyed the boy riding beside her. Warren's eyes watched the landscape unfold before him, and she knew he had more in mind than their direction.

He's worried about Ryun, she thought. Ryun's enthusiasm had waned since breakfast. It wasn't just discovering that Nick wasn't the gunfighter; it was the reminder of his homeland. Sara knew Ryun had broken the Dundain's law by riding with her yesterday. By continuing to ride with them (whether it be to Sunsetville or Sarna Mensis, Sara didn't know; that choice was Andrew's to make) he would further break that law and exile himself from his own kingdom. Sara had met Ryundain's father before—her father called him 'the old grey man.' Sara thought the old grey man wouldn't be too happy to hear of his son's travels in the last few hours. In fact, she didn't expect any welcome at all from the old grey king in the House of Dundain. Yet Ryun had insisted they ride toward it.

"There's no avoiding it," he had said as Sara bit into a

tomato she'd picked, "whether you choose to go to Sunsetville or the Sarna ranges. It's a half a day's ride north—surely you can manage that!"

"I'm not so sure your father will be happy to see us," Warren said.

"I will sway him then!" Ryun answered. "I must return home, anyhow."

"Then you're not coming with us?" Andrew asked.

"We shall see."

Sara shuddered suddenly, and felt her stomach rumble a bit. She was feeling a little queasy. She'd dealt with the sickness the last few weeks, but she didn't want to stop the company now. She closed her eyes and took a few deep breaths, tuning out the rushing world. The horse felt steady and strong beneath her. The feeling passed after a few seconds. She opened her eyes. Luke looked over at her.

"You all right?" he asked. His voice was quiet and steady in the wind. She nodded.

"Getting there," she said. He nodded back, and tried the thumbs-up sign Andrew had shown him. Sara laughed and stuck her own thumb out.

IV

Andrew's jaw dropped as he saw the House of Dundain.

He hadn't thought much about what the city would look like—Ryun had told him the name was misleading—yet Andrew could hardly believe the rows and rows of houses and buildings that rose before him. The city sat on a giant hill, and at the first sight Andrew thought the houses were stacked on top of each other. As the company drew close Andrew saw this wasn't true; instead, the houses were built *into* the hillside. Decks and patios suspended above the ground gave the city a leisurely look in the fading sunlight.

Warren began to slow his horse as they approached the outskirts of the city. He led the others past the first few houses, following a cobblestone street. The street wound a lazy route up the steep grassy hill.

"The fields we just crossed over," Ryundain said, pulling his horse alongside Andrew, "hold the graves of thousands of men."

"That's right," Warren said. He was breathing heavily from the ride. "I feel just as old as the dead after that long ride."

"Why bury 'em around the city?" Nick asked.

"The great battle of our ancestor's time was fought there," Ryundain said. "A hundred years ago. The Dundain forced droves of farmers off of the land due to a drought—the farmers couldn't produce anything worthwhile, so the king declared them useless and took the land."

"So the people rebelled," Luke said.

"It was a bloody fight," Ryundain said. "They marched on this city." He gestured at the land around him. Andrew looked at the fields below as they began to climb the steep hill.

"There's no walls," Andrew realized. "Nothing to protect the House of Dundain."

"That's right," Ryundain said, his eyes on the road in front of him. "The army of the Dundain met the rebellion in full force in front of the city. For three weeks the forces clashed at one another, gaining only a few feet of ground daily.

"They buried the bodies in the holes they fought in," Warren said. "The dead rest in shallow graves here."

"At the pace they were fighting, both sides were doomed

to dwindle and fail," Ryundain continued. "But as the legend goes, gunfighters arrived before the fighting could destroy the kingdom. They came from other worlds."

"They brought peace too?" Nick asked, while steering Home Sweet Home away from a woman carrying apples on the street.

"A hard-fought peace," Warren said. "But peace nonetheless. Everyone in the kingdom accepted the law of the gun, except the king of the Dundain—Ryun's ancestor, believe it or not."

"King Hildain eventually relented, of course," Ryundain said. "Not without bitterness of course—that's in our blood. And since the Royal Court of the Dundain refuses to recognize the law of the gun. Not that it matters, though, Andrew—no one has had a gun in this kingdom since those days. Not until now."

Andrew rode on in silence, though every time Home Sweet Home stepped over a bump in the road he felt the gun bounce in his waistband. He laid a hand absentmindedly on it as he followed Saramina and Luke, who led the way to the Hall of the Falling Sun.

V

Saramina kept her eye on Ryundain as they rode through the city. His temper had changed since the night before. He brooded quietly in a dark mood. She'd known him for many years, and knew that was not his usual demeanor. A man like Ryundain loved to ride through his city's streets, she knew. He was a proud man. Yet this afternoon no pride rode with him.

The people of the city hustled beside them. The city streets were always busy, yet today Sara felt uneasy. She couldn't put her finger on what was so different. *Maybe it's me,* Sara thought.

The Hall of the Falling Sun loomed up ahead. Sara watched it rise before them on the hillside like a palace of heaven. The tall tower rose up to the sky, painted gold and white. She'd only been here a few times as a child, yet she remembered all too well the inside of this palace.

"Have you ever been inside?" she asked Luke. Luke smiled and nodded.

"Oh yes," he said. "To the royal court? I've been. How could I forget King Hildain the fourth, and his unnecessarily high throne?"

Sara laughed. The throne was high—as a kid she had figured King Hildain simply lived up there, because there was no visible way to get down. She wasn't been paying much attention to the road, and her horse jerked quickly to the side to avoid an overturned wheelbarrow. Her hair flew wildly in her face, and she began to feel sick again. She closed her eyes and breathed in deeply. This time the feeling didn't pass easily.

Her head still spun as they reached the palace gates. She was so lightheaded she hardly noticed Ryundain swing his horse in front of her. Ryundain's eyes burned upon her. Before he could say a word, a company of guards approached. Sara recognized Frederick immediately, who led the men.

"Lord Ryundain!" Frederick called. His red hair was tied back, and he'd shaved his beard from the previous day. Sara slowly began to climb down the side of her horse, her legs shaking. "My lord, your father—the king— wishes to speak with you immediately. He is most displeased with your actions last night." Frederick stared with menacing eyes at Ryundain, who did not dismount. Ryundain looked back at him, and said nothing. Then he turned to the company.

"I must go," he said. "This is where our journey together ends." He turned his horse and began to trot toward the gates and the great tower beyond it. Andrew rushed forward.

"That's all?" he cried. "You're leaving? After everything that happened today?"

Ryundain's horse stopped. For a second he did not turn. Luke spoke up.

"We've still got a long way to go, Ryun." Luke said. The guards watched him silently. "Whether we go to Sunsetville or Sarna Mensis. Don't think you can turn away from us this easily." Sara suddenly felt the ground wobbling beneath her feet. She couldn't get her legs to quit trembling. She turned to Luke, but the man's eyes were locked on Ryundain.

Not here, Sara thought. *Oh God, don't let me be sick here.*

Ryundain at last turned his horse around to face the company. With one hand he reached into his bag. The other remained on his saddle. When he pulled his hand out of his bag, the street fell silent.

"I too have dreamed of the gun," Ryundain said. In his right hand he held up a revolver to show everyone. It was nearly identical to the one Andrew had in his waistband. "Ever since I was a boy. Ever since I was like *you*." Ryundain narrowed his eyes on Andrew, standing in the street beside the guards.

"I thought it could turn the fortunes of this world," he said. "That a gun would stop the sun from setting upon this sad place." He held the gun up, and thumbed back the hammer. "And when I saw in my dreams a gun sleeping deep beneath the Saltmine River, well… I had to have it for myself." Ryundain's eyes lit up as he aimed the gun off into the distance, to the west.

The sun had begun to fall out there over the ocean. Sara tried to focus on the scene in front of her as the man pulled the trigger.

Nick jumped beside her. Andrew never flinched. All that came from the gun was an awkward click, and silence.

"Useless," Ryundain said. He put the gun back in his bag. "That's what it always was. I've spent years trying to fix it. Every chemist and smithie in Dundain has tried to make it fire, yet it is still *useless.*"

"Enough of this!" Warren cried. He started forward. "I'll have no more this idiocy. I'm entering this Hall, and I'm having a word with your father!" Before he could continue, Frederick stepped into his path.

"None but the Dundain enter the Hall of the Falling Sun," Frederick said. "By order of the King."

"This boy is a gunfighter!" Warren cried. He stretched out a hand toward Andrew. "You and your king are *bound* by the law of the gun to let him enter!"

"The Dundain do not abide by the law of the gun," Frederick returned. His eyes burned, and he laid a hand on his sword. "We never have."

"It is childishness," Ryundain said. "The whole affair. I will have no part in your vain quest." With that, he turned his horse and entered the gate. Saramina felt her stomach drop, and she turned away. A faint ringing grew in her ears that drowned out Warren's curses behind her. She stumbled over to the palace garden and fell to her knees as she began to throw up everything in her stomach. The company turned to see the flowers and plants drowned in her vomit.

She turned and managed to say "sorry". She looked up at Luke, and saw the understanding in his eyes. She tried to say something, but no sound came out.

I

Andrew loved hotel rooms. His favorite was a Best Western he'd stayed in with his mom a year ago during a two-day stay in Point Pleasant, New Jersey. They had spent the day at the beach, and Andrew had neglected to reapply sunscreen. He was sporting a thick burn on his back when they reached their room.

Entering the room overlooking the Saltmine River, Andrew thought of that late summer afternoon he'd laid on the hotel bed and watched the TV. His mom, still in her one-piece from the beach and looking a little red herself, had gotten some ice from the vending machine and laid it on Andrew's back. She looked up and saw the show Andrew was watching.

"This nut," she said. Andrew turned the volume up. He was enjoying watching the man tight-rope over Niagara Falls. He thought it was cool and dangerous. He could feel the ice melting on his back. His mother saw him watching the show.

"Good, good. His family's there too! Wonderful." She crossed her arms. "This is just disgusting. Look at him."

"What's disgusting?" Andrew asked, keeping his eyes peeled on the screen. "It's cool! What if he falls?"

"Then his family can watch him break his neck," Patricia Tollson replied. "God, this is sad. This is a celebration of death. Good riddance, if he falls. That's what I say."

Andrew hardly heard her. The ice melting on his back was the coolest burn he'd ever felt. The bedspread under his small chest itched him a little bit, but he ignored it. The tight-rope man reached the other side easily. Andrew sipped on the cranberry juice his mom made him, and found it hard to swallow laying down. Outside the sun set over the crimson hills.

Andrew lay down now on the bed in the room, thinking of that day. As she'd tucked in him, his mom said: *You always have a choice,* she said. *Between life and death. It sounds crazy—I know—but you always choose life. Got it?*

Andrew couldn't remember whether he said anything or just nodded. He listened to the sounds of shuffling paper in the next room. Warren was back. Andrew shut his eyes, and thought of Saramina, lying in the next room.

She was pregnant—she'd admitted that much once Luke had gotten her to stand. She didn't need to admit it. Even Andrew had figured it out once she'd vomited all over the plants. According to Luke's story, Andrew figured she'd been pregnant for two months.

She said she'd be all right as they reserved two rooms. Warren figured they'd spend the night in the city. Luke and Sara were in the room adjacent to them. Nick slept cozily in the cot beside the bed. Andrew had offered the bed to Nick, but Nick declined as always. Andrew noticed he'd been quiet since the argument with Ryundain. Nick really liked Ryun, Andrew knew. He felt a little angry at Ryun for storming off like that. With all of these thoughts clouding his head, Andrew felt it was useless to nap. He sat up and saw the Saltmine River through the giant windows at the north end of the room. The river was ablaze from the light of the setting sun to the west. A tall stone bridge stretched across the valley, marking the end of the Dundain's land and the beginning of the North.

Andrew crept out of the bedroom and into the study, where

Warren sat with his nose buried in a set of maps. The boy-sage looked tired. Andrew grabbed a seat to the table Warren sat at and quietly sat down. Warren didn't notice him enter until he was sitting at the table.

"Get any sleep?" Warren asked softly. Andrew shook his head. Warren nodded, and looked back down at his papers.

"What are those?" Andrew asked.

"Maps," Warren said. A smile broke out over his pale face. "You know, I'd come to think the Dundain had forgotten about me. But the only maps they sell in the general store," Warren slid one map over to Andrew, "are the ones I wrote. Long ago, I drew these up for the Dundain."

Andrew looked down at the map and saw the signature at the bottom: scrawled in nearly illegible writing was 'As drawn by Warren of the Winds.' On the map Andrew saw deep ridges and mountains drawn in.

"The mountains?" Andrew asked. Warren nodded.

"Everything north of here. The Kirondacks, the Northfleet, and to the east—the Sarna Ranges." Warren quieted his voice. "If you so choose to lead us there, Andrew. The choice is entirely yours."

"That's the thing," Andrew said. He slid the map back over to Warren. "I don't know where we should go. We could go to Sunsetville—that's what the spider-grass is for—or we could go to the mountain. Sarna Mensa, right?"

"*Mensis,*" Warren said. "Where the door is."

"If we go to the mountain," he said, "who will bring the spider-grass to Sunsetville?" he paused. "Do they even deserve it? The people there?"

"What do you mean?" Warren asked.

"The young people there—" Andrew stopped himself

from calling them hipsters. "They… were kind of awful. They wrote hateful stuff on the walls and wanted to start a war. Joe Freeman wasn't the only crazy one there. If bringing the grass to Sunsetville means risking our lives, is it even worth it?"

Warren looked up. "Of course it is," he said. "A second chance is always worth it. These young people… they may never know what we went through to help them. They may wake up to find the world entirely changed. A new start for them. Like what you may find if you ever return to your world.

"They deserve that. They deserve life, don't you think?"

"I guess so."

Warren smiled. "This world hasn't always deserved your forgiveness Andrew. But to give it anyway—that's the hard part." He pushed the reading glasses back up his nose. Andrew decided he looked too old to be a child. "The rest is easy." Andrew stood up.

"You're right," Andrew said. "But I don't think we can go anywhere without Ryundain. That's for sure."

"Oh?"

Andrew nodded. "Nick was right—about the compass thing. We're meant to be together, the six of us. I'm going to go find him, and let him know." Andrew turned toward the door of the room. He turned the knob and stepped outside. He stopped as he felt the sun's rays hit him. He felt the gun in his waistband.

"Andrew," Warren said. Andrew stopped and turned back.

"Yeah?"

"Your gun," Warren said. "If you're going to be sneaking around the palace, you won't want to be carrying that." Andrew looked down at the gun in his waistband.

"Right," Andrew said. He took it out slowly, turning it over in his left hand. "You sure I should leave it here?"

"Quite sure," Warren said. "If anything happens, I will bring it to you." Andrew nodded. He put the gun down on the table. He felt a lot lighter without it. He nodded to Warren, who gave him a smile. Then he turned and headed out of the room. As he shut the door and walked into the street, he heard Warren's voice:

"Now, where was I? Ah yes! These damned maps!"

II

Outside the street was still. The sun had finally sunk into the ocean, the top half peering over the horizon in silence. Andrew made his way through the thick heat toward the palace. The streets were empty, which Andrew thought was strange. Everywhere else he'd been, the busiest time of the day was sunset.

The palace lay dead ahead on the cobblestone path. Andrew veered off the path and into the grass, away from the entrance of the palace. He had to find a way in, where the guards wouldn't spot him. He walked around the great walls of the palace, searching for an entrance. He heard barking up ahead and saw a dog ahead of him, running at full speed. The dog, a large brown terrier, leapt at the wall and disappeared. Andrew rushed over to the wall and saw the dog had squeezed through a small nook behind some bushes. Andrew smiled as he saw it was just large enough for a kid to fit through.

III

Andrew walked through the palace garden slowly, keeping an eye out for guards. He hadn't seen any yet, but he didn't want to be surprised. The shadows of the gigantic walls beside him cast him in darkness as he crept forward. He reached the castle itself, and saw a door ahead. Above, on the castle walls, was a gigantic portrait of a sun over the ocean. *The sun's setting,* Andrew thought.

"It's like they don't know what morning is," Andrew muttered. He reached out and opened the door.

The hall was dark—fleeting light from the sunset streamed in through the gigantic windows. Ahead a tall throne peered down upon the hall. Andrew looked up at the throne, and immediately wondered how anyone ever got up to it. Ryundain's father must sit up there. The throne sat up at least sixty feet in the air.

He worked his way toward the only exit in the hall. He made to open the door, a gate-like entrance on the left-hand side of the chamber, when a voice stopped him.

"Who's there?"

Andrew turned while his hand reached down at his waist. His gun wasn't there. He turned and saw a figure approaching him in the darkness.

"Show yourself!" the voice cried. Andrew stepped forward into the light as the figure became visible.

"What are you doing here?" Frederick asked. He was dressed up in royal armor, and his red hair shone in the fleeting light. He looked at Andrew with mistrustful eyes.

"I've come to talk to Ryundain," Andrew said.

"You're not supposed to be here." Frederick was carrying a candle in his hand, and his other hand was on the sword in his belt.

"Where is Ryundain's room?" Andrew asked. He did not take his eyes off Frederick. For a moment the two stared at one another. Then Frederick looked away at the chamber around him. After a second of surveying, the man turned back to Andrew.

"Fourth door on the left." Andrew nodded. Frederick gave him one last look. "Be quick. There's something amiss in the city tonight." Then Frederick turned away and walked toward the end of the hall. Andrew watched him go, then turned to the door.

Maybe the law of the gun isn't so dead here after all, Andrew thought. He turned the door handle and entered a long hallway.

IV

Ryun wasn't all that surprised to see Andrew at the door. He expected one of the company to show up. He guessed it would be Warren, though he supposed the old man still had his pride. Certainly he didn't expect Sara or Luke—they had other problems to deal with, as evident from the palace garden.

So he had sat at his desk, looking over some of the papers documenting what he'd missed from the royal court the last two days. His own name kept showing up with words like *misconduct* and *disobedience.* His father was not pleased with him. Ryun hadn't been able to focus on the papers, however. His mind was adrift. He kept thinking of the way Nick's eyes had flashed as he'd sat up and fired the gun into the darkness. *Gunslingers,* he thought. *In this world.* He kept thinking of tales of the gunfighters who had come to the Dundain a hundred years ago. The stories he'd read as a child. He had a book sitting under his bed written about those six men. As he sat at his desk he told himself he wouldn't grab it and start reading. His eyes continued to wander from his papers to his bed, scanning the maroon carpet beneath. He was about to get up and grab it when the boy knocked on the open door.

"Come in," Ryun said. He got up from his chair, a purple-velvet 'royal seat', as the court called it. Ryun thought it uncomfortable to sit in for long periods of time. He was so big he hardly fit.

Andrew walked in. He was still dressed in the strange garments he had worn last night. Ryun didn't doubt he was from another world—the boy dressed like he was from the moon.

"Sit down,"

"Thanks," Andrew said. He sat down in the purple chair and looked back at Ryun. "There's only one chair."

Ryun shifted uncomfortably. He never did well with guests. "Oh, right." He looked around at the room. It was a large room, with a master bathroom in the back. Shelves and shelves of books lined the velvet wall, and a huge mirror hung over the bed. "I don't know… where to sit."

"I can stand." Andrew stood up. Ryun again marveled at his eyes, which were sharp and attentive. This boy was the gunfighter, Ryun knew. He carried no gun, however.

"You didn't bring your gun," Ryun said. He was somewhat disappointed.

Andrew shrugged. "I was hoping not to have to use it." Ryun nodded.

"Right. I don't think you'll have to," he said, and stopped. He wasn't sure what to say next. Andrew cut in.

"Ryundain," he said. "You—"

"Call me Ryun, Andrew," Ryun said.

"Okay, Ryun. Look, you've got to come with us."

Ryun raised his eyebrows. "You don't even know where you're going!"

"That doesn't matter," Andrew said. "You heard Nick, and the compass stuff. The six of us... we're meant to go together. Can't you see that?"

Ryun looked away at his wall, where a long mirror hung over an antique cupboard. He saw six plates resting on the shelf.

"Six... that is a number of power," Ryun said. Andrew was nodding. "There are six kingdoms that make up this land. Legend says six gunfighters travelled to this world hundreds of years ago and brought peace."

"And six shells in my gun!" Andrew cried out. "Well... three now. But six when I came here. It's got to *mean* something!"

"Maybe it does," Ryun said. "I don't want to get wrapped up in it. I'm sorry I acted the way I did at the gate earlier—I know that was unkind on my part."

"Maybe you don't have a choice," Andrew said. "Maybe you're destined to come with us."

"I'll make the choice here," Ryun said and straightened. "I don't want to run away. That's just..." he lifted up a hand and sighed. "That's just childish."

Andrew persisted. "You love guns," he said. "You told us that. Ever since you were a kid, you dreamed of the law of the gun."

Ryun nodded. "That's different, Andrew."

"How? I've got a gun!"

"Yes," Ryun said. He tried to tell the kid what was on his mind. He raised his hands in front of him. "It's just..." he looked at his hands, and felt ridiculous. He shrugged and dropped them. "It's just not the same. Things aren't so black and white anymore." Andrew didn't say anything.

"Look, it's like this. The gunfighters of legend—they saved everyone. They were the hope and faith for this world. That this world could live on—they gave us life." Ryun smiled. "And as a kid I bought it. But when you get older, things change. It's not so simple anymore."

"I don't follow." Andrew said.

"You're too young to see it," Ryun said. "Think of it like this—those people in the forest last night? They were just protecting themselves. We invaded their homes, and Gerard scared them into thinking we were something we're not. So we killed them."

"So?"

"So who's the real villain here? Who's good, and who's evil?" Ryun spread out his hands again. "You see, it's not black and white. Not anymore."

Andrew crossed his arms. He looked puzzled. *So young,* Ryun thought. *God, I wish I was that young again.*

"I can't leave this place," Ryun said. "If I did, it would mean exile for me. And I have a *life* here. I have a title, and a woman I hope to wed. And soon!

"Let Warren lead you, kid. He's been running away his entire life, even as an adult. I've known him a long time, and it was always so clear—he hated his father, and his brother. Let him lead you."

"Then that's it?" Andrew asked. "You won't come?"

Suddenly the sound of horns echoed through the palace. Ryun looked up at the door. *Battle horns,* he thought. *Why are they blowing the city's horns?*

He turned back to Andrew. "Something's wrong," he said.

Andrew looked around wildly. "Outside, the city's giving a warning. Go find Warren and them—you'll be safe there. I've got to see what's going on." Andrew gave him one last look, then turned. He opened the door to Ryun's chamber and turned back. His eyes settled on Ryun, who had trouble meeting them.

"We need you," Andrew said. "Nick needs you. More than this city does." Then he turned and left. Ryun didn't move for a moment, thinking of Nick and his flashing eyes as he'd held the gun.

V

The blaring horns woke Sara up, who jumped with a start. Her eyes were red, Luke saw, and for a moment he worried she was going to be sick again. Then she looked around the room.

"What's going on?" she asked. Luke shrugged, and got up from his chair.

"Something's going on out there," he said. "Can you come out with me?"

The two hurried through the city streets. They pushed by scores of panicked women and children, shouting frantically over the blare of the horns. Luke had heard these horns before—he'd been in the House of Dundain when a great tempest had rolled off the ocean years ago. This was no tempest, he knew—rain had not fallen on the Dundain for months, as evident from the yellowing grass outside the city.

Street lamps led the way through the dusty streets as Luke approached the palace. Luke knew the front of the palace, at the top of the hill, would offer the best vantage point of the city. From the top of the hill, on the long street running perpendicular to the palace, you could see for miles. Already groups of soldiers scrambled in front of the palace. Ryundain attempted to organize them, astride his tall horse. The troops weren't hearing the orders—they scrambled around frantically. Luke led Sara toward the commotion, and caught sight of Warren and Nick. Warren was on his horse. Nick, standing by the horse, turned and saw them.

"Up 'ere!" the boy called. "'Ave you seen Andrew?"

"We were going to ask you the same thing," Sara said, climbing up the cobblestone street.

"He's fine," Warren said. He did not turn. He looked out the south, into the dark fields beyond the city. "We will see him soon, I am sure."

"What's going on?" Luke asked. The last twenty four hours had been a whirlwind for him—he could hardly stand any longer. He had helped Sara to the room, who had still been pretty ill. Before she'd fallen asleep on the bed, she'd looked at him.

"Luke," she said. "Luke, I'm sorry I didn't tell you."

He walked over to her and held her hand. She was already half asleep. "I want to be with you," he said. "I've always wanted that." She nodded slowly, and closed her eyes. Luke had sat on the chair in the next room, listening for any noise from Sara.

As Luke followed Warren's gaze toward the fields south of the city, he forgot all his worries. Behind him, he heard Warren say:

"My brother has done this."

In the fading twilight Luke watched the corpses sagging forward. There were so many; he thought it looked more like a great grey mass. It reminded him of fog than an army—there were so many of them, and bunched so close together.

"There's thousands of them," Sara whispered.

"Tens of thousands," Luke said. "Men who died... before the guns came to this land."

They heard the moaning next, carried by the fleeting wind. Ugly, long sounds floated out of the fields below toward the city.

"We don't have three thousand soldiers in this city," Luke heard Ryundain say from atop his horse. "We've got to take refuge—there are too many of them."

"What are they?" asked Luke. "What is this?"

"It is a terror without a name," Warren said. Luke turned to the young sage, who sat quietly on his horse. "A drought without an end. A storm without rain."

"Guys!" Luke saw Andrew running from the palace gates. "Guys, what's going on?"

"Take a look," Nick said. "It's crazy!"

Andrew stopped short as he reached the company. He stared out at the field below, watching the grey and brown mass creep toward the city.

"They're back," the boy said. He looked tired. Luke wondered when the last time was the boy had gotten restful sleep. "Those are... the zombies from the village. By the sea!"

"Yeah," Sara said. "Except there's an army of zombies now."

"Should we leave?" Andrew asked. "Over the bridge?"

Luke turned to look at the bridge, sitting behind the palace. It was still and quiet in the twilight air. *Are the dead over there?* He wondered. *On the other side of the city?*

Warren didn't answer. He continued to look down upon the advancing swarm. The fields were covered with bodies, dragging their way toward the city.

"This is what you have done!" Ryundain cried. Luke watched him calm his horse and stare down at Andrew. "Look what you've brought to this city! *Death*! Death is all you have to offer!"

Andrew ignored the raving man. Suddenly, his eyes narrowed, and he twisted his mouth. Luke watched him. *What are you thinking, kid?* He wondered.

Warren seemed to know. "Your gun, Andrew," he said, and pulled it out of his bag. He handed the revolver to the boy, who nodded and took it from the sage. The wind began to pick up. Looking into his eyes, Luke knew Andrew had a plan.

Andrew turned to Warren.

"The bridge," he said. Warren nodded.

"We need the horses," Luke said. He turned and Sara followed, running now toward the stable.

"You think it's safe to cross?" Nick asked. He regarded the bridge with a wary eye.

"I cannot say," Warren said. He led his horse toward the bridge, and Andrew and Nick followed.

"You're *leaving?*" Ryun thundered. Andrew saw him turn in disgust.

"The gun will do no one any good here," Sara called. She was astride on her mare now. Luke led his horse and Home Sweet Home behind her.

"She's right!" Luke called as he reached Andrew and Nick. Home Sweet Home snorted with delight as he saw the boys, who clambered onto the beast's back.

"If you take the bridge," Ryun said, narrowing his eyes, "you will not be safe. There is a cemetery back by the bridge— the royal cemetery. Those things…" Ryun shook his head. He looked over at the bridge again, his eyes shining in the dim light.

Luke leapt onto his own horse and looked at Ryun. His auburn hair had fallen over his face, and he was breathing heavily.

"Help us," Luke said. "If you won't come with us, then help

us get over the bridge."

Ryun regarded him for a moment. Then he turned
his horse, and began to lead the way toward the great stone
arches ahead. Luke smiled, but took a look behind him before
following Ryun. The great brown swarm and found its way into
the city below. Luke hoped the citizens had managed to evacuate
the levels below, or they'd be trapped indoors. The zombies
wanted blood, and he didn't doubt they'd break down doors to
find it.

"Come on," Nick said from behind him. "No good standin'
around, Luke." Luke watched the mob swarm between the
houses a second longer, and then he clicked his tongue against
the roof of his mouth. His horse trotted forward, following
Ryun and Warren ahead.

VI

Andrew was very aware of the gun in his belt as they closed
in on the bridge. He was also very aware that he could see the
entire city beneath him. It was quiet tonight, with the exception
of a few moans and screams. Then he heard screams in front of
him, and Home Sweet Home bucked up in the air.

"*Hold on!*" Nick cried. In a flash he was above Andrew as
Home Sweet Home bucked violently in the air. Andrew clung
tight to Nick, who pulled the reins furiously. "*Down! Down boy!*"

Home Sweet Home finally settled, and the boys managed
to stay on the beast's back. Up ahead, Sara cried out from her
horse and drew her hunting knives.

"Stay behind me, boys!" she called. In front of her, at
the entrance of the bridge, a dozen bodies blocked the way.

They swayed and pivoted in the afternoon light, fixated on the six riders in front of them. They were royal zombies, Andrew saw. They wore torn robes of maroon and grey, decorated in extravagant beads and jewelry. Their flesh, however, made Andrew's stomach turn. Once pale and proud, now the skin was a sickly dark green and grey. Eyes peered out at the riders from battered skulls covered with thin wiry grey hair. A moment of silence passed before Ryun leapt ahead of the company, bringing his sword down upon his ancestors.

"Begone!" he screamed. The two corpses in the front of the pack fell beneath Ryun's horse. Nick tried out in triumph and followed Sara, who whipped her horse into the fray. Ahead, Luke and Warren caught up to Ryun, who slashing violently at the horde of zombies. The two rode side by side, and Luke drew his own sword. He slashed at the face of one zombie and cut it in half. Blood splattered onto his horse's side as the zombie collapsed to the ground.

"Warren!" Sara called. She tossed him one of her hunting knives, and the boy had to reach up in the air to keep it from sailing over the side of the bridge. Warren grabbed it and brought the long knife down in a semi-circle that cut one lady-zombie in half. Her purple dress flopped off of her ragged body, revealing breasts and wrinkled skin. Andrew looked away and nearly gagged as he clung tight to Nick. Home Sweet Home moved triumphantly through the violence, and emerged unscathed.

Ryun pushed forward beside the boys as the royal horde diminished. He let out a cry of victory, but stopped when his eyes fell upon the other half of the bridge. Andrew followed his gaze.

A much bigger pack of zombies hung around the rest of

the way. There were at least fifty of them, Andrew decided—it was a bigger crowd than the mob Joe Freeman had accumulated in Sunsetville. The sound of gargled moans and dragging feet reached the company, who watched in utter silence.

"They came from the other side of the bridge," Warren muttered.

"You've got to be kidding." Luke said.

"Fall back, beasts!" came a wretched cry. Andrew turned and saw horses fly by him on either side. He caught a flash of one rider's red hair.

"Frederick!" Ryun called. He let out a whoop and turned to follow his mounted companions. Five horsed Dundain soldiers, Frederick included, flew toward the mob of zombies on the center of the bridge.

"Come on!" Luke screamed. He kicked his own horse and followed the assault. In a second, the world became a flash as Home Sweet Home jumped into the fray. Andrew held on to Nick for dear life as the stone bridge and the river below flew beneath their horse.

VII

Death had come to the Dundain.

Andrew had never seen so much blood in his life. Guts flew rampant as swords swung wildly. The boy could hardly see in front of his horse, but he felt it jerking beneath him. Nick was doing his best to maneuver Home Sweet Home around the calamity, without frightening the horse.

Andrew saw the man on the horse beside Frederick cry out and fall to the ground. A group of three scrawny zombies leapt on his horse, digging into the animal's meaty flesh and pushing it to the ground. Andrew didn't look down to see the other zombies pounce on the fallen rider.

"Andrew!" Sara cried beside him. "Stay behind me! I'll cut a path!" There was a long streak of blood on her forehead but no cut. She leapt ahead of the boys, and then Nick cried out in front of him. The boy whipped off of the side of the horse and onto the ground. The zombie who had shoved him moved toward Andrew, his pallid eyes focused on the boy and his horse. Andrew kicked the zombie square in the chest.

Nick cried out and fell upon the zombie, blade in hand. He buried deep in the monster's chest, and the zombie crumbled helplessly. The sword went with him, and Nick fell down on top of the tall skinny corpse.

"Get off! Get off!" Nick screamed. The zombie slapped at him with its arm, and Nick delivered a kick into its crotch. The arms quit thrashing and shot out to the side while Nick pulled Stricker's blade from its chest. Sara's cry made both boys turn.

Two zombies clung to her horse, ravaging the poor beast. Sara swung wildly with her hunting knife. The horse beneath her bucked so violently that she missed her mark. As she fell back she kicked hard against the side of her mare. The zombies clung onto their meal as the mare dragged them over the side of the bridge. The beast and its predators disappeared from sight as a group of zombies closed in on Sara, who lay helplessly on her back.

"No!" Nick cried. He rushed forward, brandishing his blade over his head. Andrew turned and saw Frederick had fallen as well; he was wrestling with a group of zombies near the edge of the bridge. A cry next to him made Andrew recoil. One of Frederick's men screamed in agony. A small zombie had

climbed on his horse and had sunk its teeth deep into his chest.
The soldier wavered a little bit, his eyes rolling into the back of
his head. The child zombie went down with him as he slid off
the horse, and continuing to feast on its prey. Its bat-like head,
covered in sweaty stringy red hair, bobbed slowly as it dug in.
For a moment its single eyeball regarded Andrew, then turned
back to the soldier beneath it.

Too many, Andrew realized. Ahead he saw Sara reaching
desperately for her sword as one zombie hovered over her. It
thrashed with Nick, who used his sword to push the menace
backwards. Another zombie, an ugly yellow pulp of a creature,
slipped past the two and reached down for Sara. She was pinned
now.

Andrew pulled the gun out of his pocket. His head swam
a little as he kicked his heels into Home Sweet Home's side.
He grabbed onto the reins with his other hands as the horse
screamed and bucked a little. Luke turned to watch the boy,
having just cut a zombie down.

"Go for it, kid," he muttered.

"*This world,*" Andrew screamed, "*is no place for the dead!*" A
hundred heads on the bridge turned to observe the boy on his
horse. The horse kicked upwards, and Andrew looked sternly
down upon the scene. For a moment, the battle stopped.

Everyone below, Andrew thought. He looked to the right
and saw the city sitting beneath the bridge. Thousands of heads
were peering up at him—from here, he couldn't see who was
dead and who was living. Ryun had told him that the bridge was
the highest point in the city. Anything he did or said now was
entirely visible, and he felt the countless eyes peering up at him.
As Home Sweet Home landed back on the stone, he turned back
to the fiasco in front of him.

"Go back to sleep!" He cried. *"I command it!"* He yelled, and dug his heels into the side of Home Sweet Home again. The horse screamed and stood upon on its back legs, suspending Andrew in midair. The boy clung on to the reins dearly with his right hand, watching the world summersault around him. Yet he didn't fall. He kept his right hand tight on the reins as he raised his left, the ancient revolver in his fingers.

Damn, he thought. *It feels good to scream.* Then he pulled the trigger.

VIII

Every bone in the boy's body rattled. The shot carried on the wind, echoing through the city and over the field. Below him he saw hundreds of soldiers and civilians staring up at him. Below them he saw the mass of corpses stop, silent. Andrew held the gun out and looked down over the city.

Don't tell me I wasted another shot, Andrew thought.

There was a great sigh as the corpses below began to drop. Andrew watched as a thousand bodies knelt before the city, down upon dry and withered knees. He couldn't hear the cracks of the joints, but he could imagine. The zombies laid down and knelt before him, dropping their heads.

Andrew remembered the way Ryun had knelt to Nick in the forest, and saw the corpses assumed the same position.

Andrew watched in silence. His eyes were wide. He heard nothing behind him. He knew the forces below were waiting. He opened his mouth, and didn't know what to say. After a moment, he shouted:

"Go back to sleep! This world is for the living!" Then he

turned away—he figured that would show the corpses he meant business. In front of him, the scene had changed. The herd of zombies (what was left of them) had begun a slow retreat across their bridge, back toward their graves.

Andrew looked up and saw Warren dismount from his horse. Luke, Sara, Nick, and the sage stared at the boy. The few soldiers remaining did the same.

Ryundain stepped in front of the company. He watched Andrew, who stood silent and watched back.

"I kneel to the gun," Ryun said. He lowered to his knees and bowed his head. Behind him his soldiers watched in silence.

"All hail to the gunfighter!" Warren cried. He too dropped to his knee. Nick followed suit, and Luke went next. Sara bowed as well, and mouthed *nice going, kid,* to Andrew. Andrew smiled a little, and Home Sweet Home whined impatiently beneath him.

Sorry, boy Andrew thought. *I don't like to kick you like that.*

Frederick looked around at his men. Then he dropped to his knee. With another great sigh the army of the Dundain followed suit. Hundreds of soldiers kneeled before the boy beneath the great bridge. Andrew looked around, his eyes wide.

Ryundain looked up. "I am in your service, Andrew Tollson."

Andrew laughed. "Good," he said. "Cause you're coming with us!"

FIVE

Six Shells

chapter twelve
smoke and fire

I

Nick slept well that night. He was exhausted by the time he got back to the room with Andrew and Warren, and collapsed. He slept through, without the worry of bad dreams. He dreamt of his home, where the great open fields and skies had once made him dream of the open road. He figured now he'd found the open road, it made sense he should dream of home. That was the way life went, he figured.

Someone began to shake him as he saw his father walking in from the fields. Nick looked around frantically but no one was near him. Still the shaking sensation persisted. He began to run around the yard of his house, a small white barn (he called it a barn, much to the dismay of his mother). He couldn't get rid of the shaking feeling, and soon he could hear his name called:

"Nick."

He opened his eyes and saw Andrew standing over him.

"It was a dream?" Nick asked, rubbing his eyes.

"Yes," Andrew said. Nick saw the sun rising in the window by his cot. The hotel room was no longer dark—someone had thrown open the shades. Nick shielded his eyes from the light. Yet the sun hadn't fully risen. Nick knew this time of day well. He got up at dawn every day during the harvest.

"Is it time?" Nick asked. Warren, who was gathering up the maps on the table, looked over. He was wearing silver and green riding robes.

"Time to go, Nickolas," Warren said. "One last day of riding ahead of us."

The three boys left the room in a matter of minutes. Warren had been out early and bought breakfast for the boys. Nick munched on his bagel as he untethered Home Sweet Home. It suddenly popped into his head that he hadn't fed the horse since they had arrived in the city. He looked at Home Sweet Home, who began to sniff his bagel. Nick laughed and broke off half of it. Home Sweet Home caught on right away, and munched the bagel right out of the boy's hand. Nick laughed and pet the horse lightly.

Now the three boys led their horses through the quiet streets. Nick watched the city sleep around him, and announced that he thought dawn was the best time of day.

"How so?" Warren asked.

"It's simple," Nick said. "Things don't seem so… heavy at dawn. Yeah, heavy's the word."

Andrew laughed. "What do you mean, heavy?"

"Well," Nick began, and stopped. "I dunno know."

Yet he did—he just couldn't put it into words. He passed the quiet houses and parks and looked out to the west where the sun climbed slowly over the ocean. He thought of home again as he led Home Sweet Home toward the palace gates, and thought of the sunsets there. He thought of his father coming in from working the fields, exhausted and disappointed. Nick always knew he was disappointed because he would sit at the dinner table with his hat in hands, waiting for food. The old man would stare at the floor, silent and lost in thought. Nick and his brothers would chat a little bit, but there was always silence at the other end of the table. Nick could feel the heaviness sitting over their table, weighing him down as the sun went down outside. There were no lights where he lived either—just starlight—so things got dark outside quickly.

"I don't usually get up this early," Andrew admitted. "I don't have to wake up til seven when I head to school. Well," he grinned sheepishly, "when I go to school, that is."

"But it's the best time of day!" Nick said. He looked over at Andrew, who regarded him with a smile. "We always get up early for the spring harvest—before it gets real hot. And it's quiet and still out, but you feel like you can do anything! Like the day is yours, and whatever happened yesterday don' matter." Nick nodded. Now he knew what to say. "It just makes you want to say, 'well, maybe today can be different.' It don' have to be like yesterday, I guess."

Nick wanted to say more, but they rounded a bend toward the gates. Sara saw them first—she dropped the reins of her horse and turned to wave. Luke was talking to Ryun, who was amidst some of the city soldiers. Yet as soon as Sara waved Luke turned his head and saw the three boys leading their horses up the quiet street. A big grin rolled over his face.

"Thought you would sleep all day, boys?" he called out. "There's riding to do!"

"Well, I would've been here *much* earlier," Warren began, "but you know how boys like to sleep." Luke shot him a grin, and Warren shrugged.

Ryundain turned to face the company. "All affairs are in order for today. Frederick and a company of our finest soldiers are going to take the spider-grass to Sunsetville today. Do you have the grass with you, Andrew?"

Andrew nodded and took his bag off of his shoulder. He handed it over to Frederick, who was dressed in red and black riding gear—the color of the Dundain. As Andrew handed over the bag, Nick realized he would have to explain to his aunt why the purse she'd given Andrew was lost.

"Wait!" Nick said. The soldiers turned to him in surprise. Frederick looked over in surprise. "That's my aunt's bag."

Frederick looked at the bag, and back at Nick. "All right," he said, and reached into the bag. He began taking handfuls of grass out of the bag and shoving them into a satchel on his saddle.

"And my explanation last night was thorough?" Warren said. "On how to use the grass?"

Frederick nodded as he took out the last handful. He tossed the bag back to Andrew. "Yes," he answered.

"Good," Ryun said. "Frederick, you'll have to be careful. Gerard may have laid a trap for you in Sunsetville, expecting the six of us."

"He's right," Warren said. "Though I doubt my brother will have done any such thing. He has very little interest in the affairs of this world—he will most definitely wait for us at the door."

Frederick nodded. He looked at the six of them, and then at Ryun. "Hard to believe you're leaving."

"I'll be back," Ryun said, though Nick thought he didn't sound as confident as usual. Frederick nodded, and bowed his head. Then he started down on the hill on his horse. A company of a dozen horsed soldiers followed. They departed, leaving Nick and his friends alone at the palace gates.

"Well, it's just us now," Luke said. He looked around at the company with a silly grin. "Though I wouldn't mind staying at the riverfront hotel there for a few more days…"

"There is no time!" Warren said. He looked at Luke and realized the man was joking. Warren sighed and began to climb on his horse.

"What's the rest of the city doing up?" Sara asked. She was watching throngs of people moving down the hill toward the fields outside of the city.

"Burying the dead," Ryun said. "Most of the corpses buried themselves underground last night, but not very deep. The royal council decided it would be best to cover their shallow graves with more dirt."

"The dead will not rise again," Warren said. "You can be sure of that. They follow the law of the gun now."

"My father," Ryun said, and rolled his eyes a little bit, "wanted to cut off the heads of the 'zombies'. But I managed to convince him that was most unholy."

"Good!" Warren said. He had managed to scramble up on his horse. The beast side-stepped uneasily beneath the child. "Then that is all. Let's be off!"

Sara led her horse next to Andrew as Nick climbed on top of Home Sweet Home. "You didn't forget your gun, did you?" she asked. Nick thought she was hiding a smile. Andrew showed her the weapon in his belt.

"Good," she said. "I think we're going to need it."

II

Luke looked over the side of the bridge as they trotted across. *We're miles up this time,* he thought. He felt the wind across the bridge and shivered a little bit.

"Get ahold of yourself," he murmured, just loud enough for Sara to hear him. "You've been over this bridge a thousand times."

The bridge was stable too—he really had nothing to worry

about. Still, he had a bad feeling. It sat in his lower stomach and tightened his entire midsection. *What am I, pregnant?* He thought to himself, and couldn't hide his nervous smile. He looked up and saw Sara's eyes regarding him.

"I'm okay," Luke said. "Just a little unsettled, that's all."

She smiled and looked away, and he took a deep breath in. Across the bridge he could imagine Gerard sitting there on his horse, waiting for them.

Oh, you've all come so far.

The end of the bridge was empty, however. The wind began to blow in their face, and Luke knew that wind all too well—it was a cold northern wind. He closed his eyes and tried not to think of home.

His mind drifted to his dream he had last night. He dreamt of the day his brothers died, and hearing the old song again— 'the last of my friends have climbed over the horizon.' This time it was a man singing it, and as he walked through the town searching for the voice, that feeling of imbalance had grown substantially. He passed a house and came upon a graveyard, and where he found the old man singing.

Except it wasn't an old man singing—it was a young man. Luke saw he had long dark hair that had begun to gray. The man had his back to Luke as he sang the song over a gravestone. Luke crept closer and read the tombstone.

'Here lies Saramina Bellsgrove, daughter of King Geromino. Loved by Lukemir of the Northfleet—her loving husband."

Luke's stomach dropped. He looked at the man standing over the grave, singing the song. *That's me,* he thought. *Oh God, —I don't want to live in a world without her.*

He'd woken up feeling empty and alone. Sara was beside

him but she felt so far away. Luke felt the despair well up inside of him. It was the same feeling he'd discovered when he learned of his brothers' deaths, and the same feeling he'd carried with him for all the years he'd wandered this land. It clung him to as the morning dragged on—he couldn't shake it.

III

Saramina felt her horse begin to grow restless beneath her. The mare didn't like to be on such narrow ground. The path they walked on wound a slender path around the cliffs north of the city. Now the path grew rocky and twisted.

"We should walk," she muttered. Warren nodded, and stepped off his horse. Beside her she heard Luke exhale slowly.

"Thought we were done with heights for today," he muttered. Ahead of them the path grew narrower and whipped around the side of the cliff.

Sara looked over at Luke. The dark rings under his eyes stood out clearly in the morning light. She hadn't gotten much sleep either. Luke's muttering in his sleep last night (he admitted to some bad dreams when he woke) had kept her up as well. As she dressed this morning he told her he had dreamed of the day his brothers died.

"I kept thinking of the letter the officer gave my mother," Luke said as he folded his shirt from the previous night's dance. "The one I never get to read. I've always wondered who wrote it."

He wouldn't say much more about it, and she didn't want to press the issue. In his face, though, she saw the melancholy returning. Sara knew that far off look all too well. She thought of her own father, standing over the open casket at her brother's funeral. The old man hadn't wept. He had simply stood over the velvet lining of his son's coffin and looked sadly into what lay inside. It could have been her father beside her today, Sara thought as Luke began to lead his horse toward the bend. Melancholy always wears the same face, she decided.

Behind them the city sat in a haze of blue and gold. Sara could still hear the Saltmine River rushing down below them.

"This is the last bend ahead," Ryun announced. "The cliff descends after this, so we will be able to ride again."

"Stop," Andrew said suddenly. He was up ahead with Warren and Nick. He bent down and examined the ground in front of them. Sara smiled, admiring the boy's keenness. "These tracks... they're fresh."

"That's right," Warren said. "Wagon tracks. We've been following the trail for a few hundred yards."

"No wagon rides on this trail," Ryun said. "It's too dangerous. Wagons take the cart road, around the cliffs."

Sara reached up and ran her finger down the bow on her back. She followed Warren's lead, who led his horse steadily toward the sharp right turn.

"Be on your guard," Warren said. "My brother may have laid a trap for us after all."

"Sara," Luke said from beside her. She turned to see his blue staring into hers.

"Yes?" she said.

"I'm with you," he said. She nodded, and reached down to squeeze his hand.

To their left, the cliff fell sharply. Sara marveled as she turned the bend how any wagon ever got around this corner. She could see the tracks of the wheel, and they veered dangerously close to the edge of the path. There was more than enough room for a horse, but a wagon was a tight fit.

Warren stopped ahead, and the boys followed. Sara threaded her way past Andrew and Warren to observe the wagon that sat quietly in the path ahead. They couldn't continue past it; it blocked the way. The coach had been turned perpendicular to the path—the front dangled lazily over the edge of the cliff, rocking slowly in the breeze. Sara saw Andrew's hand on his gun, and was about to tell him to spare his bullets. She never got the chance—at that moment the door to the coach opened.

Sara whipped the bow off of her back and aimed into the inside of the coach. She knew the face all too well that emerged from the inside, with its ugly sneer and loose skin falling over the eyes. Luke, Warren, and Ryun didn't recognize it, but she did. She fired first, before Andrew could ever draw his gun.

The sneer on Stricker's face became a grimace of pain as her arrow found its mark in his chest. He lurched forward out of his velvet seat by the door. Sara recoiled at the sight of the man in the light—her first thought was of her brother in his casket. Something was in his left hand, Sara saw. It looked like a red baton. She laughed.

"Is that all?" she asked. She began to walk toward the coach, as Stricker struggled to keep from falling out of the coach. He had a bloody towel wrapped over his right hand, and he could find no grip as he stumbled out of the coach and flopped onto the path, on his back. Sara suddenly remembered the night in the tavern, and Andrew's flashing green eyes as he had pulled the gun out from under the table.

He has no right hand, she remembered.

"Sara, get back!" Andrew yelled from behind her. Stricker

reared his head at her.

"Time to go *boom*," he snarled. The red baton, she saw, had a fuse attached to it. A small flame wound its way down that fuse. The look in Stricker's eyes, which were pure red and ablaze with hate, made her stop in her tracks. The wind hit her back with full force, and she stumbled over Stricker.

"No! It's too late!" Stricker mumbled giddily, and held the red baton up. He tried to thrust it at her, but failed. He dropped the baton and it hit the ground. The wind killed the flame on the shortening fuse, and the baton rolled down back toward the coach. It came to a rest at the wheel of the wagon.

IV

"A neat trick," Warren said, walking up behind Saramina. "No doubt my brother is behind this."

"That's dynamite!" Andrew said. He looked up at Warren, who shook his head. "It's… like an explosive. It explodes when you light the fuse."

"With all the dynamite in the coach…" Ryun said, stepping to take a look inside. He shook his head. Andrew knew what Ryun was trying to say. The dynamite would have blown the entire side of the cliff sky-high.

Stricker let out a long gargled moan. Andrew looked at him, lying on the ground. It was not the same man he had shot two days ago. Sores covered his face and neck now. His flesh hung loose and wildly off his face. Two red eyes bulged out of his sockets, peering up at Andrew.

"*You,*" Stricker spat. He began to crawl forward toward Andrew. He didn't get very far before Ryun stepped in the way, his hand on his sword. Stricker stopped short, staring up at Ryun.

"You'll get no closer, beast," Ryun said. Stricker stopped, staring at Ryun's eyes. Then he shut his eyes and let out a long, ugly moan. He rolled onto his back and began to retch, holding his abdomen. Andrew watched him sadly.

"So this is the guy from the villages by the sea," Luke said, standing over the thrashing man. "You weren't kidding, Sar— he's a creep."

"I think I feel bad for him," Sara said. "Gerard must have gotten into his head somehow."

"He did," Andrew said. "Just look into his eyes—you can see the dust there."

Warren bent down beside Stricker. As soon as the boy laid a hand on Stricker's forearm, the man stopped thrashing and looked up.

"You know my face, don't you?" Warren said. Stricker regarded him with wide eyes. His body went rigid.

"How did you get here?" Stricker whispered. His eyes began to seize.

Warren shouldn't touch him, Andrew thought. He drew close and put his hand on Warren's shoulder.

"I am not who you think I am," Warren said. "I am his brother. And I have come to give you peace." Andrew froze. He blinked and saw an image of Gerard, staring back at him.

"He found me," Stricker said. Andrew barely heard him. Suddenly he could see Gerard—two yellow eyes glaring at him—and it was night. He closed his eyes and heard Gerard say:

I've got a little job for you, my scurvy-ridden friend.

"I rode on a horse—following you." Stricker said. "But *he* found me first. And he gave me all of this."

There's a wagon, and some horses. I'll tell where you to go—kill the horses when you get there. You'll know my brother when you see him. Gerard bent close and showed him the back of his hand. *You'll see the scar on the back of his hand.* A long, purple-red scar separated the knuckles.

"Gerard sent you here," Warren whispered. Even with Andrew's hand on the sage's back, Warren sounded miles away. "Last night, he found you."

Andrew watched as Gerard got up from his crouch. He was looking through Stricker's eyes, the boy figured.

You should be dead, Gerard said. It was too dark to see much of him. *But I'm not finished with you yet. Now you get to go out with a bang!* Andrew took his hand off Warren's back. He looked at his hand. It was the same.

What in the world was that? Andrew wondered.

"The terror... waits for you," Stricker said suddenly. His eyes opened wide. "I saw it."

Warren didn't take his eyes off of Stricker. "What terror?" he asked, his brow darkening.

Andrew saw the blood soaking through the raggedy shirt Stricker wore. It was supposed to be a gray shirt, Andrew figured, but now it was soaked maroon.

Stricker shook his head slowly. "It's hungry. I don't want... to think of it." He laid his head upon the ground again. His stringy hair tangled in the dirt. He looked up at Warren and tried to say something else. Instead, blood began to leak out of the corner of his mouth.

"Goodbye Stricker, man of the sea." Warren said. "May you fare better in the next world than you did in this one." He turned to the company as he rose to his feet. No one said anything. Andrew waited for Warren to do *something*.

"For heaven's sakes, I'm just a child," Warren said. "I can't push this thing by myself!"

With their combined strength the wagon moved easily. It rolled lazily off the edge of the cliff, and somersaulted out of Andrew's view. The boy didn't watch it fall, but waited for the explosion. Instead, there was a loud crunch as the wagon hit the rocks below. Nick looked over at Andrew.

"I thought it would explode?"

Andrew shrugged. "I guess it needs fire. Or the dynamite's old, and useless."

As they began to lead their horses past Stricker's body, who lay rigid in the dirt path, Luke nudged Andrew.

"That 'dynomir', as you call it— " Luke began.

"Dynamite."

"Right, dynamite. It is not from our world. That's from yours?"

Andrew nodded. "Yeah. But it's not the first thing Gerard took from my world. Remember the walk-man, Warren?" He eyed Warren strangely, remembering what he had seen when he lay his hand on the sage's back.

I'll ask him later, Andrew decided. *Now's not the time.*

Warren nodded. "I wouldn't say he took it from your world, Andrew—he found it. Somewhere deep in the desert, he has found all of this."

"Don't forget this," Ryun said. He held out the bronze revolver in his hand. Andrew's hand instinctively fell to his belt, to check that his gun was still there. It was. "This too is from your world, Andrew. It must be. I found it in the river, though."

They began to ride away from the smoke. The path was large enough for them to ride on again, and began to descend. Ahead Andrew saw a long rocky savannah stretch into the horizon. At the horizon, he could just make out a few mountaintops.

"Hey Ryun," Nick said, pulling up beside him.

"Mm?" Ryun said, without taking his eyes off the path.

"Could I... borrow your gun?"

Ryun turned to the boy, his eyebrow raised.

"Just to see it," Nick said. Ryun nodded, and handed over the revolver. Nick's eyes grew wide as he turned the weapon over in his hands. Luke turned to look back, and Andrew followed his gaze. Stricker's body lay motionless in the dirt, with Sara's arrow sticking out of his chest. Already a vulture in the sky circled over the path, waiting for the company to move on.

V

The ride north took the rest of the day. As they approached the mountains the terrain grew rocky and desolate. The five mountains jutted out of the ground ahead like sad stone giants, overshadowed by their older brothers to the east. There the Kirondack Mountains rose up to magnificent heights, dwarfing the Sarna ranges. Luke eyed the different ranges with indifference.

The Sarnas, which Warren informed Andrew weren't truly mountains but "as close to mountains as you can get" jutted awkwardly from the rocky earth as five outstretched fingers. Luke named each as they approached: Sarna Locus, Sarna Dias, Sarna Rauros, and Sarna Luego crowded around the great centerpiece of the range. The tallest of the bunch, Sarna Mensis, sat quietly in the fading afternoon light. As the company walked their horses through the mountain path that wound through valleys and dried streams, Ryundain gazed up at the mountain.

"I have dreamed of this place," he said. "Always, since I was a child. All of the kids in the palace were afraid of it—claimed it was haunted."

"It prob'ly is," Nick said, leading Home Sweet Home beside Ryun. "T'least that's what the stories are where I come from. 'The Haunted North', the jackers called it."

"Jackers?" asked Andrew.

"Travellin' folk," Nick said. "Men without a home."

"Men *looking* for a home, Nick," Luke said. "Sometimes they find one, too." Sara smiled at him.

"Whatever the case, I've always wanted to see this range," Ryun said as he led his horse down a steep embankment. Andrew followed him, listening as his deep voice echoed through the stony hills. "But never have I been here, not in all my days. Sad to say, lordship and diplomacy hold much adventure, but only to places of civilization. Such a desolate area as this…" Ryun looked around. "I've always yearned to see it."

"They're romantic, you're saying?" Andrew asked.

"Romantic, yes," Ryun said. "When you're surrounded by lords and soldiers all day, even the Haunted North seems romantic." He turned to Warren. "I think this will be a good place to stop, Warren. Set up camp for the night."

"We're not climbin' up tonight?" Nick asked. Warren, who had trailed the company a few paces, caught up.

"This place is as fine as any," Warren said. They had arrived at the base of the mountains. Ahead the terrain turned steep and rugged, winding up a maze of stone. "And no Nickolas, tonight we camp. I would not bring us up these mountains in darkness."

"He's right," Luke said. "They don't call it the Haunted North for nothing, kid."

"Then we'll climb in the morning?" Andrew asked.

"Yes," Warren said. "Before dawn. Our journey will come to an end as the sun rises."

Luke tended to his horse as the others began to search for sticks for a fire. The horse had been scratched the night before, on the bridge. Luke looked closely at the wound and decided it was just minor. He jumped when he heard a voice behind him.

"Luke," Sara said. Luke turned and saw her standing by her bag.

"You're quiet," Luke said. "I didn't hear you coming."

"I'm sorry about this morning," she said. She looked off to the mountain behind Luke, and was silent for a moment. *Apologizing,* thought Luke, *is not her strong suit.*

"I was... stupid." She shook her head. "I got thinking about my brother, and I lost myself."

Luke moved away from his horse and came over to her. "It's all right," Luke said. "You're here now. That's what matters."

"But there's more," she said. Luke stopped. "Luke... this is crazy."

Luke nodded. "I was hoping you wouldn't say it. But you're right."

"All I can think of is Stricker's body in the dirt," she said. "And the vulture circling over it. Did you see it?" Luke nodded. "We're dealing in death now. And tomorrow... it could easily be one of us in the dirt."

Luke hadn't wanted to say so, but he thought of his dream again. The image of Sara's grave flashed through his mind, and his stomach dropped a little bit. *Hold it together,* he thought. *It's just a dream.*

Sara drew close to him now. "I think I know what I'm trying to ask," she said. "I don't know how to say it."

Luke took her hand, and stood like that for a moment. Then he nodded.

"It's time."

Warren and Andrew returned to camp first, carrying a few sticks and brush with them. "There's plenty out there," Andrew explained to Luke as he laid down the sticks. "The drought killed a lot of trees."

Warren sat down with a sigh. He looked at the bundle of sticks in front of him, and looked up at Luke and Sara. "I suppose you want me to start this, then."

"If you can put out a fire so quickly," Luke said, "I figure you'll have no problem getting one started."

"How'd you know to blow out the fuse?" Andrew asked.

Warren looked over at the boy. "Dynamite's not from our world, Andrew," he said. "But as the saying goes, where there is fire there is something amiss."

"That's not the saying," Andrew said. It was Warren's turn to raise an eyebrow. "The saying is, 'where there is smoke, there is usually a fire.'"

"Warren," Luke said. "Sara and I want to marry—tonight, if possible. Before we go up the mountain." His eyes were shining.

"Whoa!" Andrew said. "That's kind of sudden!"

"Life's too short," Luke said. "Especially with whatever's waiting for us in the road ahead." Sara stepped beside Luke, and Luke was glad to have her next to him.

"He's right," she said. "It's time."

Warren raised both eyebrows, and turned back to Andrew. "Now there's smoke *and* a fire."

VI

Nick would never forget Luke and Sara, standing face to face with their hands interlocked. Warren stood between them, reciting the vows from memory. The white field of wildflowers bloomed around them—Nick had found it with Sara while the others made the fire. The boy had been out walking with Sara when they heard the crash of the rushing water. The pair followed the sound for a few minutes and came upon the great waterfall, cascading off the sheer western face of Sarna Rauros.

Nick had never seen anything like it. The waterfall fell into a great clear pool, around which a grove of white and purple wildflowers grew rampant. The flowers rolled through the grove, creating a sea of color. They were mostly daisies and lilies, Nick knew. Sara feared this might be Gerard's treachery, but when Warren caught up to them he laughed.

"I don't think so," the boy said. "Gerard wouldn't dare go near a place of such light and life. No…" Warren looked up to the top of the waterfall. "There may be more to this place than we see, though."

"What do you mean?" Nick asked. He hated when Warren made unclear statements. Warren simply shrugged and said no more.

"Then we can have it here?" Sara asked. "The wedding?"

Warren thought that was a fine idea. The others came back to camp and listened with surprise as Nick informed them that Sara was waiting in the grove for their wedding. Nick got prepared as quickly as possible (Luke lent him a comb for his curly hair, but it was so thick the comb got stuck). Then he followed Luke, Andrew, and Ryun over toward the waterfall.

Nick quit listening to Warren after a few minutes. The sage's words became background noise as Nick watched the sun descend beneath the ocean. He'd always thought the sunset was long in Sunsetville, but out here it seemed to last for hours. He thought of the gun Ryun had lent him earlier. It was still broken, though Nick had an idea he could fix it once the wedding was over.

He looked over to Ryun, standing tall and straight behind Luke. Andrew stood behind him, and Nick stood behind Andrew. They looked funny, Nick decided; there were three best men and no bridesmaids.

"We're kind of like her bridesmaids, though," Nick had pointed out to the others on the way over. Luke couldn't help but laugh.

"Well… because we're all so close, I mean!" Nick said. "Not 'cause we're girls or anythin'."

Ryun snapped Nick out of his daze as he began to sing the Song of Ceremonies. Nick had been to a wedding before—his cousin Sal had married Fran, a girl from town— so Nick knew most of the procedure. He listened to Ryun sing and looked up to the water above, falling from the side of the mountain. The sun reflected off of the cascading falls, and Nick narrowed his eyes. He thought he saw something there, where the water fell over the side of the mountain. It looked like the shadow of some great dog, or even a lion.

"As a sage of the third order, son of Hiralyn the Great, it is my duty and pleasure to declare you husband and wife."

Nick blinked as Warren concluded the ceremony. As he did, the shadow disappeared. Still, he thought of Warren's words as they had found the grove: *There may be more to this place than we see, though.* Nick kept his eyes peeled on the top of the falls as Warren declared Luke and Sara husband and wife.

"Allow me to take a liberty and say that I am very glad for

the both of you," Warren said. "Some might think it is fitting: on a day when the east and the west unite in peace and order," and Warren nodded to Ryun, "so it is fitting that the north and the south be wed in unity in love."

"I knew you'd take the liberty," Sara said.

"Well, you're husband and wife now, and my job's done. Let the flame between you burn in love and treasure!" Warren bowed his head as Luke and Sara kissed. Andrew clapped first. Nick could've told him it wasn't ceremonial to clap until after the kiss, but Nick didn't think ceremony applied here. He joined in with Andrew's applause, clapping fervently and laughing. The sun fell beneath the hills, casting the lovers in orange and yellow. Nick closed his eyes and felt the sunlight hold him quietly in its fading embrace.

VII

Ryun led the three boys back to camp. He was in a hurry to start dinner—he had left the stag he had killed earlier roasting over the fire. Sara and Luke stayed behind in the grove to celebrate their marriage, and Ryun figured even Andrew and Nick knew what was going to happen amidst the flowers. It made him think of a woman he met in the royal court, when he had begun to come of age. Her name was Lady Guinessen, and the way her red hair fell over her bare shoulders when she wore a dress had made the young Ryundain's head spin. She had gone off to live in a convent, and Ryun always thought that was the world's greatest shame.

They waited for the lovers to return before they dug in, but it didn't take long. A single horse carrying two riders passed by the side of Sarna Rauros before an hour passed. Luke and Sara trotted back into camp, riding bareback on Sara's horse. The mare eyed the company lazily and snorted.

"Good thing your back," Ryun said.

"Yeah," Andrew said. "I'm so hungry I could eat a horse." Warren looked at Sara's mare in surprise, but Andrew laughed and shook his head. Ryun dug into the meat—he loved deer meat. Luke had something to say as soon as he began to eat.

"This isn't bad," Luke said, as he munched down a huge chunk of meat. "Looks like the city boy can cook after all."

Ryun laughed, and returned Luke's grin with a grin of his own. It felt good to laugh, he decided. "I am glad a man so hardened by years of the road can enjoy it."

"First he gets married, now he's makin' jokes," Nick said, and shook his head. "What in the world's next?"

Soon they were all laughing and talking. The sky grew dark and the mountains above became tall silent guardians watching over the company. Ryun hardly noticed—the light of the fire was enough for him. He figured Gerard could probably hear them, high up on the mountain, or wherever he was hiding out. Ryun thought that it must be lonely up there, all by himself. He thought of his father, sitting up on his high throne in the Hall of the Falling Sun, and decided that Gerard probably felt the same way. Suddenly he was very glad to be around these five people, around this fire.

Nick lay back on his hands and stared up the stars above. The boy tucked his hands behind his head and smiled.

"You know what'd make this meal just perfect?"

"What's that?" Sara asked. She leaned back against Luke, who sat on a log Ryun had found earlier.

"Dessert. My ma', she makes a terrific apple cruster," Nick

claimed. "I haven't had it in so long, though. Not since the drought started. Since then I've had to put up with city cookin'."

"The cruster," Andrew said. "It's like pie? It's round and doughy?"

"Oh yes," Nick said. "The best cruster in all the southlands. With all due respect, Ms. Saramina."

Sara waved it off. "I'm sure its very good, Nick," she said.

"All our cousins and their cousins gather around at our farm durin' Whisper-Fest." He looked over at Andrew. "When summer ends, that is. They come to get a taste of that cruster," he paused and closed his eyes. "Tastin' that, that's when I know I'm home."

"What about you, kid?" Sara asked Andrew. "What are you going to do? When you get home, I mean."

"Have a catch with my dad, I guess," Andrew said. "That is, if everyone hasn't gone bugshit at home." Warren, sitting cross-legged next to Ryun, looked up at this. "Crazy, I mean."

"I know what it means," Warren said. Andrew smiled.

"After all, I've been gone for five days. Around here, that might not be a big deal. But in New Jersey, the entire state police force will be out searching trunks and looking for me."

"What's a 'catch'?" Ryun asked.

Andrew explained it to Ryun, who thought it sounded like a waste of time. He was about to say so when Warren looked up into the fire.

"Listen closely," the sage said. His silver-blonde hair shimmered in the firelight. "Our path has been clear of danger for the most part. Some might call it luck, others fate. Whatever the case, do not expect tomorrow morning to be so easy. My brother has underestimated our company before. Do not expect him to do it again."

"But we can beat him, right?" Ryun asked. "If the six of us stay together?"

"That's right," Warren said. His eyes lit up and he looked around. "Gerard knows he does not have the strength to stand against all of us. Even the power of the dead has failed him, as you have all seen. There are great forces at work here, and not all of them are evil." Ryun nodded.

"Luke," Andrew said. Luke looked up from across the fire at the boy. "You'll fight? Tomorrow?"

Luke nodded. Nick asked the next question.

"Why'd you fight in the first place?" the boy asked. He had sat up while Warren had talked, and now he mimicked the sage's cross-legged style. "I thought you weren't ever going to fight, after what happened to your brothers."

Luke nodded. "True," he said. "But I decided to follow on my own compass this time." Sara looked up at him and offered him a smile. Nick suddenly got up and walked back toward his bag. "Besides, sometimes you have to fight. For the people you care about."

Nick hurried back over to the camp, his bag in his hand. Ryun recognized what the boy was looking for.

"Nick," he said. "I think you have something to show me."

"That's right!" Nick said, and nearly stumbled over Warren. "Sorry—I got so excited over the wedding I forgot to tell you. I think I've figured it out." With that the boy pulled a familiar gun out of his bag.

"Watch this," Nick said. He showed Ryun the gun, and at first Ryun didn't think it looked any different. He became aware five sets of eyes were on him as he reached out for his old toy. Holding it in his hands, he immediately felt the difference.

"What's this?" he asked, and held the body of the gun up

close. Right next to the cylinder a gear was attached to the metal.

"It's a piece I foun' on the back of my compass," Nick said. "It just popped right off, and I thought it might fit on your gun."

Ryun looked at the gear for a moment more, then back up at the boy standing before him.

"You know I've had hundreds of people look at this," Ryun said. "Scientists, smiths… even alchemists. Ever since I found it, as a kid. You think it'll work now?"

Nick shrugged. "Give it a try!"

Ryun's knees popped as he stood up. *I'm getting too old for this,* he thought. Still, he could feel his heart pounding a little bit. The shells were loaded into the chamber—he had them forged by a blacksmith years ago to fit the gun exactly. He looked up from the fire at the mountain above, and thought again of his father sitting on his throne.

"Here's to years of incompetency," Ryun muttered, and pointed the gun off into the darkness. He thumbed the hammer back (in his mind he saw Andrew on the bridge, gun in his hand) and pulled the trigger.

There was no bang, but an audible pop. Everyone at the campfire jumped from their seats. Ryun jumped too; he'd half expected the gun to explode in his hand. A smile spread on Andrew's face.

A wooden stick stuck out of the muzzle, extending about two feet forward. At the end of the stick a white cloth hung, rendering the stick a flag. On the cloth the word *POW!* was written in giant red letters.

Ryun was the first to laugh. Soon the entire mountain echoed with the sound of the company's laughter.

VIII

Andrew lay next to Nick. The two boys' sleeping bags (hides, Andrew reminded himself) were close enough where Andrew could see the boy out of the corner of his eye.

"So you're finally headed home," Nick said.

"Not yet," Andrew said. "I'm nervous about going home, anyway. It's been a week since I left—my parents are worried sick, I bet."

Nick shrugged. "I know what you mean. My own parents are prob'ly scared. I snuck away too, you know?" Andrew nodded, thinking of Margaret Smith and the chicken he had eaten his first night in Sunsetville.

"We'll be in some kind of trouble, huh?" Andrew said, placing his hands under his head. He could feel the rocky ground beneath the hide.

"Home's like that though. It's where we're all headed anyway." Nick said.

"Yeah," Andrew said. "I'm going to have to face the music when I get back."

"Sure, we've got to face the music," Nick said. "But home is where you can be forgiven too." Andrew saw Nick close his eyes, and within a minute Andrew heard the boy's steady breathing. He was asleep.

Andrew turned over on his side, and saw Sara and Luke lying together on a mat a few feet away. He heard Sara whisper:

"Luke of the north, king of the south." She laughed as she said it.

"Saramina, princess of the south, lady of the north." He smiled, and pulled his blanket over them as a cool breeze whirled through the camp. The remnants of the fire scattered away from the mountain with the wind. "We're crazy, Sara. Backwards, too."

"Backwards? Yeah, I'd say we're all backwards. Backwards for a kid with a gun." Then she drew in close and whispered: "But if you keep walking backwards, I'll follow." He nodded and kissed her. Soon they were quiet, asleep in one another's arms. Andrew turned over and saw Ryun sleeping on the other side of camp. His gentle snores wove through the quiet night.

"They say those who sleep often are lonely," Warren said. He was sitting on the one of the logs by the dead fire pit, on watch.

"And those who can't sleep wish they were," Andrew said, remembering Luke's words from a few nights.

"Come and sit with me, Andrew," Warren said. Andrew climbed to his feet and ambled over to the fire pit. "Perhaps talking will put your mind at rest. You've come to know this world quite well, haven't you?"

"Yeah," Andrew said, sitting down in the dirt next to Warren. "I can hardly imagine leaving it." The breeze picked up a little, tossing Andrew's light brown hair from his forehead. He turned to Warren. "What happened today, when you touched Stricker? I saw your brother when I put my hand on your shoulder."

Warren closed his eyes and nodded. "I thought you saw something. I suppose I should explain." He looked down at his hands. "When I touch someone, I… I see their memories."

"Any memory?" Andrew asked.

"No," Warren said, and shook his head. "Just the one that's on their mind. Like a word that's on the tip of your tongue."

"When Stricker saw you today…" Andrew thought of the back of Gerard's hand. "He thought you were Gerard. He saw the scar on the back of your hand."

"And so the memory on the tip of his tongue was last night, when my brother found him."

Andrew nodded, then looked over at Warren's hand. "And how did you get that?"

"This?" Warren raised his hand for Andrew to see. In the dim moonlight he could see the outline of the scar. "Funny, I hardly remember. I think Gerard was fooling around when we were kids, and cut his hand climbing up some rocks."

"That doesn't explain how you cut your hand," Andrew said, shifting in the dirt. "Unless…"

"Unless what?" Warren asked. He took a pipe out of his shirt pocket and began to fumble around in the dark for tobacco. "His cuts are my cuts?"

Andrew shrugged. "I figured anything could happen on this side of the door."

Warren smiled. "You're right. Take this scab, for example." He pulled his pant leg to show a crusting scab on his right shin. "I stumbled in the forest a few nights ago, before I found you in the grove." Andrew looked down at the bruise, then back up at Warren.

"You mean…"

"Gerard has the very same scab on his right shin."

"No way!" Andrew said. "How does that happen? I mean, when did it start?"

"I will tell you," Warren said. "But you must promise not to tell the others. If they knew, they might… hesitate. And we cannot have that." Andrew nodded. He wasn't thinking of the others—his mind was racing with this new discovery. "Gerard and I are not only brothers—we are twins." Warren lowered his head and the wind picked up. "We were one fetus, originally. Hiralyn, the sage, sensed great darkness in my mother's womb. He concocted a potion that would kill this fetus and save my mother's life.

"Instead, my mother suffered. The fetus separated in two, and Gerard and I were born. My mother died, and Hiralyn decided he would raise us. Yet we were strange twins, and soon it became apparent that whatever Gerard suffered, I suffered as well."

"Does he see memories like you do?" Andrew asked. "When he touches someone, does he see their past?"

"No," Warren said. "It is a troubling gift to have, one that I have borne since birth. In fact, the moment I truly knew Gerard killed my father was when I touched him that night on top of the clock tower and saw what he had done. Before that I had refused to believe it." Warren sighed and looked up at the mountain. "It is not always so magical, this gift of mine. The past tends to be darker than the future. I have seen one of your memories as well, Andrew."

"Which one?" Andrew asked. "When?" Yet he thought he knew. "Was it… the night in the forest? When I was stuck in my world?"

"Yes," Warren said. His blue eyes shone. "When I pulled you out, I saw what you were thinking of—the day you ran away."

Andrew said nothing as he stared into the dead fire pit.

"I know you're worried about going home, Andrew," Warren said. "Things seem to fit for you here."

"Then why should I go back?" Andrew asked suddenly. "Why can't this be home?"

"Because it's not."

Andrew said nothing. He got up and turned toward his sleeping bag.

"One more thing, Andrew." He turned back to Warren, sitting quietly on the log.

"Yeah?"

"If you kill Gerard tomorrow," Warren said, "the door will close. Forever."

"I know it," Andrew said. He looked at the boy sitting before him on the log.

Warren nodded. He put the pipe in his mouth, and the flame within lit up his face. Andrew nearly laughed—here was a wise sage, over a hundred years old, looking no older than thirteen with a pipe in his mouth.

Andrew shrugged. "I'll see what I can do." He was too tired to think anymore. He walked over to his hide and lay down, resting his head on the rocky pillow.

chapter thirteen
the rauros vale

I

Luke woke them long before sunrise. The night sky had
only begun to fade to a dark grey-blue, and the birds hadn't
begun chirping. Andrew pulled on his shoes, sitting on the same
log Warren had sat on the night before. Saramina walked over to
him, her blue eyes sparkling and alert.

"Ready, kid?" she asked, offering him a hand. He took it,
and she pulled him to his feet. "It's the last climb. I guess we'll
miss you, maybe." He laughed at that.

"You can miss me when I get through the door," he
answered.

They set off, Luke leading the way. Warren followed him,
wearing a dark blindfold over his eyes. Nick asked him why he
wore it, and he answered that Gerard had a way of seeing his
movements. Andrew knew there was more to it than that, but
didn't say so. Warren grasped Nick's hand and asked him to lead
the way.

"Luke knows a special path around these mountains,"
Warren said. "One that not even I know. If we follow his lead,
we may be able to surprise my brother and take the door by
force."

Nick led the blindfolded boy, their hands interlocked, and
Sara went after him. Andrew followed her, with both revolvers
tucked into his belt. Ryun had insisted the boy carry his faulty
gun. As a gunslinger, he had a right to, Ryun had claimed the

night before as he handed the gun to Andrew. Even if it was just a toy, Ryun wanted Andrew to take it. Ryundain followed Andrew, taking the rear of the company. Luke led them left on the mountain trail, and they began to ascend Sarna Luego. Andrew asked Sara why they weren't climbing Mensis, and Sara laughed.

"Trust Luke," she said. "He doesn't usually know where he's going, but just trust him on this one."

Sarna Mensis and Sarna Luego ran next to one another, but they began to split after a few minutes of walking. In front of him, Nick grumbled about how he wished they had brought their horses.

"It's too steep and narrow, Nickolas," Warren said. "We were better to leave them at camp."

Nick sighed, but pressed onward. Soon the two mountains separated by a distance of twenty yards. Andrew looked into the valley below and saw a great chasm separating Mensis from Luego.

Luke led them north, winding up and around Luego. Their path (which became less worn as they climbed) was hilly and rocky, sloping upwards. Andrew had to look down as they crossed through a great bed of rocks, nervous about turning his ankle. Below them the world dropped away; above them the sky regained its color. Morning was less than an hour away.

They had been walking for nearly an hour when Warren looked up and stopped. A great shriek echoed over the mountainside. Andrew saw the same vulture that had stalked Stricker's body yesterday flying through the air. It was joined by two other vultures, gliding through the valley.

"Gerard!" Warren cried, looking off to the south despite his blindfold. "He's looking for us!" Luke turned and looked for a place to hide, but the mountainside was void of boulders and brush where they were. Before anyone could move, the vultures cawed in surprise. A flock of doves descended from the above, flying northward. Sara cried out in joy as countless doves fell upon the vultures. Black and white collided in the air, with countless birds spiraling downward in the great clash. Andrew thought the doves brought some morning light, even with the dawn so far away. The vultures squealed and fled. Andrew didn't doubt their master atop Sarna Mensis was watching. Andrew hoped he was upset.

Saramina turned to Warren. "Not often do doves fly north!" she cried. Warren, still blindfolded, smiled.

"Neither do princesses of the south. The world is full of wonders."

II

Luke led them close to the peak of Sarna Luego. They stood upon the north face of the mountain, and Andrew saw Sarna Mensis. It towered high above Luego by at least three hundred feet. Even in the darkness, Andrew could see tiny figures at the top of Mensis. The peak was flat; Sarna Mensis was truly a plateau, Luke informed them. The boy squinted, trying to make out what those tiny shapes were.

"The dead," Ryun whispered. "Gerard has raised them here as well."

"There's so many!" Nick cried. "What'll we do?"

Warren looked up at the dead, assembled high on the mountaintop above them. "We'll decide when we get there."

Directly ahead was Sarna Rauros. The south face of the

mountain sat between Luego and Mensis. Andrew thought he knew Luke's path; he would lead them over to Rauros and then onto the north side of Sarna Mensis.

A great waterfall fell from Sarna Rauros' northwestern face, and the company slowly approached it. Down below, in the chasm between Rauros and Luego Andrew could see the white and purple grove where Luke and Sara had been wed. The waterfall fell into the pool in the back of this natural garden. Sitting on the cliff ledge beside these magnificent falls was the biggest lion Andrew had ever seen.

It looked to be at least five times greater than the lions he had seen at the Bronx Zoo, when he had visited with his second grade class. Though the chasm between mountains separated the company from the great beast, Andrew didn't doubt it could leap the gap with its giant legs and bear down upon them. Warren knew the beast was there.

"The spirit of these mountains awaits—Sarna Leone," the sage said in a low voice. "I've long heard legends of the Leone pride, who tend the mountains to the north, but never in my years have I seen one."

"What does he want?" Luke asked. He stopped and looked back at Warren.

"He will not harm us; more likely he has sensed who we are, and has come to witness it for himself."

"I don' mind what he's come to do, cause with jaws that big we'd be smart to turn round," Nick said quietly. Luke paid him no mind and continued on the path.

Now less than twenty feet separated the company from the lion. The beast sat still, observing with gigantic grey eyes. The cliff it sat upon was so drenched from the Rauros falls that it was impossible to safely navigate. Still, the beast sat close enough to the falls that it could easily reach out with one magnificent paw and touch the falling water. Andrew gazed at the falls wonder as a mighty voice filled his head.

Name yourselves, travelers.

Andrew instantly thought of Gerard's voice, which had filled his head in Sunsetville. Yet this voice was ancient and mighty, not thin and hateful. No one in the company spoke.

What brings you to my mountains?

"You know who we are, and why we come to this place!" Luke called. "We follow the law of the gun! We have come to send the boy-gunslinger to the door!"

The gun has not come to this world in hundreds of years, the voice said. *And what of the door? That door is closed, and it always has been.*

"Speak not so, Sarna Leone!" Warren called out. "The door has opened! Dark and white magic have opened the path between worlds!"

Warren the Wise, the voice said. *The boy-sage, it appears. It has been long since you were of any use to this world, and now you return as nothing but a child.*

"A child I may be," returned Warren, "but my power is not diminished. That much you know, mountain-spirit, so mock me not!"

Andrew watched the falls, seeing their spray and mist obscure the lion from sight briefly. *But do they even drench you, Master Lion?* The boy wondered. *I don't think so. I think the water passes right through you.*

The lion's grey eyes met his. *Do you admire the falls, boy-gunslinger?* The voice asked. Andrew said nothing, watching the lion carefully.

They were once much greater, o wanderer, the lion continued.

The river that once fed so great a stream now dries with each passing day. Some blame it on the drought, but I know better; no drought could cause this world to decay. This world is drying up, Andrew Tollson. Don't you think so? Andrew said nothing, his hand on the butt of his gun. He didn't like being mocked, but he wasn't sure what to say. The lion turned its glare to Luke.

You lead your company through a path only you and I know. Yet there is another who may know if it, fleetman. Be forewarned, for an ancient terror has returned to this mountain.

"What terror?" Warren asked. His voice cracked a little bit.

It is a nameless fear, responded the lion. *And it answers to your brother.* Now the lion stared at Warren with accusing eyes. Though Warren couldn't see them through the blindfold, Andrew bet he could feel them.

"Will you answer our call?" Andrew asked. The others looked at him in surprise, then back at the lion. Two great grey eyes locked onto the boy. "We're in trouble. We've got to get to the top of the mountain, but I think we need some help." The lion regarded a boy for a moment longer, then turned back to Luke.

It is folly, the voice said. *Do you really believe a boy and his gun can save this world from darkness? This world is cursed.*

"I'm not going anywhere," Luke said.

"The men of the west stand by him!" Ryundain added.

"So do the women of the south!" Sara said.

"You owe him your allegiance, spirit," Warren said.

"You saw us last night!" Nick said. Andrew turned to him in surprise. "You saw our wedding from the waterfall. You know who we are!"

Andrew smiled. He stepped forward, feeling strong. He pulled out his gun and held it up in the air. The lion turned back to him.

"Aid us, spirit!" Andrew called. "Or face my wrath!" The lion reared its great head, still regarding the boy. For a long time the two stood there—the beast beneath the falls, and the boy holding his gun. A mist settled over the lion from the falls, obscuring Andrew's view. When the fog cleared the lion was gone. Andrew had heard one last thing before he had disappeared.

Have faith, little one.

Luke turned back to them. "Do you think he'll come?" Warren shrugged, but Andrew knew better. They had stood together as one. No living creature could ignore that call.

"If he comes he comes," Andrew said. "If not, we're on our own."

"We've done all right this far, right?" Nick said, looking around. Everyone nodded. Andrew was suddenly very glad to have his friends around him, at the top of this world.

"Let's go then," Luke said. "We're almost at my path."

"If we hurry," Warren said, his eyes skyward, "we can reach Sarna Mensis before daybreak."

"And then?" Andrew asked.

"Then," Luke said, "comes the end-game."

III

The company reached the peak of Sarna Luego not long after that. Above them rose the peak of Sarna Rauros, and Sarna Mensis above that. Luke led them over to a rock wall on the north side of the peak, descending in breakneck fashion. On the bottom of the drop sat the slopes of Sarna Rauros. Ryun fished through his bag and brought out a long coil of rope. He tied it to a stone atop the wall and then fastened the loop around Warren, who descended first. Luke followed, then Andrew, Nick, and Sara. Ryun was the last to descend, and he untied the rope around his waist as the company prepared to move on. They left the rope there, however—it was still tied to the stone above. Luke led them up the slopes, leaving Sarna Luego behind.

"Hasta Luego," Andrew said.

"What's that?" Ryun asked, walking behind the boy.

"Nothing," Andrew said. They pressed on.

Sarna Rauros was not quite as steep as Luego, but Luke knew it was wide in girth. The climb was slow. Luke followed the river, winding past them down the mountain toward the falls below. Luke peered along the side of the mountain, and anxiety began to grow in his gut.

Pull it together, he told himself as he stepped over an outcropping of rock. *We need a leader right now.* Yet up above he could see Sarna Mensis, peering down at him. He felt naked.

After half an hour of climbing, Luke paused. He was glad the others only saw his back—he was sure his face was covered in sweat. They had nearly reached the top of Rauros, which was flat and round like Mensis' peak.

"What's that?" Andrew asked. A great stone structure sat on the top of the mountain, circular in shape. It was rotted and decayed. A few eagles had made this building their nest, looking disapprovingly at the realm below.

"That's a lighthouse," Warren answered. Luke stepped forward, running his hand on the rock wall to their right. "Before the law of the gun came to this land, three great lighthouses stood upon the Sarna Range: one atop Rauros, one atop Mensis, and one atop Sarna Dias."

"But they're built so far from the sea!" Nick cried.

"Keep your voice down," Luke said from ahead.

"Sorry," Nick whispered.

"These aren't ordinary lighthouses," Warren said. "These were lighthouses built to spy enemy movements in the Dustroll and the Fleetgap to the south and east. Eventually they were abandoned when the gunfighters brought peace to this land."

"This one looks kind of eroded," Sara said. "What about the others?"

"The one atop Sarna Dias still stands," Luke said. "In the morning light we'll get a look at it." *If we see the morning light,* Luke thought. "But there's no tower left atop Sarna Mensis. Only ruins."

"That's where the door is," Andrew realized. "Among the ruins."

"What happened to the tower?" Nick asked.

"No one knows for sure," Warren said. "I've heard many stories. Some say a great gust of wind blew it from the mountains and into the heavens. Others say the spirits of the tower became angry with its disrepair and tore it down. Either way, it is a haunted place."

"Great," Luke said. "I've found the way there. Follow me." He grabbed ahold of the notch in the stone wall he had found, and climbed up. The wall was short—hardly four feet tall. He reached the top and had to catch his breath—the sight always amazed him. The entire realm of Romini spread out before him. He turned and looked down to the company.

"This is it," he said. "This is the path." In front of him, the trail became a ledge. It led over Sarna the north face of Rauros, which dropped in breakneck fashion to the left. Behind him, he heard Ryun boost Warren up. Nick followed.

"Wow," Nick said quietly as he climbed up. He walked over

beside Luke. "And over there—that's Sarna Mensis?"

"That's right," Luke said. "Just follow the ledge and you'll be there in no time." His voice wavered a bit. The peak sat a few hundred feet above where they stood now, yet a huge stone wall of rock to the right of the ledge shielded the company from any onlookers on Sarna Mensis.

"That's brilliant," Sara said. She was beside Luke now. "How did you ever find it?"

Luke shook his head. "Just wandering up here one day, I stumbled on it. It's a tight squeeze though, Sar—be careful." He wanted to say *be really careful*, but he didn't need to. Sara nodded and squeezed his hand. Her hair flew wildly in the breeze.

"No time to waste then," she said, and started along the cliff ledge. The gorge below sat quietly as she walked along the ledge, and Luke thought it was waiting to swallow her whole. He gulped—the end-game had begun.

IV

Andrew's stomach dropped when he saw the look on Luke's face. He climbed up the stone wall with Nick's help from above. He looked at Luke, who was watching Saramina walk slowly along the cliff ledge ahead, and saw the mixture of pity and horror on his face.

"I'll go next," Warren said.

"You're all right to go?" Nick asked. "You can't see!"

"I'll be fine." Warren turned to Andrew and Luke. "Remember the six of us are a great force, if we stand together. Our stand must be on the top of the mountain—not on it's slopes."

"Then this is it?" Andrew asked.

"Once we cross," Warren said, nodding, "it will be a race to the peak."

Andrew started to nod, but then he stepped forward and wrapped his arms around Warren. They remained like that for a moment, as Nick and Luke watched in silence. Andrew let go and Warren sighed as he turned toward the vale.

"Something's wrong," Luke said. "I've got—I don't know."

"What it is?" Andrew asked.

"I've got the worst feeling," Luke said. "I should go." Nick beat him to it. The boy followed after Warren, who ran his hand gently across the stone wall to his right for balance. The wind picked up again, and Sara began to sway a little.

"Warren, can you turn that down?" Luke called with a thin voice. The wind drowned it out, and Andrew didn't think Warren heard him. The boy-sage was already at least fifty feet ahead.

Dark curly hair hung over Luke's sweaty forehead. His eyes burned a bright blue in the morning light. Andrew heard a grunt behind him as Ryun climbed up the stone wall.

"Luke," Andrew said. Luke turned to him, and the look in his eyes nearly made Andrew forget his words.

Tell him to go, Andrew thought.

"It'll work out," Andrew said. "Just have faith."

Luke looked at him for a moment longer. His chest rose and fell sporadically under the thin jacket he wore. Finally, he turned to follow. Andrew watched him go.

"You next," Ryun said. "I'll follow you." Andrew nodded. After a few seconds of watching Luke cross, he started across the ledge.

The path felt jagged and uneven beneath his feet. He saw

Sara reach the other side safely as he left Sarna Rauros behind.
Andrew told himself not to look down, muttering it under his
breath. He imagined Luke was thinking the same exact thing
ahead. Andrew stumbled a little over a stone on the path, which
fell softly off the ledge. The boy raised his eyebrows as he saw the
stone tumbling down a thousand feet of nothingness toward the
slopes below.

He looked ahead and saw Sara standing on the slopes of
Sarna Mensis. Warren had nearly reached the other side as well.
Luke was about halfway there, and that was a relief, Andrew
decided. Ahead Nick passed beneath the shade of the great rock
wall to their right. Then a gust of wind blew, and Andrew saw
what was sitting on Luke's shoulder.

V

Andrew wavered a little in the wind, but it wasn't his loss
of balance that made him cry out. He watched the silky spider
land on Luke's shoulder with eerie speed and grace. The spider
was nearly the size of a basketball, and Andrew decided that was
eerie too.

Behind him, Ryun cried: "Above! They're falling from
above!" Nick, twenty yards in front of Luke, called:

"Luke! Your shoulder!"

"Wha—" Luke began, and then the spider bit in. Twin
stingers protruding from the front of its mouth sliced into Luke's
shoulder. Luke cried out, his hands falling limply to his waist.

Spiders were falling all around them now, mostly missing
their mark. The wind picked up again, blowing the silver-green
monsters from their course and to their doom thousands of feet

below. Behind him, Andrew heard Ryun slashing with his sword. A spider landed at Andrew's feet with a soft plump, but Andrew hardly paid it any mind. He had eyes only for Luke, who began to sway uncontrollably in the wind.

The boy's hand dropped to his gun as he delivered the spider a quick kick. The beast flipped over the edge of the vale. Andrew saw orange markings on the spider on Luke's shoulder, and the boy knew this spider was different. *It's going to kill him,* Andrew knew. *It's poisonous, and it only needs a few seconds.*

Nick cried out and sprinted back along the ledge toward Luke. Luke's mouth foamed and his eyes were blank. Andrew knew Nick couldn't get there in time—he was too far away.

The boy whipped his gun out of his belt. In the same movement his right hand pressed back the hammer, and his left hand pulled the trigger. A great BAM! echoed off the cliff wall as the beast on Luke's shoulder disintegrated in a purple cloud. Blood and guts splattered on the side of Luke's face and neck, but Andrew didn't think he noticed. Luke began to sway in the wind, his tall body moving back and forth, teetering toward the edge of the vale. He turned a little bit, and Andrew saw his eyes roll into the back of his head. His body went rigid as he collapsed toward the edge and into the arms of Nickolas Smithson.

Above them the spiders stopped falling. The gust of wind had blown the rest astray, over the edge of the cliff and into the gorge below. Ryun and Andrew looked up at the mountain ahead; a great roar passed over the slopes.

"They heard the shot!" Ryun murmured. He put his hand on Andrew's shoulder. "Hurry!"

Andrew and Ryun scurried over the pass, following Nick. Nick still held Luke in his arms, and the boy bent low to carry the weight. Andrew watched Nick carefully, ready to grab him in case he swayed toward the edge. Nick stepped in the remains of a dead spider, and continued forward. Andrew wondered if he even noticed.

Nick reached the other side of the pass and collapsed as Sara took Luke from his arms. She lay him down on a bed of dirt and tore off his jacket. Andrew arrived as she took a look at the wound.

His jacket was so thin, Andrew remembered. *The spider bit right through it.*

Andrew's stomach spun a little bit as he saw the wound. It was a deep gash, and it was colored yellow and orange. Pus leaked lazily into Luke's blue shirt. Sara picked up Luke's hand, looking for a pulse. Her eyes were wide and alert. Warren took off his blindfold and turned to Andrew.

"That was a nice shot," he said quietly. Andrew nodded, but didn't take his eyes off Luke.

"I knew I had to," Andrew said. "A few more seconds and…" He looked at Sara and stopped himself.

"Will he be all right?" Nick asked as Ryun helped him to his feet. The five of them gathered around Luke, whose skin was turning a pure white.

"He's alive," Sara murmured, though her hands were trembling now. "The pulse… it's there. It's just slow." The hardest part, she decided, was that she had to watch the whole thing. Warren and Nick had been in her way, and she had frozen. She had simply watched.

"Strangest thing," Ryun said. "There's no one on this side of the mountain." Sara didn't look up, but the others did.

"The lion," Andrew murmured. "Sarna Leone. He must have distracted them—"

"We must hurry," Warren said. He began to walk forward, up the slope. "If we hurry, we can make it up the slope. Sara, can you carry Luke?"

Sara looked up and blinked. The peak stood before them, bald and empty. The zombies had disappeared from the mountain. "But how did—" she began. Warren cut her off.

"Sara! Your husband!"

Sara looked up at Warren. Ryun stepped beside her, and began to bend down to pick up Luke. Sara put her hand on his arm.

"I've got him."

Ryun's eyes grew wide, and he stepped back. Then he nodded, as Sara bent down and picked Luke up from the dirt. His body was still rigid, and she had to force his back to bend over her shoulder.

Hold on, Luke, she thought. Then she started after Andrew, who pocketed the gun with one bullet left in it.

I

The north face of the mountain fell below their feet as the company rushed toward the peak. Ryun figured they were lucky; their path was clear. He could see an opening to the peak ahead, among the sharp rocks that surrounded the summit. This was the opening Luke had told him of last night—it was the only entrance to the summit. The rocks were otherwise too difficult to climb.

Sara carried Luke ahead of him. She moved with surprising speed and grace. Ryun could see Luke's face, as he was slung over her shoulder. His eyes were a pure white, and they reflected the rising sun to the east. Foam leaked gently out of his open mouth. Ryun ran close behind Sara in case she lost her balance, and much of the foam that leaked out of his open mouth landed on Ryun's pants.

They were nearly at the summit when a terrible voice encompassed the mountainside. Ryun knew that voice all too well—he had heard it in his own court before. Years ago, before the drought and Gerard's madness. Even then, it had been a voice of fear, hate, and terror. He supposed the zombies on the other side of the mountain knew the voice as well: it was the voice of their master.

"FOOLS! THEY'RE ON THE OTHER SIDE! GET BACK TO THE FUCKING NORTH FACE!"

Ryun thought Andrew had been right about Sarna Leone;

the spirit must have distracted the zombies on the south face. Yet the ruse was up now.

"Run!" Warren yelled. He led the company. Now Ryun could hear soft trampling. Sara picked up on it first—she had sharper hearing than he did.

"The dead!" she cried. "They're coming!" Ryun looked up and saw the horde.

The first few zombies came lumbering over the mountainside. A few tripped and fell among the jagged rocks. The horde scurried past the fallen, trampling them. Ryun put his hand on his sword. They were still a hundred feet away, rounding the eastern side. Yet he heard moaning to his right and saw another pack of zombies rounding the western side. Ryun saw a freak leading the pack, a corpse standing over seven feet tall with blue-grey skin and long bony arms. *He has no lips,* Ryun saw as he looked closer. He drew his sword from his sheath.

Warren reached the jagged boulders directly below the summit and turned. Ryun saw his eyes and nodded. He knew what he had to do. There could be no other way—the dead would follow them to the summit otherwise. Warren shifted his grave gaze to Saramina, but she didn't need explaining either. She turned to Nick, who stood beside her.

"You carried him once," she said. "Can you do it again?" The boy nodded.

"Hurry!" Andrew called. He ran in front of Warren, toward the plateau. Ryun turned and saw the zombies drawing in. The pack to the east would reach them first. No matter, he thought—he and Sara could fend them off from their vantage point among the boulders.

It could have been different, he thought as Sara handed Luke to Nick. The boy bent low again to balance. *If Luke hadn't been bitten—if it was the six of us standing together—the dead wouldn't have dared followed us to the summit.*

"Take care of him," Sara said. Then she turned and came to Ryun's side, drawing her bow as she came. Nick took one last look at his two friends as the horde of zombies descended upon them. There was a great clash as the tall zombie fell beneath Ryun's sword, and then Nick turned away. With Luke in his arms, he wheeled around and scurried up the peak. To the east, the first rays of sunlight broke over the Kirondack Mountains.

Daybreak had come.

II

"Nick!" Andrew called as the boy climbed up onto the summit. "Take my bag!" Nick looked up and saw the bag flying through the air toward him. He tried to reach out and grab it, but Luke's weight was too much. He collapsed, Luke's body falling at his feet. The bag hit him in the face.

He looked up and found himself sitting in a grove of wildflowers. He thought of the grove Sara and Luke had been married in, except these flowers grew long and tangled. They were red and orange, and grew in throngs. The ruins of Sarna Mensis sprouted out of them. Great silent slabs of stone sat sadly in the morning light. Among the ruins, directly ahead, stood a door. It was separate from the ruins, simply standing in the flowers on the other side of the summit. Nick remembered Luke's story; he had expected the door to be glowing. Instead, it sat quietly and stared at the three children atop the summit.

The bag, Nick thought. *Why'd he throw it at me?* He sat up and looked at the bag, sitting amidst the weeds and flowers.

Then he remembered—this was the bag Andrew had stuffed all the spider-grass in.

"But he gave it all to Frederick," Nick muttered. Yet he wondered—perhaps there was a strand or two Andrew hadn't grabbed. If there was, he could use it to wake Luke up. The boy grabbed the bag and opened it wide. It was empty.

Just reach in, Nick thought. *It doesn't have to be empty. Oh please, don't be empty.* He reached his hand into the bag and closed his eyes. He felt the rough leather against his small hand, but felt no strands of grass. He ran his hand along the inside of the bag—his aunt's bag—and felt a small crease.

"A pocket," he muttered to himself, his eyes still closed. His hand dove into the pocket, and at first it felt empty. His heart sank, but his hands passed over something smooth. He grabbed it and drew the strand of spider grass out. Ahead, Andrew and Warren stood before the door, talking amongst themselves. Nick didn't pay them any mind. His heart was racing. He leaned over Luke, the strand of grass in his hand.

"I hope this works, Luke," he said. "You're not lookin' so good." He pulled Luke's blood-stained shirt off of his shoulder and crushed the strand of spider-grass against the wound. At first Nick thought he couldn't stomach it—the wound was grinning up at him in the most vile way—but he took a deep breath and plunged his hand into the wound, rubbing the grass along the swelling.

Please, don't let it be too late, Nick thought. *Don't let it be too late.*

III

Andrew didn't turn around to see Nick after he threw the bag. He raced through the ruins after Warren, who headed straight for the door. The weeds brushed against his ankles and shins, but he hardly noticed. The door sat placidly amidst the weeds and stones.

Warren turned to him as he reached the door. "Andrew," he panted. "Hurry."

Andrew stopped and faced the boy. "Hurry," Warren said. "We don't have much time. Gerard is close."

"I've got one bullet left," Andrew said. "I'll put it right between his eyes."

"No!" Warren cried. The word echoed through the ruins, like an ominous chant. Andrew looked at the tall stones above, and then returned his glare back to Warren.

"Don't be a fool," Warren said. His blue eyes locked on Andrew's, though his voice grew soft. "The door is right here."

Andrew wasn't thinking about the door. He was thinking of the rush that had come when he drew the gun and blew the spider off of Sara's shoulder. *That door,* he thought, locking his eyes on the bronze handle. *That door means the end of the rush. The end of being a gunslinger.*

"You're going to kill him," Warren said suddenly. Andrew met his sharp blue eyes, and saw pain there. "You're not going through the door. You're going to shut it against yourself."

"Never mind the door!" Andrew said. "We're talking about Gerard here! You want me to let him live?"

"If I can't get you back through this door," Warren, "we will *all* have failed." The sage's eyes looked past Andrew. The boy knew he was looking at Luke, lying in the grass at Nick's feet. Andrew regarded Warren, narrowing his eyes. He felt strange suddenly—like there was sunburn on his forehead.

"You're afraid of dying," Andrew said. Warren's eyes flashed back to his, and grew wide. "You know that when I kill him, you're going to die too."

"Never think it!" Warren cried. "Andrew, we have no time for this!"

"Sure, we do," Andrew said. He put a hand on the gun in his belt and offered Warren a smile that didn't feel like his own. "All I've got to do is put a bullet in his head, and I'll have all the time in the world. But you don't want that, do you?"

"*Andrew!*" Warren snapped. "If you kill him, you can't go back!"

"If I go back," Andrew responded, "no one will kill him!"

Warren met the boy's gaze, and his face became calm. "I won't raise my voice to you, Andrew Tollson." Then he stepped forward, into the weeds.

"If killing Gerard meant saving us all, don't you think I would have killed myself a long time ago?"

Andrew was about to turn away when he saw Warren's face. Andrew stepped forward toward Warren.

"You…"

Warren regarded him with wide eyes. "You… you don't want to see it, Andrew." Yet Andrew didn't stop. He reached out and touched Warren's small white hand. It was thin and old, and full of life.

IV

He was staring at a river, winding a clear path through the trees. The river was low—the drought and his brother had seen to that—but still lively enough to float in. A single question ran through his old mind.

His left hand ran along the long smooth blade of the knife he held in his right hand—he could feel the ridges from where he'd sharpened it. He thought of the long nights he'd stayed up in the grove, running a stone along the blade, dreaming of this day. Now Warren looked into the water and back at himself, staring at the child in the reflection. He heard the question again.

Wouldn't it be so easy, he asked himself. The water ran slowly along the banks. He dipped his bare toe into the water, and confirmed what he already knew: it was warm. It would be so painless. The question ran again through Warren's mind, the one that kept him up at night as he slept on the cold forest floor.

How many times did you come here? *Andrew wondered.* How many times did you ask yourself this question?

Too many times, *came the response.*

The boy stared up at the trees that hung over the river. The Southwoods hung over him like a deadening blanket. He had once thought nature so beautiful, so lively—the source of immortality. It had all changed, though. The question ran through his mind again. It ran like a river, running south through these old woods.

How easy would it be, *the boy wondered.* How easy would it be to float away in the warm water, float until the troubles were gone? Until the water turned red and the doors shut?

The lion's words, Andrew thought suddenly. Warren— faith! Have faith, little one. *And somewhere in this forest, the trees whispered the words his mother had once said to him as he lay under the blankets of a Best Western bed:*

Between life and death. You always choose life. Got it?

I choose to live, *Warren said. He dropped the knife into the river as he turned away.* I choose to live. I choose to—

Two strong hands gripped the back of Andrew's shirt, and the world became a blur.

V

The world became a blur. Andrew was vaguely aware of a splitting pain in his right shoulder and head, and he tried to open his eyes. At first he only saw blinding light. Then he felt weeds against his face, and the numbness in his right arm. A black image stepped in front of the sun.

"That's a trick I learned a long time ago," he heard Gerard say. His voice sounded miles away. "The art of *tossing*." Andrew felt stone against his back. He pieced it together as he saw Gerard's face bent over his. Gerard had thrown him against one of the stone pillars in the ruins. He could no longer feel his right shoulder. He tried to move and stop Gerard from taking the gun, but it was no use. Gerard plucked it from his belt and held it in front of his face. "A good trick for short range combat, especially if there are stones to throw people against." Gerard began to walk away, gun in hand.

When Andrew saw what Gerard was wearing, he blinked. The boy decided he looked like a joke cowboy. Gerard donned bright blue jeans, a tight fitting leather vest, and two rawhide boots pulled up to his knees. Everything was so tight that Gerard nearly squeaked as he walked over to Warren, who hadn't moved from the door.

"Greetings, brother!" Gerard called. "Admiring my handiwork?" He gestured to Luke, laying the grass beneath Nick. "Didn't quite get all of you, but it did the trick, don't you think?" Warren said nothing, regarding his brother with a solemn stare. "I'm ready for the next world, Warren. I've even made some clothes, based off of the pictures I found. In a 'photo-album'."

Warren didn't say anything, but Andrew knew he was thinking of the dynamite and the walk-man.

"The game's over, Warren," Gerard growled. He cradled the gun in his hands. "You and the boy have managed to pull a fast one on me, I guess. Putting the zombies back to sleep was a real trick."

You haven't seen the greatest trick of all, Andrew thought, climbing to his knees. He wavered a little, but he could at least see straight.

"But with this?" Gerard said, holding the gun out in front of him. "With this, I could really have some fun. Learn a few new tricks, that's what I'm going to do first. Want to see one, Warren? I'll show you a wonder." He cocked the trigger and held it out in front of him. "Something this world hasn't seen in a thousand years."

Years of incompetency, Ryun had said. Andrew couldn't help but smile.

"Don't do it," Warren said. "If I die, you go too."

"NO! NO ONE DECIDES WHO DIES BUT ME!" Gerard shouted with glee. "THE GAME'S UP, WARREN! I WIN! I WIN! I WIN! I—" He pulled the trigger, and his mouth dropped.

POP! coughed the gun.

POW! read the flag.

The silence was ear-shattering.

VI

Luke saw it all.

He could see the ruins around him, though it was veiled. He didn't know what happened to him, or why he couldn't move or speak. He simply floated in the weeds, observing the scene play out before him.

The end-game was here. He'd thought about it so much these last few days as the mountains drew closer. The door was there too. He could see it behind Gerard and Warren. The toy gun was between them now. Luke watched them and felt an urge to rise, and step between them. Yet he couldn't move.

This is it, he thought. *Some good I'm doing, laying here.* He tried to reach out to Nick, whose hand he could vaguely feel rubbing through his shoulder. His body was numb, but he could feel Nick beside him. It was almost as if he was dreaming, and Nick was trying to wake him up.

This is it, he thought. *This is what we all signed up for.*

Andrew had, when he'd come through the door.

Nick had, when he'd followed Andrew into the sewers.

Warren had, when he'd shown up in the forest and broken his staff.

Ryun had when he'd knelt before Andrew in his own city, the gun still smoking in the boy's hand

Sara had, when she'd found the boys in the tavern.

Luke had, when he'd cut down the pregnant woman in the forest.

Luke wondered where Sara was—his eyes searched frantically around the grove. Then he saw The Terror—and he tried to scream. Yet no sound came out. He couldn't make out what it was—like the stone pillars it was veiled and covered in the darkness—but he could see it was ugly.

He looked over to Andrew and tried to yell to the
boy. The sun was climbing over the hills, and The Terror was
descending upon the boy. Luke saw Nick over him. The boy was
concentrating on his side and shoulder, and Luke tried to yell.

Andrew! It's above Andrew! Help him, not me!

No sound came out.

VII

Gerard stood still for a few moments, arms still outstretched.
The gun lay calmly in his palms, the joke flag protruding from
the nozzle. Andrew did his best not to laugh as he reached out for
his own gun, tucked safely in the rear of his belt-loop. Andrew
marked the man in front of him, but this time the rush didn't
come. He heard Warren's words again:

*If killing Gerard meant saving us all, don't you think I would
have killed myself a long time ago?*

Andrew felt the smooth grips on his left palm. Yet he
didn't draw. Warren made the first move. He looked at his twin
brother, with the toy gun outstretched in his arms, and smiled.
It was a slow smile, one that Andrew had never seen on Warren's
face. It was a smile from one brother to another.

At last, Gerard snapped. He let out a cry of anguish and
whipped the gun at his brother. It glanced off Warren's tiny
shoulder, who stumbled backwards in surprise. Warren back-
peddled past the door, tripping through the dirt. Gerard rushed
forward and pounced upon his brother. Andrew watched as the
two tangled on the ground, throwing punches and rolling in the
dirt.

Andrew! It's above Andrew! Help him, not me!

The cry shot through his head, and Andrew started. He felt as if a bolt of electricity had seared through his head. He turned to Nick and Luke and caught something strange out of the corner of his eye.

"Who—"

Then he saw the spider.

If he had not turned, it would have had him. It hung two feet above Andrew, and it was the biggest spider Andrew had ever seen—it was nearly the size of the Lexus Sedan his dad drove to work. Its legs were splayed out. Andrew pictured those legs wrapping around him, encompassing him in a ferocious strangle as the two long pincers protruding from its mouth (both longer than Andrew's arms) dug into his chest and neck.

Andrew saw the hair on the beast's arms as it lowered closer to him. This was the hair, Andrew realized, that would prick him into paralysis as those long legs folded around his little body. Andrew dropped his arms from his gun, unable to move.

It's body, he thought. *Those are the same symbols from the walls. In Sunsetville.* The world became distant and faraway as Andrew watched the symbols on the beast's belly come to life, full of radiant color. They were written in a different language and pleasing to the eye, but Andrew knew what they really were: malice.

It doesn't want to eat me because it's hungry, Andrew thought as the legs opened in front of his face, splaying around him. *It hates me. It—*

The world became a blur again, and his body whipped to the side. His right shoulder hit the ground, and he rolled over a few times through the flowers. He lay over on his back, and felt the gun against his back on the ground. He looked up and saw Nick standing before the hanging monstrosity. Nick lunged forward with Stricker's blade as Andrew realized what had happened: Nick had pushed him over.

The spider flipped around as Nick lunged forth, and the boy's blade smashed against the top of the spider. A loud metallic screech echoed through the ruins as the long hunting knife fell into the weeds and Nick sprawled backwards. The spider's armor on its backside had deflected the blow, and now Nick was helpless to the beast that crawled toward him on eight long legs.

Not helpless, Andrew decided, pulling out the gun as he sat up. To his left he heard a yell-- Gerard was mounted over Warren, raining blows upon his child brother. Andrew watched as Warren lay defenselessly beneath Gerard's wrath. Blood poured from Warren's nose, and Andrew saw the same blood spilling from Gerard's nose.

He's like an angry child, Andrew thought. *He refuses to admit that his blood is Warren's blood.* He felt hot again, and raised his gun toward Gerard. Yet he turned to Nick, crawling backwards from the spider, who was nearly on top of him. He swung his head in both directions, not sure who to shoot.

"No time to think," Andrew said. Still sitting in the grass, he thumbed the hammer back. Andrew closed his left eye to see straight and fired.

VIII

Sara hadn't had much time to think about Luke. The zombies clamored and moaned as they poured over the rocks around her, swinging wildly with bony rotten arms. One arm glanced across her head as Ryun stepped in front of her and drove the horde back with his sword. Sara fell back, stars falling over her eyes. One of her hunting knives dropped from her hands, and she heard it slide down the slopes below her. She put one hand on the earth below her, her head spinning.

"Sara!" came Ryun's call. She shook her head and turned back to him. He was standing in front of her, holding back half a dozen corpses with his sword in front of him. One reached a hand (with fingernails much longer than Sara's) and clawed at Ryun. Sara whipped the bow from her back and fed an arrow into the zombie's face. The corpse recoiled violently backwards, stumbling over the rocks.

"I'm fine," Sara said. She took Ryun's side, swinging her remaining hunting knife at the zombies. They began to fall back, but Sara knew they would surge forward in a moment. There were too many of them, and she and Ryun were losing ground.

Andrew! It's above Andrew! Help him, not me!

Sara froze as the voice she knew so well ripped through her head. In that instant she blinked and saw a gruesome image: some huge darkness hanging over Andrew above. She couldn't make out what that black blur was, but she could feel its malice. She turned to Ryun, who was looking at her.

"You heard it too," Ryun said. Sara nodded.

"We've got to help him!"

As she shouted the horde surged forward, closing in around Sara. She thrashed violently backwards with an emaciated woman whose eyes were buried in her skull. The woman opened her mouth and snarled at Sara, revealing long sharp teeth. Sara thought they were the most sickening shade of green she had ever seen.

Sara grasped the woman's arms. The two were locked in a close embrace now, and Sara saw Ryun couldn't help her. He was fighting off four or five that had broken through the pass. Sara let out a cry of anguish and drove the dead woman backwards, toward a boulder to their right. The woman's head smashed against an outcropping. Sara grabbed the zombie's head and broke it against the outcropping again. Blood splattered all over Sara's arms as the woman's head shriveled into a ball of pus and blood. The cold hands on Sara's arms became limp and slid off of her. Sara turned and saw three more zombies lumbering toward her. She groaned and raised her hunting knife, aware that she was unable to help Andrew or anyone else on top of the mountain.

The entire mountain froze as the sound of the gunshot thundered above.

IX

The monstrosity seized backwards, as if it had been struck by a baseball bat. Black filth poured from its eye and rained down at Nick's feet, who was too dazed to move. The flock of vultures sitting atop the ruins took off all at once, frightened by the crash of the gun. The thunder echoed down the mountainside, and left a ringing in Andrew's ears. The spider lurched backwards, scrambling toward the ruin walls. Nick watched it fall away, and Andrew saw his eyes light up.

Gerard didn't seem to hear the gunfire, for he continued to beat his brother relentlessly. The lord of spiders failed to notice Nickolas Smithson get to his feet. When Nick's eyes fell upon the wrestling brothers, he roared:

"*Get off, you brute!*"

Then the boy rushed toward the two brothers, bending low to pick up the hunting knife he had dropped. Nick ran past

Andrew, and Andrew was too slow to stop him. Gerard was perched on his knees now, his mad yellow eyes burning down at his twin. Warren opened his eyes when the blows stopped suddenly, and looked up to see a blade inches from his face. It was protruding through Gerard's midsection.

Gerard had raised both arms in the air for his next blow, but he never got the chance to strike. His arms dropped slowly to his sides, twisted and open, as if to say, *Why, God?* He rolled off of Warren and into the dirt, staring incredulously at the blade sticking through his torso. It was Stricker's hunting knife, come back to betray its master. Gerard twisted awkwardly, afraid to let the handle in his back touch the ground. He tried to scream as it did, but no sound came out.

Nick stood over the two brothers with a look of utter disbelief on his face. Warren tried to get up, but Andrew saw a great blotch of red growing right below the chest of Warren's silver shirt.

"Andrew!" Warren sputtered, and pointed. At first, Andrew thought Warren was pointing at him. When he turned, however, he saw what Warren saw. The monstrous spider wasn't dead, and it was moving toward Luke for one final meal. Andrew cursed. The black filth of the beast's left eye still ran from its wound, but Andrew knew what he had done. He had missed the monster's brain. He ran forward now, the empty gun still smoking in his hands. Yet the spider was quick, and reached Luke before he did.

"Get away," Andrew said. He pointed the gun at the spider. "Get away from him."

The spider regarded him with its remaining black eye, but didn't move. Andrew stepped closer, and rotated the gun in his hand. He couldn't shoot it, but he could at least smash it with the butt of the gun. He stopped as a cry rang out through the ruins.

X

Sara hurried to catch up with Ryun, who was already on his way up toward the peak. She turned and saw the dead falling back, terrified by the sound of the gun. They knew that sound, she knew—it was the sound of the gun. To her it meant that Andrew's chamber was empty, but the dead didn't know it.

"*Run!*" she screamed at the zombies. Her voice was hoarse and sharp. "*The law of the gun has come to this land, to punish you all! Run, and never return!*"

The zombies heard her clearly. They turned and scrambled down the mountain. Many fell in the attempt, and soon the mountainside was an avalanche of tumbling bodies. *Good riddance,* Sara thought as she turned to catch up with Ryun.

As soon as the dead had heard the gunshot, they had begun to retreat. Ryun had seen it first, and moved for the mountaintop first. Sara scrambled now as Ryun disappeared over the peak. When she caught up with him, he was already climbing one of the ruins.

"What are you doing?"

Ryun ignored her, and pulled himself up on top of the stone support. Sara looked past the ruin and her mouth dropped. The largest spider she had ever seen was standing over Luke. It was orange and black, with some color under its monstrous belly.

She forgot about Ryun, climbing up the stone pedestal above her. She sprinted forward into the ruins, toward the backside of the spider. The beast sensed her coming, and turned to meet her. As it did, Sara shouted and tossed her hunting knife to the ground. It was too thin to cut through its legs anyway. They were thicker than tree trunks.

The beast let out a wicked cry, so inhuman that Sara

shivered to hear it. It sounded like a dying bird, trapped beneath a boulder. Then it turned back to Luke, who was lying at Sara's feet. She looked up at the beast and met its eye. Andrew watched the scene unfold, standing behind the spider with the gun in his hand.

"You'll have to go through me," she spat. The spider lowered its head, and more filth splattered onto the dirt. Then it charged.

Sara squatted down and caught the beast's front legs as it arrived. She drove upwards with all her might, and the days she had spent flipping wheels with the men in her court paid off. The spider lurched upwards, jumping on its hind legs. Sara held the spider there, locked in a deadly embrace.

She had grabbed the right part of its legs, she saw: the stinging hairs were further up than she had grabbed. The skin felt rubbery and thick where her hands were. The spider let out a call and thrashed its pincers at Sara, but they were too short. A full foot lay between their reach and Sara's body.

Sara felt the spider weakening in her grasp. As she did, her legs began to slip a little bit in the dirt. She grunted as she pushed the spider backwards, refusing to give up any ground. Behind them Luke lay peacefully in the weeds.

The beast, Sara saw, had been horribly wounded. A gunshot the size of her hand ripped open its eye, and purple and grey blood leaked out of the torn flesh. Sara thought of Stricker, missing his hand with an arrow buried in his chest. She had wanted to feel him squirm under her sword, watch him die. The same way her brother had died—painfully. She knew she could do the same thing to this spider now—as large as it was, it was at her mercy. She looked into the remaining black eye of the beast, and said something else entirely:

"If you come back for him, I will break you in half."

The beast's eye blinked in understanding. It knew what she knew: she currently had the ability to tear its front legs off, the way she held them. Sara stared into the eyes of the beast a moment longer, and then shoved with all her might.

The spider squealed and flipped backwards into the weeds. It struggled to regain its balance, with eight legs thrashing violently. Sara watched it struggle back to standing position, and back away from her slowly. Then she saw Ryun falling from the stones above.

"FOR THE BOY!" Ryun screamed, and brought his sword down upon the beast's spine. The sound of the beast's shattering armor rippled through the ruins. Ryun landed on top of the beast and bounced off into the weeds. He lay there, watching the spider thrash and buck wildly. His sword was buried in its back, and stuck through its belly. The spider flopped helplessly at its mortal wound, and Sara watched as it stumbled carelessly over the edge of the ruins. It slid off and fell down the boulders, where it met its demise. Sara heard it screech below, hungry in its death.

XI

It took Andrew a few seconds to realize his ears were still ringing. He sat down in the spidery weeds, his curly blonde-brown hair falling over his forehead. He put his head in his hands, and began to massage his temples. Sara bent down beside Luke's rigid body in the weeds. She ran her hand along his pale cheek.

"He doesn't stir," she said. Her arms, Andrew saw, were covered in blood.

"He will," Andrew said. "He has to." Sara sat down beside her lover, folding her legs and watching Luke grimly. Andrew watched with a feeling of dread in his heart. Luke had to be all right. If anyone was in trouble, it was—

"Warren!" Andrew leapt to his feet and swung around toward the door. Ryun and Sara looked up and gasped to see the brothers on the ground, covered in each other's blood. Gerard still lay on his back, looking up the sky with an ugly grimace. Nick knelt beside Warren, his head down.

"What have I done?" Nick sobbed. "I've killed you, Mr. Warren! I didn't mean it, not me. But careless Nick, stupid old Nick stuck that sword right through the both of you!" He buried his head in his hands.

Ryun caught up with Andrew, and the two stopped just short of the scene.

"We came as fast as we could," Ryun sighed. His boots and jacket were splattered with blood, but his jeans had managed to stay dry.

"The zombies?" Andrew asked.

"They fled," Ryun said. "That's when we headed up. But now I see that we were too late." Warren, who had been lying peacefully still, opened his bright blue eyes. He drew in a deep breath and said weakly:

"Not too late, Ryun… Never think it."

Then he turned his head to Nick. He lifted one small hand and pressed it against his abdomen, where the blood was growing. Nick watched as the sage grasped his hand next and pressed it against the boy's silver shirt.

"Feel… that? The cloth, it's…" Warren trailed off, unable to finish.

"It's not torn!" Nick called out in surprise. "But my

sword…your hurt… it should have passed right through you!"
Warren only shook his head, and looked up to Andrew. *Explain,*
his eyes said. *I am too weak.*

"He and Gerard have a special bond, Nick," Andrew said,
blinking away his own tears. "They… hurt together. They will
rest together."

"Rest?" croaked an ugly voice to the right. Andrew turned
to see Gerard, resting up on his elbows. His eyes, once pale
and yellow, were now streaked with fiery bloodshot veins. "The
dead… don't rest… there is nothing for the dead." He coughed a
bit, and black phlegm spilled out onto his chin. He was a pitiful
sight, but he still had a wretched grin on his face.

"Still your tongue, foul brother," Warren snapped,
displaying a surprising amount of energy. "You've… failed. And
now you're off to face your maker. May he have more mercy on
you than this world has." Gerard's eyes widened, and he shook
his head incredulously.

"I'd cut that tongue from your mouth," Ryun said,
advancing. He pulled out his hunting knife, but Warren stopped
him.

"Leave him be, Ryundain. He's lost enough today. His
hope, his breath… even his miserable pet." Ryun stepped back,
but spared Gerard one final look that was not so kind. Warren
turned onto his side, and looked at Gerard.

"I… forgive you brother." Warren said. "For everything."
Gerard looked as though he was going to be sick. He turned
away, leaning on his side, and watched the sun rise to the east.

Andrew walked over beside Nick, and put an arm around
his friend. Nick's eyes moved out to the sunrise, and Andrew
followed his gaze. The sun had risen over the endless slopes of
the Kirondacks, which stretched all the way to the horizon.

"My friends," Nick said. "They're leavin', like in Luke's song. 'The last of my friends have climbed over the horizon.' Remember it, Andrew?" His voice was heavy, and Andrew felt his own gut sink. Warren looked up at Nick and smiled.

He reached up again and grabbed Nick's arm, and Nick bent close so he could hear what he had to say.

"I may be leaving, Nickolas," Warren said. His own eyes were watery now. "But that doesn't mean the wind will stop blowing."

Andrew closed his own eyes, and saw the boy sitting on the side of the river with the hunting knife in his hand. He heard Warren's voice again:

If killing Gerard meant saving us all, don't you think I would have killed myself a long time ago?

Andrew opened his eyes and saw Nick still bent over Warren. Warren's hand was still planted firmly on Nick's forearm, and Andrew wondered if Warren was showing Nick the same memory—the one of the boy by the river, holding the hunting knife. He hoped not; some memories were better left forgotten.

"That was something else, kid."

Andrew spun around and saw Luke standing before him, a dumb grin on his face. He looked a little tired and worn, and his shirt was almost entirely torn off (his jacket was still somewhere in the weeds). Sara walked up beside him, and took his hand.

"You saw it all?" Andrew asked. Luke nodded. Andrew saw a strand of gray in his hair above his right temple.

"Heard it all too," Luke said. "That thing... the spider... it sent its *children* down on us when we were crossing the pass." He shuddered at that thought. "When one of them bit me... I could *hear* its thoughts."

"What was it?" Ryun asked.

"It grew up on this mountain, as a pretty big insect," Luke said. "But then it went east, to the desert. It met him." Luke stuck his thumb out at Gerard. "The same stuff that drove him mad made that spider what it was today."

"And it came back for us," Sara said, her eyes wide. "When the door opened."

Luke nodded. "It hated you, Andrew. It knew you were from another world, and it hated you for it." Andrew nodded, and knew Luke's grey strand wasn't from being bitten; the strand had turned color the second Luke heard the monstrosity's thoughts.

Warren turned to Andrew at last, and let go of Nick's arm.

"You've... got to go," Warren said, looking up at the sky. "It's going to rain. And when it does... the door closes. Forever."

All six of them looked up, Warren included. For the first time in nearly a year, storm clouds were rolling over the realm of Romini. A sky that had been clear through the dawn was darkening now. Tall grey clouds rolled off of the sea, and Andrew hardly heard Gerard moan as the wind picked up.

"Warren," Andrew said. "When we first met—in the grove—"

"I told you it was all a dream," Warren whispered.

"Did you mean it?"

"No. This all... has been better than any dream I could have ever had." Andrew saw Sara nodding out of the corner of his eye. Tears welled up in the boy's eyes, and his throat began to hurt. Warren looked up at Andrew and tried to smile, but it was so weak. "Go."

Andrew nodded. "Goodbye, Warren." Then he straightened, and walked toward the door.

XII

Andrew stopped when he reached the door, and turned to his companions. Luke and Sara stood hand in hand, watching the boy with a pair of sad smiles. Ryun rose slowly from Warren's side, nodding his head three times and bowing his left shoulder. Andrew figured that was the sign of mourning for the people of the west. Nick stood sheepishly, his head bowed and his hands in his pockets. It suddenly occurred to Andrew that he still had the gun tucked into his belt. He took it out and turned to Ryun.

"Ryun," he said. "The gun. You've got to—"

"Bury it. On he mountaintop." Ryun nodded slowly. "Do you think someone will find it? Someday?"

Andrew nodded, a smile on his face. He couldn't be sure, but he had a faint hope. Would there be six more bullets in the gun when that day came, six more shells to spend? Andrew thought so.

Ryun nodded as Andrew handed him the revolver. The man bowed. "It has been an honor, boy-gunslinger."

Andrew bowed himself. Then he turned to Nick. "You were brave Nick. You stood the tallest of us all."

Nick met his eyes. He was holding back more tears. "It's time to go home," Nick said. "Face the music, remember?"

Andrew nodded and put his hand on the boy's shoulder. "And you get to go home too, Nick. When that first raindrop touches the dirt, it will be time for you to go back."

"He showed me home too," Nick said. He wiped a tear away from his eye. "Warren did. I saw myself going home to a great green orchard, and rolling green hills. The way it used to be."

"He can't see the future, Nick," Andrew said. "Just the past."

"Then maybe there don' need to be no difference," Nick said. A single tear rolled down his cheek, glistening in the morning light. "Maybe what's happened and what's bound to happen can just be the same. And I can be happy, and just go home."

"Nick," Andrew said. "You'll be all right." Nick took in a deep breath. He nodded slowly.

"It's been a real honor, Andrew," Nick said, shaking his head. "I mean it." He bowed low in a comical kneeling position.

"No, Nick," Andrew said, "the honor has been mine." He bowed himself, and Nick raised his eyebrows.

"You're kids!" Sara cried with a laugh. "Nobody needs to bow to anybody!"

"Yeah," Andrew said with a grin. He got up and put his hand on the doorknob behind him, but not before he turned to look at Luke and Sara.

"You'll be all right?" Andrew asked. "You'll get on okay?"

"We'll get on like we always have," Luke said. "Through strength."

"Through honor," Ryun chipped in.

"Through faith," Sara said, looking at Luke. Their blue eyes met.

"Just kiss her already!" Nick cried. Luke did, wrapping her in his arms and kissing her on the mouth.

Andrew smiled. He turned and thought of his five friends in this world—he remembered Ryun, holding the toy gun in his hand and the rest of them laughing together—and knew he couldn't stay. He turned the brass doorknob and the door opened before him, revealing a blinding white light. He heard Sara's voice behind him.

"Hey kid," she said. He turned, his face illuminated by the brilliant light.

"Don't be afraid to show up to school every now and then," she said, with the grin on her face Andrew loved to see. Were there tears on those cheeks too? Andrew thought so. "You might learn something."

Andrew laughed, and nodded. Each of his friends nodded back.

"Well, goodbye," he said. Then he stepped into the light, and closed the door behind him.

EPILOGUE

Washed Up Beds

Andrew stepped out of the light and into darkness. He thought it was night, but one look around told him it was overcast. The air was still and hot, but it wouldn't be for long. There wasn't a patch of blue above him.

He was in his mother's garden. The weeds and flowers lay quietly at his feet, turned upwards at the sky. He saw the spider grass across the stone path—it was lying flat on its back. No strands waved delicately in the wind, as they had when Andrew had visited a few nights ago. The patch of weeds lay quietly beneath the stone white porch ahead.

Andrew looked back once. He saw the short stone wall in his front yard, and the outline of a door etched onto it. It was faded now, and closed forever. A piece of magic, good and evil, had passed from the universe.

Maybe it's better that way, Andrew thought, walking toward his house. *Just walk away.* His steps were short and uncertain; he was walking the tight rope again, as he had over Sarna Mensis. He stopped short of the stone steps when he saw someone standing on the porch, her back turned to him.

"Mom?"

She turned around. Andrew let out a short breath when he saw her standing in the dawn light. She looked older than he remembered. The black circles beneath her eyes had deepened alongside a sea of furrows and creases on her brow. Her blue and yellow dress hung loosely off of her. She regarded him slowly, like in a dream.

"Andrew."

He didn't move. Above the rain began to fall. He felt the first drop sizzle on his arm, and jumped a little. It was cold. He looked down and saw the drop sitting on his arm—he expected to see some dried blood on his arm too. There was none—he had come out of that world unscathed.

In a moment he could hardly see in front of him. The rain drove down upon the earth and pummeled him. He looked down again at his shirt and it was soaked through. In a matter of seconds he was drenched, and the rain poured down on his face. He looked up at the sound of steps creaking and saw Patricia Tollson walking down the steps.

"Mom," Andrew said. "Mom, don't. It's wet." His hair clung to his forehead. He would have to get a haircut, he decided. It had been a while since his last cut. He began to laugh—he couldn't help himself. He looked up and saw his mother laughing too. "Now you're wet too!"

His mother walked out into the rain. Beneath her the beds began to flood. Dirt and soil loosened and swayed in the pounding water, before sliding beneath their feet. The stone path became a flowing river of earth, and Andrew walked through it to meet his mother.

"You're home," she shouted over the rain. Yet she didn't hold out her hand, or embrace him. "The police—everyone has been looking for you. You're father's not home—I should call—"

"Mom," Andrew said. He was done laughing now. His shoes were lost in the watery earth.

"Forgive me."

She smiled, and the creases and lines on her face disappeared for a moment. She took his hand, and at last Andrew felt the wind pick up. The rainy air became a tempest raging around them, and he smiled back.

"Yes," she said. "I do."

She turned and he followed. The wind followed as well, guiding the two toward the house and up the steps. Andrew turned once and saw the blowing storm outside of the porch.

The river across the street began to run again—it was flowing upstream, pushed by the north wind. Andrew watched it move a second longer, and then he turned and followed his mom through his front door.

Apprentice House is the country's only campus-based, student-staffed book publishing company. Directed by professors and industry professionals, it is a nonprofit activity of the Communication Department at Loyola University Maryland.

Using state-of-the-art technology and an experiential learning model of education, Apprentice House publishes books in untraditional ways. This dual responsibility as publishers and educators creates an unprecedented collaborative environment among faculty and students, while teaching tomorrow's editors, designers, and marketers.

Outside of class, progress on book projects is carried forth by the AH Book Publishing Club, a co-curricular campus organization supported by Loyola University Maryland's Office of Student Activities.

Eclectic and provocative, Apprentice House titles intend to entertain as well as spark dialogue on a variety of topics. Financial contributions to sustain the press's work are welcomed. Contributions are tax deductible to the fullest extent allowed by the IRS.

To learn more about Apprentice House books or to obtain submission guidelines, please visit www.apprenticehouse.com.

Apprentice House
Communication Department
Loyola University Maryland
4501 N. Charles Street
Baltimore, MD 21210
Ph: 410-617-5265 • Fax: 410-617-2198
info@apprenticehouse.com • www.apprenticehouse.com

Thanks to Evan, April-Ann, and John for lugging the door through the forest, and many thanks to Kate for capturing it on film.

CPSIA information can be obtained
at www.ICGtesting.com
Printed in the USA
FFOW02n1138220316
22514FF

9 781627 200042